Alfred Rochefort

Vladimir, the Nihilist, or, the Czar's Spy

A story of Russia today

Alfred Rochefort

Vladimir, the Nihilist, or, the Czar's Spy
A story of Russia today

ISBN/EAN: 9783337298807

Printed in Europe, USA, Canada, Australia, Japan

Cover: Foto ©Andreas Hilbeck / pixelio.de

More available books at **www.hansebooks.com**

ROBERTSON'S CHEAP SERIES.

POPULAR READING AT POPULAR PRICES.

VLADIMEER, THE NIHILIST ;

OR

THE CZAR'S SPY.

A STORY OF THE RUSSIA OF TO-DAY

BY

MAJOR ALFRED ROCHEFORT.

TORONTO:
J. Ross Robertson, Corner King and Bay Streets.
1881.

VLADIMEER, THE NIHILIST;

OR,

THE CZAR'S SPY.

—

BY MAJOR ALFRED ROCHEFORT.

CHAPTER I.

IN THE PALACE.

January 1st, 1878. The short winter days of 60° north latitude made it dark as at midnight in the imperial city of Saint Petersburg at three in the afternoon. The sky was inky black, and a biting wind swept down from Lake Ladoga. But cold and dark though it was, the people of the city seemed determined that the elements should not interfere with their enjoyment. The frozen Neva was covered with skaters, and lit up by countless bonfires and myriad lamps. Fur-lined sleighs, filled with happy people, flew along the streets to the music of their own bells. Every lamp was lit, and it looked as if every house were illuminated; even the watchmen, on the towers and in church steeples, made fiery circles with their blazing torches. The five thousand windows in the Winter Palace seemed aflame with colored lights that fell with kaleidoscopic patterns on the surrounding snow. The great quadrangular square of the palace was filled with thousands of men and officers in the brilliant uniforms of the Guards. Through the massive gates squadrons of mounted gens-d'armes were coming in from their posts, or marching out, with a great jingling of arms, to relieve their comrades on patrol.

That it was a night of festivities, even the beggars, cruching under shelters from the biting wind, knew full well. From the churches came the pealing of organs; from the Admirality and the Hermitage the rhythmic din of brass bands; from the steeples the chimes; and from the Winter Palace the soothing cadences of stringed instruments, attuned to dancing measures.

Even those out of pleasure did not loiter along the streets, but walked with a brisk step, and a hospitable roof in view. Among these pedestrians one man was so conspicuous that even the most hurried stopped to look after his tall, muffled figure. That he was young and vigorous his long, quick stride told : but the fur cap drawn low on his face, and the fur collar meeting it, hid every feature but his sharp, bright eyes. The dress was unmistakably that of a noble, and the bearing was unquestionably that of a soldier. Glancing neither to the right nor left, he made his way from the Troitskoi Bridge to the illuminated palace.

As he entered the north gate the sentinels came to a salute, which he acknowledged by mechanically touching his cap. Avoiding the groups of officers, and the light-flooded, open doors of the quarters of the Guards, he crossed the square and entered that part of the Hermitage occupied by the Chapel of Peter the Great. 'A dim religious light' was reflected from the pillars of colored marble and verdant malachite, and lit up the tattered battle flags, wrested from Russia's foes by her redoubtable warriors. French eagles, dimmed by six decades of rust and captivity, pashas' horse tails, the guidons of Turkey's sleeping legions, Circassian shields, the keys of fortresses that had yielded to Slavic prowess the batons of leaders captured in battle, and the rusting swords of defeated but historic foeman, met the eye on every side, and gave the chapel the appearance of an arsenal or military museum.

The man removed his cap and turned down the collar of his fur cloak, thus bringing to view by the light of the lamp under which he stood, a well-shaped head covered with nut-brown hair, and the handsome, aristocratic face of a man of five and twenty. He took a position at the entrance to one of the covered galleries that connects the Hermitage with the Winter Palace.

He was evidently expecting some one, for he stood in an attentive attitude, and kept his dark eyes fastened on the further end of the colonnade. He had been there about ten minutes, and began to show his impatience by biting his mustache, when hearing a step behind him, he instinctively laid his right hand on his left hip, where the hilt of his sword usually met his grasp, but he had no sign of arms now.

He turned and saw before him a short, stout man, with very light hair and eyes, and wearing the resplendent uniform of aid-de-camp to the Czar.

The aid-de-camp saluted and asked:

'Have I the honor to address Prince Gallitzin of Novgorod?'

'That is my name,' replied the gentleman addressed.

I am Count Kiseleff, aid to his Majesty the Czar.'

The young men shook hands, and Count Kiseleff continued:

'I come from Prince Gortschakoff.'

'He told you, you would meet me here?'

'He did,' replied the count, 'and bade me escort you at once to his presence.'

Count Kiseleff was about to lead the way when the prince stopped him with a restraining gesture and the question:

'Is General Gortschakoff with the Czar?'

'He is in attendance, and now awaiting an audience,' replied the count.

'The general's message being peremptory, I hastened hither without making any change in my toilet. I am in undress.'

As the prince spoke he threw open his sable outer garment, and displayed his splendid figure in the close-fitting undress of a colonel of artillery.

'Ah!' laughed the count, 'General Gortschakoff will prefer that you answer with the promptness of a soldier, rather than appear later in the garb of a courtier. The time has come when our imperial master needs men, not array. Be pleased to follow me.'

Count Kiseleff bowed again, from his hips up, and with a very stately bearing for one so short of stature, he led the way down the long gallery and into a deserted but brilliantly illuminated hall of the Winter Palace.

Cold as it was outside, here the air was of a tropical warmth. Dark as was the wintry sky, here a soft, mellow light flooded every niche. Lite-sized figures of mediæval warriors, in silver and bronze, lined the walls on either hand, their drawn swords tipped with flame, and their polished shields, held high above the head, answering for reflectors.

Soft carpets and softer rugs deadened the fall of the feet; there was an odor of flowers in the air; and from the distance came the faint, delicious ripple of music. The jingling of the count's trailing sword smote the ear of the prince as harsh and out of place at this time, though even in the cradle the sound of spurs and arms had been his lullaby.

By a narrow winding stairs the count led the way to an upper hall, the sky-blue ceiling lit by blazing stars, and the wall hung with pictures that had made the name of their painters immortal.

At the further end, and to the right of this hall, Count Kiseleff opened the door, and conducted the prince into a suit of magnificent apartments, the furniture of which showed they were designed for private use.

'Be pleased to remain here, and I will announce to his excellency, Prince Gortschakoff, your arrival.'

The count waved his hand, and without stopping went into another apartment.

Before the door of the room by which the count vanished a tall soldier stood, with a drawn sword at the position known to military men as a 'carry;' and but for the winking of his eyes he might have passed for a life-like figure that should have been with the bronze soldiers in the lower hall. In a few minutes the count returned, and said:

'His Excellency awaits you.'

The prince followed him into the next apartment, and was brought face to face with a long, thin, sharp-faced man, whose gray hair, shriveled hands, and wrinkled face bespoke great age. He wore the court costume of his rank, and looked like an animated mummy in masquerade. This was Prince Gortschakoff, the premier of Nicholas, and the giant subject in whose shadow the throne of Alexander was shrouded.

'I come in obedience to your excellency's order,' said Prince Gallitzin, when the count had announced him, and the old man, without rising, looked up from the papers he was examining.

At a signal from General Gortschakoff, Count Kiseleff withdrew.

'I have much of import to say. Pray be seated.' The general waved a shriveled hand, and the prince sat down.

'Our imperial master has been pleased to

notice your many gallant deeds in the Balkan passes and beyond,' said the general.

'It has always been my desire to permit the approval of my imperial master, and to lend me every effort for the honor and integrity of all the Russias,' replied the prince.

'And,' continued the general, as if he had not heard the interruption, '*I* have watched your course with delight; for though your long absence from Russia has prevented my knowing you as I should desire, your father, I was proud to call a friend, and your grandfather, and I were at college together, and wore our first epaulets in the wars with Circassia. You hold a responsible position; the glory of two great names hangs on your acts.'

'As yet,' said the prince, proudly, ' no act of mine has tended to dim the lustre of their honoured names.'

'Spoken like a true Gallitzin !' The old man drew his chair nearer, and after an asthmatic fit of coughing, went on in a more confidental tone : ' It is not only in the field that you must continue the course so brilliantly begun, but also in counselling and upholding the empire, which is now threatened by those fanatics the Nihilists, who aim to reduce to chaos the structure crystalized by centuries of honored custom and wise laws. General Gallitzin, you must henceforth be nearer the person of our imperial master.'

'I stand ready to obey; but your excellency mistakes ; I am not a general,' said the prince.

A smile passed over the old diplomat's withered face, and leaning forward he took from the table a parchment, from which depended two golden seals stamped with the double-headed eagle of Russia.

'Read that,' he said, handing the young man the document.

It was a commission appointing Wladislas Gallitzin General of Brigade in the Imperial Guard, and it bore the sign manual :

'Byt po siemu.
    CZAR ALEXIS.'

(Be it so. Czar Alexander). The young man bowed, and stood for some seconds in silence, the old, sharp eyes reading his face the while.

CHAPTER II.

IN THE GARRET.

Within sight of the Winter Palace, and on a little, dim, snow-blocked street running back from the Neva, there stands a very high, narrow house, with very small windows, and over the dingy door is a sign in Russian characters : ' Apartments to Let by Week or month. There are other houses of a similar character on either side of the street, and all have the appearance of having seen better days, and of having shrunk under the combined influence of bitter cold and biting poverty. All these houses appear to have sunk below that state of poverty know as ' genteel,' for there is no attempt to conceal the spectre of Want that seems to have made his headquarters in this street. On the very top floor of the very high, thin house referred to, and in the corner most exposed to the fury of the north, wind, the family of Madam Ruloff, wife of the exciled general of that name, lived. In the principal apartment, which was at once sitting-room and kitchen, a lard lamp burned on a pine table, and a handful of charcoal burned in the little white stove.

At the table Madam Ruloff and her beautiful daughter, Elizabeth, sat sewing, as if more lard from the lamp and more charcoal for the stove depended on their efforts. At a little window that comanded a view of the merry skaters on the river, and the thousands of warm lights in the imperial residence, a young man of twenty two or three stood looking out at the city, but seeing nothing. He was of medium height, but so finely proportioned as to seem smaller. His yellow hair was cut after the military style, and the carriage of the head and the square shoulders bespoke a man trained physically, at least, for war. His close-fitting dress was that of a student professor of the School of Mines, but it had seen better days. Turning abruptly from the window he stamped his foot on the bare floor, and with clinched and raised face, hissed :

' A curse on them ! Heaven's most terrible curse on the houses of Paulowitsch and Romanoff !'

Madam Rulofi looked up from her sewing and fastened her patient, blue eyes on her son. She had been a very handsome woman, but there were lines of care on the white forehead, and traces of pain about the well cut mouth. The dead gold-hair, visible under her snowy cap, had threads of silver in it, and the small white hands looked as if they had not long been familiar with the heavy coarse work on which they were now engaged· In a low musical voice she said :

' Patience, patience, my son. Do not give up until we have heard of the efforts of our old friend, and your old schoolmate, Gallitzin of Novgorod.'

At mention of the soldier-prince's name Elizabeth Ruloff glanced up from her work, and a crimson wave passed over the pale face and white throat. She looked as her mother must have done at eighteen, less the expression of care which her mother, the petted daughter of a rich noble, could not have had. Elizabeth Ruloff might have passed for the heroine of an old Norse romance, the veritable daughter of a Viking. Without comment she continued her work, while her brother, retaining his attitude, eloquent of youthful passion and manly indignation, said, with manner of a man speaking his fiery thoughts rather than addressing those present:

'It may be Gillitzin's turn next. But an hour since I met him on his way to the Winter Palace, in obedience to a peremptory summons of that monster Gortschakoff. To-morrow Wladislas Gallitzin may drag a chain through the snow, with his bowed face turned to Siberia.'

'Oh! no, brother! No!' interrupted Elizabeth Ruloff.

'But why not he as well as our father? Is the house of Gallitzin of better blood, or more prolific in warlike patriots, than that of Ruloff?'

'But,' urged Elizabeth, 'Wladislas Gallitzin is fresh from victories in the Balkans.'

'True; but did military service save our father or the scars received in a hundred battles plead in his defence when the spies of the Czar confronted him with their false but well-matured charges of conspiracy? One year ago no name stood higher in the favor of Alexander Paulowitsch, our lord and master, than that of General Count Ruloff. No man had finer ancestral estates; no man was happier in the midst of his family. But where is he now? An exiled slave, dressed in leathern garb, shackled, and only unhandcuffed that he may the better ply the pick and use the spade in the dark, death-breeding mines of Siberia.'

'Oh, my son! my son! Do not! do not make darker the sombre picture in my heart?' wailed Madame Ruloff.

'Pardon me, my mother,' said Vladimeer bending and kissing her. 'I would not willfully add a pang to your agony; but I cannot keep back the expression of the feelings that haunt me night and day. Confiscation has impoverished us, and I am helpless to save you from mental labor and biting want. Men acknowledge my education, and concede I have abilities that should win bread; at least, for my loved ones; but those who could employ me shrink from having in their service the son of the falsely-charged conspirator Ruloff. The minions of the Czar would inform him that those who gave me work were Nihilists, and ruin would come to them with the suddenness of a Caspian storm. Again, I say a curse on the house Romanoff! Let them encircle the throne of the autocrat with conscript bayonets ten thousands deep; let them mount a Cossack lancer on every horse, from the Neva to the Don: let them man the batteries of Cronstadt, and plant cannon in the streets of Saint Petersburg; let them rob the people of the last vestige of this mockery of liberty, and fill every town and hamlet with cringing spies—yet they cannot keep the dagger from the heart of the tyrant, nor the torch from his throne. Fifty millions of the downtrodden await the signal! Throughout all the Russias, eyes hungry for the God-given light of liberty peer through the darkness, to catch the first sparks of the coming conflagration. Wait! wait! Patience, and the air of Russia, now filled with the clatter of arms and the groans of the enslaved, will become musical with the crash of broken shackles!'

On the face of Vladimeer Ruloff an inspired light burned. His right hand was raised, and his flashing eyes were turned to the ceiling. Even the mother and daughter looked with feelings of admiration and awe on this embodiment of virtuous vengeance, this personification of the fiery, desperate element that smouldered under all the ramifications of Russia's power.

'Vladimeer, my son! my son! Know you not that they are watching you, and that a breath of what you have just said, if heard by other ears, would result in their tearing you also from me! As you love me, Vladimeer, continue to suffer, and learn from our dear Elizabeth the heroism of patience.'

The mother was on her feet, and her arms about her son, and the blue eyes larger for the tears that dimmed them.

'Patience, my mother, is a womanly virtue, and the men of Russia have learned it from their mothers. If I could talk as boldly on the streets as I do here, there would be freedom and peace in the land. But you mistake if you think the sentiments I utter are mine only. What here I say aloud, ten thousands — aye ten millions of people are thinking or whispering into fai hful ears this night.' Then kissing his mother and speaking with an affectation of cheerfulness, he continued: 'But I will be cautious, for your and my sister's sakes. Have I not been prudent? Did I not, when discharged last month from my beggarly professorship in the School of Mines, bury my nails in my palms, and my teeth in my lips, as I smiled and bowed myself out? Oh! I have patience. The Ruloffs never rushed so blindly into a danger that they did not see their way out.'

'But you father! bear in mind, my son, that if the advisers of the the Czar decide to destroy you—like the wolf with the lamb—

they will not want for an excuse. Do not give them the shadow of one, by any association with the revolutionary element. And above all, cease companionship with Michael Pushkeene,' said Madam Ruloff.

' Well, Michael is not fair to look on, I concede, but a braver, truer heart never beat. I do not encourage his admiration for Elizabeth, though the fondness argues well for his taste. But his most assiduous court is paid to freedom, and his country is the only bride he desires.'

Vladimeer Ruloff had scarcely ceased speaking when a cautious tapping was heard at the door. Elizabeth tooked up, and her face grew paler as in answer to her brother's ' enter,' a small, lean-faced man, with black hair and eyes, walked in and stood bowing before her.

Without looking at the man Elizabeth inclined her fair head and bent lower over her work, while Madam Ruloff placed a chair, and said something about its being a cold night.

' A very cold night, Madam Ruloff, but you look warm here." Michael Pushkeene turned his back to the stove, and his little black eyes on Elizabeth ' Thanks, I will not sit down,' he said ; ' Professor Vladimeer and I have an engagement with some friends to night, and it is nearly time we were with them."

' And I,' said Vladimeer, ' came near forgetting it, in watching from the window the illumination along the Neva. It is the first of the new year ; some are no doubt wishing their friends happy new years, but it is a mockery.'

' A great mockery,' rejoined Michael Pushkeene, bringing his hands from behind and rubbing them.

Vladimeer Ruloff put on a long, heavy overcoat, any a fur cap, the visor of which concealed his face.

' I will be gone but a few hours," he said to his mother, as he kissed her affectionately.

' And you will keep clear of danger, my son,' she whispered.

' I promise you that,' he replied.

Michael Pushkeene bowed again to the ladies, and made as if he were going to shake hands, but seeing no disposition on their part to meet him, he turned and went out with Vladimeer.

CHAPTER III.

IN WHICH A VERY REMARKABLE GATHERING

IS DESCRIBED.

Vladimeer Ruloff and his friend Michael Pushkeene kept in the darkest, narrowest streets. Before turning a corner they would stop and listen for the patrol, and only move on when assured they were not observed by any of the many men in uniform on the streets. After half an hour's turning and doubling in the shadows they came to a sombre-looking structure that stood back from the street, and before which burned two huge lamps. The space in front of this barrack-like house was railed off from the street, and the snow-covered shrubbery and fountain showed the inclosure was a flower garden in the summer season. The two young men must have been seen as they approaced, for as they neared the massive front door it swung open. They entered a wide, dimly lit hall, the door closing noiselessly behind them. Into the farther end of the hall poured a cataract of stairs, and up these stairs the young men went, the cushioned steps giving no sound, and no evidence of life meeting their eyes. Entering a dim upper hall they traversed half its length and were brought to a halt by a tall figure, wearing a black mask.

' What seek you here ?' demanded the mask.

' That which we have lost,' replied Vladimeer Ruloff

' What have you lost ?'

' Something hidden in the heart blood of our masters,' replied Vladimeer, in an intense whisper.

' Its name ?'

' Liberty !'

' The answer is correct. Follow me.' The mask replaced the dagger in his girdle, and led the way to a room in which sat a figure attired like himself. The walls of this room looked like a giant honey-comb, filled with black bundles. The man rose, and taking two bundles, handed them to the new-comers, whispering as he did so:

' There is no time to spare.'

Each bundle contained a black mask and a long black gown, which Vladimeer Ruloff and his friend at once assumed.

' Are you ready ?' asked the guard, in the same cautious tones.

' We are ? responded Pushkeene.

The guard tapped on the wall, and an answering tap came from the other side. Then the wall slid back without noise, and closed, as the two young men stepped through the opening.

They were in a room filled with figures dressed like themselves. These people were talking in low tones, and despite the disguise it was evident not a few of them were women.

' Fifty-two ?' called out a voice at the further end of the room ; and all the maskers turned to Vladimeer and his friend, who now advanced and stood by a long table that ran down the middle of the apartment.

'The pack is full," said Vladimeer, looking along the table.

There were fifty-two chairs, and on the table, before every chair, a playing card was fastened.

'Then let the game go on. Here is the box; draw.' This was said in a woman's voice, and a short slender figure laid a box on the centre of the table, and inserting her hand, drew out a card. Holding it up so all could see, she called out, 'The queen of hearts!' and took the chair opposite that card. In the same manner the others drew. The knave of clubs fell to Michael Pushkeene's lot and the ace of diamonds to Vladimeer's. The ace of hearts was at the head of the table, where there was a larger chair. This place was drawn by a tall man, whose long, red beard showed under his mask.

For some minutes after all had taken their places they sat with their heads bowed on their hands as if in silent prayer. The ace of hearts broke the spell of thrilling silence by rising and saying:

'It falls to my lot to preside at the game to-night. It is the first game of the year. It should gladden us to know that one hundred thousand games are being played at this hour by our brothers from the White Sea to the Black, from the quarries of Siberia to the salt mines of old Poland. During the past year many of our brothers and sisters have fallen before the rifle, under the knout, or died on the gallows; but each death has been a crop of dragon's teeth from which armed men swarm up for liberty. During the past year many of our friends, and those suspected of being our friends, have been dragged down from positions of honor and sent to Siberia, while their families, deprived of means, are left to famish. This has been notably the case with my old friend and master, General the Count Ruloff. But though the father is gone, the edict that banished him sent into our ranks Vladimeer, the Nihilist.

A murmur of applause ran round the table, and the masks looked from one to the other as if trying to find General Ruloff's under the disguise.

'The word Nihil means 'nothing;' meaningless in itself, is significant of the replies given to all our petitions and pleadings. Three days since Paul Rudier went to Ghourko to plead for his father's life. To-day the father is dead, and Paul Rudier is on his was to Siberia. Action must be taken on this case at once.

The ace of hearts sat down, and looked from mask to mask.

'There is but one course to take.' Michael Pushkeene rose, and was recognized as the knave of clubs. 'Ghourke comes within the forfeit. Remember, an eye for eye, and a tooth for a tooth; the dagger for the knout, and death for exile!'

Michael Pushkeene sat down and the presiding officer asked:

'What say you, my friends? The game moves slowly.'

'It is a forfeit,' said the woman representing the queen of hearts. 'Let us draw lots.'

'Hold!' called out a deep bass voice at the foot of the table. 'Ghourko left Saint Petersburg to-day to join his brother in the Crimea; but the man who takes his place at the head of the Czar's secret police becomes responsible for the sins of that office. This has ever been our rule. Our brethren in the Crimea will will care for Ghourko; it is our duty to deal with his successor.'

'Who is his successor?' asked the presiding officer.

'I know not,' replied the deep-voiced man. 'But to-morrow's Gazette will announce his name. Gortschakoff sees that the offices near his imperial master are not long vacant.'

'Would it not be well,' asked Vladimeer Ruloff, rising, and speaking in agitated tones, 'to defer all action in this matter for the present?'

The queen of hearts again rose, and said, in a low, intense voice:

'We must not defer until to-morrow, what can be done to-day. I know Ghourko's successor, and have known it since yesterday.'

'Who is he,' demanded a number of voices.

'Wladislas, the Prince Gallitzin of Novgorod!' she replied.

'Gallitzin of Novgorod!' ran from lip to lip.

'Gallitzin of Novgorod!' she repeated, adding, with thrilling fervor: 'And now I insist that lots be drawn.'

'Our sister is right in her demand. Let all the cards be again placed in the box,' said the presiding officer.

'Before this step is taken, I, the ace of diamonds, appeal to you to postpone action in this matter. You may not know, but I do that Wladislas Gallitzin was, for many years before the war with Turkey, a resident of America; and he is not now, and never has been, a friend of the tyrant, or a foe to his own down-trodden countrymen—'

'He will prove your words if he refuses the position this day tendered him by Gortschakoff,' interrupted the woman. 'But whether he accepts or not, some one will fill the place. It is against the man who becomes chief of the Czar's spies that our blows must be aimed. Again I insist on the drawing.'

'And again I oppose it,' said Vladimeer Ruloff, hotly.

'You cannot oppose a rule of the game,' sneered the woman.

'Draw if you will; but know now that I will not respond should the lot fall to me.'

A hoarse murmur ran round the table, followed by a chorus of 'Draw! Draw! Draw!'

'Will you abide by my decision?' asked the presiding officer.

'Yes,' was the response.

He inserted his hand in the box, rattled the cards round for fully a minute, then, with thrilling deliberation, he pulled out a long dagger, and with it a card. Turning a card, he called out:

'Can you all see it?'

'We can,' they replied.

'What is it?'

'The queen of hearts!' came the response.

The woman rose hurriedly from the chair, and going to the head of the table, she picked up the glittering weapon, and holding it high above her head, she said, in the thrilling accents that characterized her words:

'I pledge my life to bury this blade in the heart of him who holds the office of the Czar's spy!'

She hid the blade inside the long, black gown, and walked back to her chair with a bearing that denoted inflexible resolution.

'What other business have we?' asked the presiding officer.

'A case to investigate?' said the deep-voiced man. 'It is rumored that one Michael Pushkeene, a member of our order, has been seen in consultation with our foes.'

'I deny the charge, and demand, in behalf of Michael Pushkeene, an investigation,' called out the owner of that name, as he held up the card he was known by at that meeting.

The deep-voiced man repeated the charge, and at his request three were appointed to hear the defence, and mete out such punishment as the case, if proven, demanded.

Verbal reports were made of recent 'outrages' on the part of the government, and of the success that had attended the plans of the Nihilists.

A remarkable thing in connection with this meeting was that there was nothing documentary about it; not a record that could be found if the police were to burst in on the moment. The members were disguised, and by a curious lot, they were designated as cards, and only by the merest chance could any one represent the same

card twice in succession. The guards without were the only persons that saw the Nihilists unmasked, but as those guards could not possibly bear anything that took place, and were changed by lot every night, a profound secrecy was assured. But apart from these precautions there was the still stronger one of death against treason; not to mention the still more potent one of a common league against a common wrong.

The people left the room one, or at most two, at a time. It was ten o'clock at night when Vladimeer Ruloff and Michael Pushkeene unmasked and went to a hall on the first floor, where a large number of ladies and gentlemen were engaged in merry, social converse. Not a few wore the imperial uniform.

CHAPTER IV.

THE CZAR'S SPY.

The official *Gazette* of Saint Petersburg contained, the day following the events narrated in the preceding chapter, this notice:

'It has pleased his majesty to promote Colonel the Prince Gallitzin to the rank of general of brigade, an honor well won by distinguished service south of the Danube during the war that has just closed with so much honor to Russia. The foregoing is given as official. It is whispered in the best informed circles, that the young prince is to be detailed for a position of secret trust, that will bring him into close and intimate relations with our imperial master. It is even intimated, among the officers of the Guard, that Gallitzin of Novgorod is the successor of the vigilant General Ghourgo, who has won for himself the sobriquet of the Russian Argus, etc.'

Vladimeer Ruloff read this passage to his mother and sister, and asked their opinion,

'I am glad,' said Madam Ruloff, 'that one of our friends is meeting with the favor he deserves.'

'A favor, to fill the place of the perfidious Ghourko!' exclaimed Vladimeer. 'I would rather hear that he was dead—or worse, sent off to Siberia!'

'You may depend, my brother, that Prince Gallitzin will occupy no position that reflects not credit on himself, and do no act that does not become a gentleman, a patriot, and a soldier,' said Elizabeth Ruloff, a beaming light in her wonderful blue eyes.

'I fear, dear sister, you are not in a condition to judge impartially of your young friend's acts.'

Vladimeer Ruloff smiled sadly and began pacing the room.

'I believe I am still of sound mind, Vladimeer,' she said with dignity.

'Aye, and of sound heart; but with your feelings it would be hard to make you believe that General Gallitzin, as we can call him now, could do anything that was not right Hark! a step on the stairs!'

Vladimeer went to the door, just as a rap was heard on the other side.

On the door being opened, a young man in the uniform of a Cossack lancer, strode in, and assuming a military attitude, stood with his hand to his hat.

'Ah, Ruryk! What news bring you from your master, General Gallitzin?' asked Vladimeer.

The corporal removed his hat, but still maintaining his rigid attitude, he said:

'My master bade me present his compliments and profound regards to the Countess Ruloff and her daughter. He is their obedient servant.'

The soldier stopped suddenly, and the ladies bowed, when he continued at the same pitch:

''Ruryk, say you to Professor Ruloff, the son of the Countess, that I desire to see him at my quarters to night at seven; I will be alone, and supper will be set for two.' These words the general spoke, and I have reported.'

The soldier replaced his hat, wheeled, and was about to walk out, when Vladimeer called to him:

'Did the general send a note?'

'Not a line,' replied the soldier.

'Present the compliments of myself and daughter,' said Madam Ruloff, 'and our congratulations on his deserved promotion.'

The soldier repeated her words like an echo.

'And say to the prince that I will call at the hour appointed,' said Vladimeer.

Ruryk the Cossack saluted, wheeled, and strode out, as if on parade.

'I wish I could see General Gallitzin,' said Madam Ruloff, when the sound of the soldier's feet died away on the bare stairs. 'Being so close to the Czar, he might be able to secure a pardon, or, better still, an impartial hearing of your father's case.'

'A pardon from the Czar would imply an offence on the part of my father; a new trial would imply the possibility of error on the part of the tribunal that sent him unhear l into exile. No, my mother, I have no hope, General Gallitzin would subject himself to suspicion if he whispered a word in our behalf. We can ask from him no sacrifice,' said Vladimeer, gloomily.

'Would it not be right for him to plead our father's cause?' asked Elizabeth Ruloff.

'Yes, sister, right in the abstract; but, like every other abstract right, it is dangerous to assert it in this land.'

'I will see the Prince Gallitzin and beg him to plead for my father,' said Elizabeth, with unusual energy. 'I care not what the reasons or the policy may be against the act. I would bend, yes, bow my head in the dust to save my father.'

'And so endanger the life of the man you love?' said Vladimeer, preparing to leave.

'Men do not risk their lives blindly. Wladislas Gallitzin will not. He must judge, if it be right and safe to help us, as he has often promised he would.'

'It will do no harm to try. Now I must be going; first to see about the clerkship with the American merchant, and then to keep my appointment with the general.'

Vladimeer kissed his mother and sister and went out. It was nearing the close of a very short day, and though only half-past two the shopkeepers and lamp-lighters were making ready for darkness. The flat streets, bordered by high flat buildings, looked particularly gloomy, and the muffled figures passing back forth seemed anything but cheerful. Vladimeer Ruloff entered a comfortable-looking house, within a stone's throw of the Hermitage, and handing his card to a white-capped servant-maid, said:

'I desire to see Miss Radowsky. Please to say I will not detain her a moment.'

He was conducted into a cozy, well-furnished parlor. On the low grate burned a hard coal fire. The chandelier was lit, and the portraits of the present Czar, his father Nicholas, and several members of the royal family adorned the walls.

He had been seated but a few minutes, when he heard the rustle of a dress behind him, and turning he saw a young woman of twenty, petite of form, with the complexion of a child on cheek and brow, and the iron resolve of a soldier in the thin red lips and keen brown eyes.

'Oh! Professor Ruloff, your visit is not unexpected. How are you to day?'

These words were uttered in the low, thrilling tones that distinguished the queen of hearts at the Nihilist meeting; it now belonged to Miss Helen Radowsky, an instructor of German in the imperial family.

After a few complimentary commonplaces, and the assurance that he could speak without danger of being overheard, Vladimeer Ruloff asked:

'Have you read the *Gazette* of to-day?'

'What past?'

'That pertaining to Prince Gallitzin?'

'I have.'

' And you believe the unofficial statement, that he is to be at the head of the secret police ?'

' I do,' she replied with emphasis.

' I do not.'

' Even the Czar cannot prevent a difference of opinion,' laughed Helen Radowsky.

As if he had not heard her, Vladimeer Ruloff continued in his impetuous way :

' I cannot believe it ; the Prince Gallitzin is incapable of doing anything that is not bold, open and manly. He comes of a family honored for noble deeds—'

' Hold Vladimeer Ruloff ! I am willing you shall utter your opinions and give vent to your feelings—Heaven knows how you have been provoked ; but you must not attempt to teach me about the House of Gallitzin. Did you know I was born in Poland ?' She leaned forward, her dark eyes burning into his face.

' I think your name would indicate a Polish origin.'

' And rightly. Up to 1832 the Radowskies were in Poland what the Ruloffs were in Russia until one year ago. My father's father resisted the partition and fell with the immortal Radzivil. My own father ever cherished thoughts of freedom for his beloved land, and he was permitted to retain the feudal estates of our family ; but in the year named a futile revolution broke out. The Prince Gallitzin—father of the Czar's spy —was sent to our country. He seized my father, threw him into prison, and there he was left for twenty-two years, until Alexander came to the throne and sought éclat by breaking a few shackles, in 1855. My father came out an old man, his estates confiscated, his family destroyed. He went to London, married a French lady, and survived ten years—a teacher of languages. When my mother died three years ago, I came to Saint Petersburg, and by constant effort obtained the place I now hold. Of course I love the imperial family, of course I love the gallant descendant of the jailer Gallitzin. But,' she drew near and lowered her voice, without decreasing its terrible intensity, ' but I dreamt last night that Wladislas Gallitzin fell by a woman's hand, before he had been twenty-four hours in the place. Would it not be horrible if my dream came true ?'

' Very horrible ; but, then, it was only a dream. Curious, but I, too, had a dream last night, Miss Radowsky. Methought Prince Gallitzin pleaded successfully for the life of my father, and that I, in recognition of it, placed my life at his service," said Vladimeer.

' Ah !' she laughed, all dreams are absurd ; but yours is more absurd than mine.'

The entrance of the white-capped servant with another card broke up the conversation. As Vladimeer rose to go he whispered :

' Permit me to call again at ten.'

' Impossible !'

' Impossible ?'

' Yes, I have an engagement with Prince Gallitzin at that hour.' She bowed and turned to the new comer, and Vladimeer Ruloff took his departure.

After stopping for an hour at ' The American Store,' as a large warehouse on the Great Side was called, Vladimeer made his way to the most magnificent of European streets, the Nevskoi Prospekt. Here the wide, straight concourse was filled with gay sleighing parties, and the palatial structures on either hand, were ablaze with light. He stopped near the confines of the Second Admiralty District, at a house which, unlike the others, seemed deserted. The only sign of life came in the shape of a colored crescent above the massive door. In answer to the bell, Ruryk the Cossack admitted Vladimeer.

' Is the Prince in ?' asked Vladimeer.

' *General* Gallitzin awaits you,' replied the rigid orderly, saluting and leading the way to the upper floor.

The prince met his visitor at the head of the stairs, and after greeting him with boyish heartiness, conducted him into a comfortably furnished apartment that was at once a sitting-room and military office.

The prince's first inquiries were for Madam Ruloff and her daughter ; and the heightened flush on his bronze cheek, as he mentioned the name of the beautiful Elizabeth, bespoke a more than friendly interest.

' I saw the *Gazette* to-day, and congratulate you on the new military grade,' said Vladimeer, when they were seated and waiting the announcement of supper.

' I think it was not undeserved. But what think you of my being detailed for—'

The prince hesitated and Vladimeer added :

' For the duties lately discharged by Ghourko.'

' Something like that,' said the prince, blushing. I am aware that you have no cause to like the man, nor have I any relish for the duties for the place but I have thought that I might be able to use the office for the benefit of the discontented, without neglecting the duties I owe my imperial master.'

' I hope you may,' said Vladimeer, musingly.

' I propose continued the prince, ' to have the case of your father reviewed at once. My position will give me power in this way ;

ﾑ

and I assure you this was the strongest reason that prompted me to accept—'

'Heaven bless you !'

Vladimeer took his friend's hand and bent over it with emotion.

At this point Ruryk announced supper. The meal was plain as camp fare in front of the enemy—plainer, indeed, for there was no liquor on the table.

The meal over, they went back to the office, and while they smoked they talked over plans for the restoration of General the Count Ruloff; and so sanguine was the prince of success that he insisted on loaning Vladimeer a thousand gold roubles. 'Your father will repay me with interest,' he said, 'before the year expires." They talked on till the bells in the many steeples tolled the hour of ten. Then the ringing of a nearer bell was heard, and Ruryk entered with I card. The prince read it, and rising, said : 'You must pardon me, Vladimeer; but a have an engagement with a lady at this hour. She has information of importance to communicate, and for this purpose I granted her an audience.'

'A lady ? Do not go ! I beg you do not go ! It may be a plot! Let me accompany you !' gasped Vladimeer, reaching out his hand to restrain his friend.

But the prince did not hear him, else surely he would have stopped. Vladimeer saw him vanish ; heard him descending the stairs ; and then with a shout of alarm he started after him.

CHAPTER V.

HELEN RADOWSKY AND THE PRINCE.

Vladimeer Ruloff ran down the stairs, and caught the arm of General Gallitzin, just as he was about to enter a salon to the right, which a servant was now lighting up.

The general saw, with surprise, the pale face and excited manner of his friend, who seemed unable to speak.

'Are you ill, Vladimeer ?' he asked.

'Yes, yes ! Come with me ! Let me speak with you before you see that woman !' gasped Vladimeer.

The prince drew him to one side, and said in kindly tones:

'My dear friend your recent troubles have made you nervous and suspicious ; pray calm yourself, for there can be no danger in seeing this woman. It is not an unusual occurrence.'

'Do not ask me my reasons ; do not attribute my fears to an excited brain, nor inquire as to the source of my information. Be assured that there is a plot to take your life,' said Vladimeer.

'To take my life !' exclaimed the prince.

'To take your life,' persisted Vladimeer.

'But what have I done to incite the wildest to do such an act ? Who is there, north of the Balkans, that would desire me dead ?'

'Many,' replied Vladimeer, drawing him still further away from the light now streaming through the door of the salon.

'Many !' repeated General Gallitzin, in amazement.

'Very many. Pledge me to keep secret, until death, what I am about to say, for in doing it I risk my own life to save yours.'

The general took the proffered hand, and said ;

'I pledge myself to secrecy, on the honor of a Gallitzin.'

'There is a plot,' Vladimeer spoke, in an intense whisper. 'There is a plot to keep the place lately occupied by Ghourko vacant, by means of the dagger. Hush ! you promised not to ask me how I know. Apart from this, you have one bitter, fierce unrelenting foe—'

'When and where have I done a wrong that would call for a moment's enmity ?'

'The sins or acts of the father are often visited on the children in this day. Your father governed a province of Poland, after the revolt of 1832, and there placed in prison the Count Radowsky, father of the woman now awaiting you in the salon. He was kept in prison, till the death of the Czar Nicholas, in '55, and then went to London, where your visitor was born and the old man died. For the house of Gallitzin she has a rich heritage of hate. I have told you enough to put you on your guard.'

Vladimeer moved as if about to take his departure.

'Will you not wait until the interview is over ?'

'I cannot. She must not know I was here when she came.'

'Then I will call on the countess to-morrow at noon. Be pleased to convey kind remembrances.'

The young men shook hands, and Vladimeer took his departure.

General Gallitzin, as a soldier, was the bravest of the brave. At Plevna he made a charge with his regiment of artillery, and carried his guns and caissons into the very camp of Osman Pasha ; and held his place, though every horse was killed, and one-half his men were cut down by the murderous fire of the S warming Turkish legions. It was he who, at the passage of the Danube, built a raft, placed on it a battery, and boldly sweeping out with the current, engaged, sunk one of Admiral Hobart's gunboats and so opened the way for the safe crossing of the army. His valor was that of high chivalric order that inspires the dullest of followers with his martial spirit, and makes the most indifferent a patriot and a hero. The thunder of the enemy's guns made for him sweeter music than the band attached to his regiment. He would not say so himself, for he had that modesty that ever accompanies the highest courage; but every man in the army believed that he was insensible to anything like fear. Now, as he stood stroking his brow, before entering the salon where Helen Radowsky awaited him, a dread that he could not comprehend came upon him; and had the choice been offered he would have chosen to charge a battery rather than meet this strange woman. Like the memory of an early dream, he recalled having heard his dead father speak of the Count Radowsky of Poland, and that his incarceration was by the order of the Czar.

'Oh! I am becoming a woman,' mused General Gallitzin. 'A foolish, nervous woman; and this before I have even entered on the duties of the office I have assumed, that I might bring a better understanding between my countrymen and their ruler. I almost wish I had remained amid the fresh, characters and unconstrained freedom of Western America. But I am here, and have duties to perform.'

He turned, and after surveying his splendid form and handsome face in one of the mirrors that lined the hall, he entered the salon.

A lady, young and handsome, rose to meet him.

Waving her to the chair from which she had risen, he said :

'I am General Gallitzin.'

'And I am Miss Helen Radowsky—'

'The lady from whom I, to day, received a letter, promising important information, if I made an appointment ?'

'The same.'

Helen Radowsky fastened her deep, burning eyes on him, and thought :

'How wondrously handsome the man is ! Can this be the son of such a father ? Can this demi-god be the Czar's spy ?' she drew her hand across her eyes, and sinking her voice, asked :

'Can we not talk in a more private place ?'

'My house is private from top to bottom. You cannot utter a word here that is not as secret and sacred, if you command it, as in your own room,' he replied.

'We cannot tell whom to trust in this land, in these times,'

She glanced at the door, where stood Ruryk, the Cossack, as if on sentry, and drew her chair closer to where the general sat.

'You can trust those whom I trust, in my

own house. Be pleased to state the object of your appointment,' he said, his eyes holding hers, until she became nervous, and fumbled, with her right hand inserted in the folds of her fur wrap.

'I am a teacher in the imperial family—'

She hesitated and cast down her eyes under his burning gaze.

'I am aware of that. I know what you are, and who you are. Pardon me, but my time is limited.'

General Gallitzin rose, and stood with his left arm resting on the malachite mantel, and his right arm thrown gracefully behind him.

'You are imitating your predecessor in obtaining information about people, and your excellency is right.'

She rose. and coming nearer, said, with a sudden intensity :

'I know of a plot to assassinate the Czar.'

'To assassinate the Czar I repeated the general, completely thrown off his guard.

'And to assassinate you !'

She took a long, quick step, toward him, and the hand in her breast was so far withdrawn as to show the glitter of the dagger hilt.

The general did not move. He saw and understood all, but for the moment he stood spell-bound by the woman before him. He could see her flashing eyes, and the white teeth gleaming through her thin, scornful lips ; and he felt her hot breath on his hand, as she shot out the words :

'To assassinate you, for the crime of your father in Poland !'

Another instant and the hand clutching the dagger would have been withdrawn; but short as was the time, another form forced itself between her and the general, and looking up, she saw before her Ruryk the Cossack, and the dagger hand was powerless in his clutch.

'Pardon me, my master, but the lady will talk better without this.'

Ruryk, with wonderful dexterity, possessed himself of the weapon, and striding back to the salon doors, resumed his stolid, military attitude.

'What does this mean ?' demanded the prince, now recovered from the daze that came over him.

'It means that your henchman has been rude, that in his brutal zeal he mistook my earnestness, my anxiety for your life to mean danger ! Give me back that weapon !' she cried, turning to the Cossack. 'I walk the streets alone, and it is my sole protection— that on my honor !'

'Give her back the dagger, Ruryk,' commanded the general.

The Cossack let the weapon fall, and in picking it up he placed his foot on the blade, grasped the handle and snapped it off like a pipe stem. Picking up the fragments he walked over and placed them in her hands, saying to the master:

'It was a brittle blade, General, and if the lady must have a dagger to walk the streets, I will fetch her one from your collection of Turkish and Circassian weapons.'

Helen Radowsky dashed the broken blade to the floor, and glared fiercely at the imperturable soldier.

'I regret that my orderly misunderstood your acts,' said the general, motioning to Ruryk to withdraw. 'Yot can depend on me for protection for your home, and secrecy as to what has happened here. I am convinced you mean to be my friend, and I propose to prove myself not unworthy your confidence. Pardon me for a moment.'

Searce knowing what she did, Helen Radowsky, as it under the wand of an enchanter, dropped into a chair, at the motion of his arm; and General Gallitzin left the salon, with a courtly bow.

He went to his military office and tapped a bell. Before the reverberation had died out, a stout, heavy beared man in the livery of the prince made his appearance, and said in a deep bass voice:

'I await your excellency.'

'Order my sleigh at once, Varwitch.'

'Yes, your excellency,' with an abject bow

'And send my Valet.'

'Yes, your excellency.'

Varwitch waited an instant, and no other order coming he stepped backward and vanished.

'You called me, your excellency.'

'Yes, Paul. Bring me my cloak and gloves—and my belt with the light pistols.'

The valet withdrew, but soon came back with the desired articles and helped his master to assume them.

General Gallitzin went down to the salon, where Helen Radowsky was still sitting with her hands clasped and her eyes on the floor.

'My sleigh is at the door, Miss Radowsky. Mine must be the honor of escorting you home to night.'

He offered her his arm and she tried to resist the impulse to take it. She drew back, yet yielded to the stronger will. Her hand trembled as it touched his sleeve, and she coughed to clear her voice. She found herself in the sleigh, by the side of the man she came to kill. She saw the horses, three abreast, dashing off; and she heard the bells, and still more musical voice of the Czar's spy. Her brain was in the whirl of incipient intoxication. She was left at her own door, and the prince had forced something into her hand. She staggered into the house, turned up the light, and saw it was a jewel-hilted dagger.

CHAPTER VI.

MICHAEL PUSHKEENE BECOMES JEALOUS.

Michael Pushkeene was the son of a pawnbroker and aspired to be a physician; but he had not yet completed the long course of study necessary to obtain a doctor's diploma in Russia. Years ago he had made the acquaintance of Prince Gallitzin and Vladimeer, son of Count Ruloff. while attending lectures on Chemistry at the Mining School. At that time Michael Pushkeene, with more ambition than brains, and more presumption than manhood, toadied to the young nobles, and aspired to belong to their executive class. It did not take him long to discover that the acquaintance of the class-room did not imply the friendship of the salon.

Michael Pushkeene secretly rejoiced when the tongues of Saint Petersburg became busy with discussing the 'Ruloff Conspiracy,' as it was called. During the mockery of a trial he was a constant attendant on Vladimeer Ruloff, and when the count was sent into exile Pushkeene was cautiously loud in his denunciation of the 'outrage.' He succeeded in winning the confidence of the generous and impulsive Vladimeer, and he felt that he had gained an important step in the ladder of advancement when he was introduced to the Countess Ruloff and her beautiful daughter.

Among the many absurd proverbs in circulation, is that, that 'like begets like.' In his way, Michael Pushkeene loved Elizabeth Ruloff from the first; and in her way she had a feeling of loathing for the man no rank or wealth could have banished.

'I am richer, far richer than she now,' he thought. 'She has sunk away below the son of the Troiskoi pawnbroker; but I will lift her up; she shall be the wife of Doctor Pushkeene; but I must have her all to myself—no mother, no brother to interfere.'

It was Michael Pushkeene who made Vladimeer Ruloff a member of the Nihilist organization, and who took care that every other member knew of the important acquisition. Before his acquaintances he spoke of the Ruloffs with a coarse familiarity, and ever aimed to create the impression that his wife should be the daughter of a count.

'And where are you going now?' asked shrunken, shrivelled, swarthy old Michael Pushkeene, as his son descended from the living rooms over the pawnshop. 'Why can't you stay home and stick down to your books? In wasting your time, you waste the money I have saved up through five-and-twenty years to educate you. I never spend a kopeck on myself, nor have a moment to spare.'

'I am going to a private clinic, father,' replied young Michael Pushkeene, as he drew on his black fur gloves, ' and on my way I shall drop in, for a moment, to see my poor friend, the Countess Ruloff.'

'Yes,' whined the old man, ' and I'll be bound you'll see the countess's daughter, too.'

· Well, father, I cannot help seeing the beautiful Elizabeth if she forces herself into my presence. You must not forget that you were once young yourself.'

Young Michael laughed and showed his prominent, yellow teeth ; and old Michael, with a shriller whine, retorted :

' When I was young, I went with people of my own class. Your mother, sold fish in the Gostinoi Dvor, and she was'nt ashamed of it.'

' If you intended I should marry a fish woman, you should not have set your mind on making me a doctor. You gave me wings, and I propose to fly higher than my nest. Now, good afternoon.'

Young Michael went out, twirling his cane with one hand and a ragged moustache, that looked like a case of black mildew with the other, while the old man adjusted his big spectacles and peered through the dingy window after his son, with an expression of pride on his yellow, miserable face.

' I want to keep the boy's pride down, but he is as good as the best. Why shouldn't the son of rich Michael Pushkeene, the pawn-broker, aspire to the hand of the daughter of a disgraced and exiled count ? Why not, indeed, when he's too good for her !'

After this soliloquy the old man refreshed himself with a pinch of snuff, and turned to wait on a woman who came in to pawn her own rags that she might get food for her starving little ones.

The doctor in embryo, with a self-satisfied air, wended his way to the abode of Madam Ruloff.

Vladimeer was out, Elizabeth said.

' Will he be in soon ?' asked Pushkeene, his hand on the back of a chair, as if hesitating whether to sit down or not.

' He should be in by this time,' said Elizabeth, glancing at a little clock that ticked with amazing vigor and frequency on a stand near by.

' Then, with your permission, I will wait for him a few minutes.'

Michael Pushkeene, sat down, and pulling out a monstrous gold watch—an unredeemed pledge from his father's shop—he surveyed its face for fully a minute, and compared it with the clock, and volunteered the inform-ation that the latter was just two minutes and a half slow. The little clock ticked louder as if it heard and understood the comment, and was determined to catch up and even get ahead of the regular time.

· Our clock is set by the Hermitage bell,' said Madam Ruloff, speaking to break the awkward silence rather than from any desire to engage Michael Puskheene in conversation.

She gave him a text, and for some minutes he went on to show her why the Hermitage bell and all the other city bells were wrong, and positively perplexing in their varied announcements of time. It was impossible that it should, as he regulated his time every day—when the sun shone at noon—which certainly was an unusual occurrence at this season of the year.

Putting away his watch, for the second time, Michael Pushkeene, with a view to appearing quite calm and comfortable, crossed his legs, and with the little black eyes taking an observation on the top of Elizabeth's golden head, he began milking his chin with his right hand, the elbow supported in his left palm.

'It is a source of constant grief to me, madam, to see that you and your accomplished daughter are reduced to the necessity of this drudgery and privation,' said Michael Pushkeene, after he had finished his observation on the golden head and brought his eyes to bear on the face of the mother.'

' We do not complain,' said the countess, with a tinge of hauteur.

· Of course you do not ; you are too noble and heroic for that, and that's why your case seems harder to your friends.'

' Our friends ?' repeated Elizabeth, without looking at him.

He was so elated at being noticed, even in this scornful way, by the proud girl, that he quickly unfolded his legs, placed his palms on his knee, with great emphasis, and went on :

' Yes Miss Eliz—Miss Ruloff, your friends. Do not think because a cruel court has sentenced your noble father, and that be. cause the double-headed eagle has ravenous-ly seized on his estates, that you have not friends. You have friends that pray for and think of you all the time ; friends that would give up their heart's blood, and their fortunes, to show their devotion.'

' I hope you are right,' said Elizabeth, still plying her needle.   ' But we never could test the friendship of people, so faithful, in the way you mention.'

' Not if you knew it would be an honor and a delight for them to serve you ?'

' In that event it would be wrong to avail ourselves of their devotion.'

' You will see that I am right; that I know

well, at least, one man who would lay down his life to help the noble family of Vladimeer Ruloff,' said Pushkeene, with pathetic earnestness.

He waited, evidently expecting that the countess or her daughter would ask who this self-sacrificing person was, and prepared to announce himself as the hero. If either of them had any such purpose it was prevented by a step in the hall, and a military tap at the door.

The madam opened the door, and discovered Ruryk, the Cossack, standing at a salute.

'My master, General Gallitzin, is without. He presents his compliments to the Countess Ruloff and her daughter, and asks if they would kindly grant him an audience?'

Elizabeth Ruloff's blue eyes darkened, and a crimson wave swept over the fair face and white throat; but she did not rise, nor lay aside her work to prepare for the reception of the man whose presence was the brief sun of her dreary, wintry life.

'Be pleased to inform General the Prince Gallitzin, of Novgorod, that the Countess Ruloff and her daughter will see him at once,' said Madam Ruloff.

Ruryk saluted, wheeled as if he were on a pivot, and stalked off with a thirty-two inch cavalry stride.

'I fear,' said Michael Pushkeene, rising, and looking from Elizabeth to her mother, 'that my waiting for Vladimeer may make me an intruder.'

To this neither of the ladies made reply. A light, quick step was heard outside, the door opened, and the handsome General Gallitzin, was in the room.

He kissed the Countess on the cheek, then took both of Elizabeth's hands in his, and the admiration in his fine black eyes showed he resisted a temptation in not greeting her in the same way.

Elizabeth's face was now aflame with confused delight, but the well-bred self-possession never left her. She placed a chair for the prince, and said:

'You have not changed in appearance.'

'Nay, fair Elizabeth, nor in heart.'

At this instant General Gallitzin, who was about to sit down, became aware of the presence of Michael Pushkeene, and drawing himself up he glanced over at that person in his princely way.

Pushkeene, now feeling as much out of place as a fish out of water, stammered as he picked up his hat, and made a crab-like movement toward the door.

'I am Michael Pushkeene. I was waiting to meet my old friend, and yours, Vladimeer Ruloff.'

'You are Pushkeene, the pawnbroker's son?'

'The same, General,' replied the cringing Pushkeene.

'I remember having seen you before,' said the prince, with an elevation of his fine brows that indicated no pleasure at the meeting.

Pushkeene swallowed a lump in his throat and made his way out. On the street he stood for some time watching Ruryk and the prince's sleigh; and, as he left, he muttered:

'A prince for a rival, eh! We shall see if the pawnbroker's son does not win.'

CHAPTER VII.

AN AUDIENCE WITH THE CZAR.

'I would have been to see you sooner,' said the prince when the door closed behind Michael Pushkeene. 'but my time has been wholly taken up at court: and then I wanted, if possible. to be the bearer of comforting news.'

'It would have been a pleasure to see you under any circumstances,' said the madam. 'Myself and Elizabeth have both been anxious for an opportunity to congratulate you in person on your well deserved promotion.'

'Yes,' added Elizabeth, 'the hero of the Balkans earned even more than he has received.'

'To know that you believe my advancement merited gives more pleasure than the sign manual of the Czar. I speak of course, of my military position,' said the prince, hesitating; then adding: 'The office vacated by Ghourko is in no respect congenial. I accepted it, first, in obedience to the imperial will, and reconciled myself to the inevitable with the belief that I could do good by creating a better understanding between the authorities and the disaffected elements; and, I may add, that I rejoiced to think that my vicinity to the Czar would enable me to obtain an impartial re-hearing of Count Ruloff's case, which I am satisfied will result in an acquital, and a restoration to his estates and the high dignities which he so adorned.'

'From my heart I thank you, General Gallitzin,' said the madam, in tremulous tones.

'Still call me Wladislas, as you did in the happy days of my orphaned boyhood, when no place on earth seemed so much like home as the castle of General the Count Ruloff.'

'Then, Wladislas Gallitzin,' she said, taking his hand and pressing it between hers, let me thank you again; not all the old-time friends are so faithful in this the day of our tribulation.'

'Ah! my dear madam, you mistake. All the old-time friends are just as faithful.

Those who neglect you now were never friends.'

'I fear you are right,' she sighed.

'I fear I am becoming something of a misanthrope. But I have learned one thing since my school days, and that is, that there is an immeasureable distance between the warmest personal acquaintances and friendship. We can count a quaintances by the thousands ; he is lucky who does not exhaust the list of his friends in trying to number them on the fingers of one hand.'

'Then you are very fortunate,' said Elizabeth, with a smile that seemed to light up the room ; it certainly brightened the deep, dark eyes of the prince.

'Why so, my lady ?' he asked.

'Because,' she answered, 'even I can name friends of yours that will take the fingers of one hand·'

'Then make me happy by doing so.'

'The Count Ruloff, his wife, son and daughter, four ; and I think I will ennoble Ruryk by elevating him to the position of little finger,' said Elizabeth, the smile breaking into a musical laugh.

'Yes be my faith ! Ruryk has shown his fidelity many a time at the risk of his life,' said the count. Then more thoughtfully : 'There is one on the list on whom I never have and never can look as a friend.'

'As a foe, then ?' asked Elizabeth, with an effection of lightness she did not feel.

'Nay, nor as a foe. There is a feeling higher than friendship. It has been with me ever since as a boy I saw the baby Elizabeth Ruloff in her nurse's arms,' He gallantly raised the white hand to his lips, and he felt it fluttering like a bird.

The entrance of Vladimeer caused the curtain to drop for the time being on what promised to be a scene of tender if not romantic wooing.

'Ah, Vladimeer, I am glad to see you,' said the prince, rising and shaking hands with the fiery young Nihilist.

'And I am glad to see you—looking so well,' repled Vladimeer, with a meaning glance.

'I work hard and live temperately, so there is every reason why I should appear in good health. By the way, Vladimeer, do you know what our sister here has just been telling me ?'

'What is that, General ?'

'Why, that she is my friend.'

'And so she is,' said Vladimeer—' the very best friend you have in the world.'

Then the very best friend I have in the world mus' sacrifice herself for me.

'She will do it, laughed Vladimeer.

'I dread to ask her, and must be going.'

The prince took up his fur cap, and Elizabeth, rising, gave him her hand.

He bent and looked into her beautitul, downcast face ; he bent lower and she raised her eyes. Their lips met, and in that simple, honest act there spoke the love of a lifetime. Elizabeth Ruloff was the bethrothed of Wladislas Gallitzin,

He kissed the madam, shook hands with Vladimeer, who insisted on seeing him to the sleigh, and drove off to the Winter palace the very happiest man in all Saint Petersburg.

He went straight to the quarters where he was to meet Prince Gortschakoff, and, on the way, Count Kiseleff, the Czar's aid overtook and accosted him.

'I have not yet had an opportunity to congratulate you, General Gallitzin—permit me to do so now,' said the count.

'I thank you very much. Others more deserving has been less fortunate,' replied the prince.

'It is well to believe that the powers that grant honors are the best judges. Your new position will be a trying and, I may add, a dangerous one,'

'I shall endeavor to do my best.' said the prince, modestly.

'Of that every one is certain. But my theory is that luck is often better than exertion.

They had reached the entrance to General Gortschaoff's apartments, and the count passed on with a courtier's smile on his lips and anything but love in his heart for the latest favorite at court.

'Like a true soldier, you are prompt to the second, said General Gortschakoff, as Prince Gallitzin, stood before him.

'I have no right to other people's time, General,' replied the prince.

'That was a motto with your grandfather ; I never met a prompter man. We were, Captains in the same regiment during the retreat of the French from Moscow, and though often hungry, and always so cold and weary that we felt like tumbling over in the snow, yet he never seemed tired. I have known him to wake the exhausted bugler that the calls might be sounded. He was lieutenant-colonel of my regiment when we marched into Paris after the fight at Waterloo, but the fetes and festivities had no charm for him. He was a soldier in every tissue of his body. And then your father was a most vigorous, rigorous man. I remember when he was sent to Warsaw. He did more to quell the Polish revolt than any other man. He made a great many enemies, yet he always went unguarded. Thadeus, Count Radowsky, tried to assassinate him ; but the curious part was that, when the count was tried and condemned to death, your father pleaded for his life, and the would-be murderer was sentenced to imprisonment for life. Ah, well'—the general sighed, and replacing his glasses, added—'we old men live more and more in the past.'

'It is a pleasure to hear you speak of those so dear to me,' said the prince, evidently moved by the old man's words and manner,

'And a pleasure for me to have one near me who can suggest the past. Sit down, General ; there are yet twenty minutes before the time set for the audience with our imperial master.'

The prince sat down, taking his dress sword on his lap, and the old man continued:

'I feel a more than friendly interest in you, and am anxious that men like you shall fill places like mine when I have passed away, as I soon must, and giant Russia looks for strong, steady hands to guide her, through the fermented sea of unthinking agitation, to calm prosperity and merited success. You should marry,' said the general abruptly.

'I have thought so myself,' replied the prince.

'You should marry a lady who will bring to you wealth and family strength. Such an one I know.'

'There are many such,' coughed the prince.

'Nay, nay ; there are but very few such as the Countess Alexandrina, daughter of Admiral Rekoff.'

'Your niece ?'

'Aye, my niece, and none the worse for that, I trust.'

'On the contrary, your excellency—all the better for that. But I have heard it rumored about the court that the Countess Alexandrina Rekoff is already bethrothed,' said the prince, hesitating whether he should speak of his own betrothal to Elizabeth Ruloff.

'And with whose name, pray, does rumor connect that of my niece ?' queried the old man.

'With that of the noble Count Kiseleff.'

'So ho ! Well, as usual, rumor is mistaken, Before the well-merited disgrace of General Ruloff there was a boy's and girl's intimacy between my niece and the son of an exile ; but that has, of course, long since vanquished into thin air, ' and General Gortschakoff spread out his lean fingers and illustrated in pantomime the dissipation of all the love that has ever existed between Vladimeer Ruloff and his niece.

At this moment Count Kiseleff entered and announced that the Czar's pleasure was to see General the Prince Gallitzin of Novgorod at once.

The old man rose unsteadily, but once on his feet he held himself erect, and walked with a vigor surprising in a man of over four-score years.

Count Kiseleff led the way along a series of magnificent halls, and through suits of these gorgeous apartments for which the 'Winter Palace is famous. At length they passed through an ornate door, the arch being formed by the extended wings of a double-headed eagle, two officers of the guard standing with drawn swords at the entrance to the imperial reception room.

The decorations of this superb apartment were barbaric in their magnificence, but an examination of each portion would have shown that, from frescoed arch to the carpeted floor, the highest art had exhausted its beauty and all its invention of decoration. On a chair at the farther end of the room sat a gentleman in evening dress, with a single order glittering on his brea t, and a broad blue ribbon over his left shoulder. He would have been a tall man if erect. His face was pale and of a melancholy cast, and the brown side-whiskers and moustache were tinged with gray. He had the high, narrow head that distinguishes the houses of Panlowitch and Romanoff, and the dull eyes that come of introspection.

This was Alexander, Czar of all the Russias. About him Courtiers, in resplendent uniforms, were grouped, some of them soldiers who had won renown while yet the stern Nicholas, father of Alexander, was on the throne.

Walking directly in front of the Czar, General Gortschakoff, and the prince bowed, and the latter bent on the right knee, as the former said :

'By the kindly permission of your majesty, it becomes my duty and pleasure to present to your majesty General the Prince Wladislas Gallitzin of Novgorod.'

'We are happy to meet so brave a soldier so faithful a subject,' said the Czar, in a low yet sweet, strong voice. He reached out his thin white hand, and taking it, the prince raised it to his lips.

'Rise, General Gallitzin ; from you we expect great things,' said his majesty : adding, when the prince had risen to his feet, and stood in a respectful attitude before him : 'The house of Gallitzin has ever been among the strongest pillars that support our throne. We feared that Russia had lost you when you left for America, but our heart was rejoiced when, at the first sound of w r, you fled back, to battle for the honor of the empire.'

'I cannot express my joy at knowing that my humble deeds have attracted the attention and won the approbation of your maj-

·esfv.' said the prince, with characteristic
mc d :sty.

'.. will be our pleasure to see you often,
and to advance your interests with your
growing strength and deserts.'

The prince, mindful of his promise to plead
for General Ruloff, was about to speak, when
the Czar arose wearily. It was the signal
that the audience was ended,

The prince, though never presented before
and unfamiliar with the ways of courts, knew
it would not do to press the claims of his
friend now. Waiting till the Czar had passed out through the ranks of bowed heads, he
retired with the General Gortschakoff.

'You are the most fortunate man in Russia,' said the old man, as they went back.
'His majesty as in ill health, but I could see
that you created the very impression I hoped
for. Get married as soon as possible, and
there is no position under the throne beyond
your reach.'

General Gortschakoff shook hands with
him warmly at parting, and made an engagement for the morrow, when the prince should
dine with him, and see the beautiful Countess Alexandrina.

General Gallitzin drove home with his
brain in a whirl, and anything but joy in his
heart, at the morrow's engagement.

CHAPTER VIII.

MICHAEL PUSHKEENE AND HELEN RADOWSKY
HOLD A LONG AND SERIOUS CONSULTATION.

As Michael Pushkeene sauntered along,
twirling his cane and feeling particularly
bitter toward the prince, he heard a light
step behind him and felt a light hand on his
shoulder. Turning suddenly he found himself face to face with a veiled lady.

His first thought was, that this lady was
one of his conquests—for he drew great comfort from the belief that he was irresistible
with the fair sex ; but the sound of the intense yet even voice of the queen of hearts
undeceived him.

'I am glad to meet you, Mr. Pushkeene.
Are you busy ?' asked Helen Radowsky,

'Never so busy,' he answered, with imi-
tative gallantry, 'that I am not hand and
heart at the service of Miss Radowsky.'

'You are very kind. Come with me. I
will take your arm.' She led him to the
house, and into the room, in which she had
received Vladimeer Ruloff, the evening before.

Laying aside her fur bonnet and veil Helen
Radowsky, with a laugh that chilled Pushkeene as a plunge-bath in the Neva would
not have done, said :

'I saw General Gallitzin but now, going
to the apartments of the Countess Ruloff—'

'Yes,' gasped Pushkeene, 'he was at college with me and Vladimeer.'

'They say,' she continued, 'that as children the prince and the beautiful Elizabeth
Ruloff were betrothed.'

'I don't believe it !' snapped Pushkeene.

'The prince is a man of his word. Her
poverty would only strengthen his desire if
he loved her. She is very lovable, I
believe ?'

'Oh, very lovable, indeed,' echoed Pushkeene.

'And, I have understood, Mr. Pushkeene,
and your heart was smitten by the fair en-
chantress.' said Helen Radowsky, arching
her fine brows, and uttering another tantal-
izing little laugh.

'I think my visits are not objectionable to
her,' said Pushkeene, with an effort at com-
placency.

'The visits of a plebeian cannot long be
welcome, when a prince presents himself as
a rival. Ah !' she said, with a sigh, 'even in
love the many base-born must yield to the
noble few.'

'I'd die first !' hissed Pushkeene.

'What, for love ?'

'And he'd die. He ought to be dead, if
the Nihilists made good their threat to keep
the office vacated by Ghourko vacant.'

He lowered his voice and fastened his little black, beady eyes on her, with an expression intended to imply that he meant more
than he would dare express in words.

'I heard of those threats, and heard one
was selected to do the work, but—' she hesitated, and Pushkeene interposed,

'The one lost heart.'

'The one thought of a destruction more'
certain than the thrust of a dagger, more
terrible than sudden death ; a destruction to
life, name, fame, love, prospects, everything !

'And that can be brought about in his
case ?' queried Pushkeene, his little eyes
snapping with delight.

'It can be brought about as certainly as
that you are sitting in that chair. If I had
one man of nerve—one brave, true man, who
would obey me implicitly and ask no questions—I would in less than one year so crush
the proud Prince Gallitzin, that the meanest
wretch in our prisons would not feel honored
in being chained to him. He is favored and
mighty at court now ; but if I had this brave
friend—and I felt like destroying this man —
the name Gallitzin, would be stricken from
the list of Russian nobles ; and this one
should be the last of the race.'

In conclusion she clenched her hand, and
her thin lips came together like the lips of a
vice,

'If I was anxlous to get him out of the

way, I know just the man for the place,'
said Pushkeene.
  'You do?'
  'I am certain I do.'
  'It would require a prudent man ; one
who could comn and him e f, and never be led
into anything rash or dangerous,' she said,
musingly.
  'Oh! such a position would just suit this
man,' said Pushkeene, giving his yellow hands
a vigorous dry wash.
  'When could I see him ?' she asked abruptly.
  'Oh! any time you make an appointment.'
  'I want to see him now.'
  'Now!'
  'Yes; there is no time to lose.'
  'Well this man would want to know all
about the plan before he went into it. He'd
want to know first what danger there would
be' to himself, and what the reward in the
event of success ; then he would want to know
just what course was going to be taken in
the case of General Gallitzin.'
  'Ha! ha! ha! Yes, he is, in truth, a
cautious man, and if his nerve and persistency
be commensurate, his success is assured.
Now, my dear Mr. Pushkeene,' she said, with
an increasing confidence in her voice, enforced by laying her beautiful white hand on
his arm, ' let us suppose you are the man who
is to help to do the work, and I am the one
who directs.'
  'Yes, let us suppose that—for the sake of
saving words,' he acquiesced.
  'Very well ; I shall answer your questions
in the order asked.   First : if you won, Gen-
eneral Gallitzin would cease to be a rival—
a great point, you will concede.'
  'A very great point.'
  'Then you might be enabled, by the act,
to gain the favor of the government, and be
rewarded with honors and wealth, if not
ennobled.'
  'I see, I see,' chuckled Michael Pushkeene.
  'The only danger would be in the event of
failure, Of this you can judge by my answer
to the second part of your question : ' The
course to be taken in the case of General Gallitzin,' I can reply to that in one sentence :
Make the authorities believe he is an Nihilist!'
  ' Make the authorities believe he is an Nihilist ! repeated Pushkeene, in amazement.
  Helen Radowsky compressed her lips,
nodded her pretty head, and watched her
companion.
  'Could it be done ?' asked Pushkeene,
after a painful pause.
  'As easily as that, if prudence be exer-
cised,' she said, turning her hand, palm up.
  'Oh, you can trust me for prudence. But
would it not make the Nihilists our foes ?'

  'Our foes !' she laughed. 'It would do
more to strengthen the cause of the Nihilists
than anything that has happened for a gen-
eration !'
  'You amaze me.'
  'I can see I do ; but I speak the simple
truth nevertheless. You know that Gallitzin is the idol of the young soldiery ?'
  'I do.'
  'The tenants, but yesterday serfs, on his
vast estates are numbered by tens of thousands, and so far they have remained true to
the house of their master.'
  'I know that.'
  'Can you not see that the sympathies of
all these will go to the cause for which the
prince is convicted, and that hundreds of the
nobles, dreading that it will be their turn
next, will combine to overthrow the autocrat whose will is the law of Russia ?'
  'Why,' he exclaimed, with admiration,
' you are as long-headed as Gortschakoff !'
  'Thanks for the intention, but you have
uttered no compliment. If I were a Nihilist'—she laughed and showed her little white
teeth—' I would bend all my powers to fast-
ening suspicion on the people of prominence
who do not belong to the order.   That was
done in the case of Count Ruloff, and it
drove his son into the Nihilists ranks.   Persecute a man on suspicion, and the chances
are a thousand to one that he will retaliate
by giving you grounds for your suspicion.'
  'You speak wisdom, Miss Radowsky.'
  'I speak common sense. In the execution
of this plan it would be necessary to link the
names and fates of Vladimeer Ruloff, and
General Gallitzin.'
  'Of Vladimeer the Nihilist and the Czar's
spy,' laughed Michael Pushkeene.
  'Exactly so, Now, could you, to accomplish
your object—to win the object of your love—
sacrifice your friend, Vladimeer Ruloff ?'
  'I could sacrifice my father,' replied Pushkeene.
  'As you are his heir, the world might not
think that a sacrifice. Could you work
against Vladimeer ? answer that.'
  'I could !'
  'You swear you could follow my directions—implicitly—in the plan proposed !'
  'I swear it !'
  They shook hands on this understanding,
and made an engagement for the morrow.

CHAPTER IX.

HELEN RADOWSKY SETS TRAPS.

  After Michael Pushkeene left, Helen Radowsky sat for some time before the fire,
with her little white hands firmly clasped
on her lap, and her unwinking eyes fixed on
the fire. The face, usually so intellectual

and pretty—even beautiful—had an aged expression; there was a deep perpendicular line between the brows, and the firmly set mouth was drawn down, as if trying by force of will, to kill a pain at her heart.

'He looked so like a demi-god, so held me with his wondrous eyes, that my arm became paralyzed, and my mission a failure. I called up the sufferings of my dead father, and the vow I made as a child and repeated so often as a woman, to be avenged on the house of Gallitzin. But I could not draw the dagger from its sheath in my breast to bury it in his. I must not go near him, must never see him again, else it will weaken the purpose of my life.'

She began stroking her brow and patting one of her dainty feet on the rug before the fire. A low, mocking, self-deprecating laugh burst from her lips as she continued:

'Am I such a fool as to feel anything like love—I, who have steeled my heart against men that I might the better carry out the purpose of my life? I am weakest where I felt sure of my strength. My father's avenger has become a forgetful child in the presence of the man whose sire subjected mine to torture, and threw him, aged, and weakened, and poor, and homeless, on the unfeeling world!'

She rose to her feet and spoke, with all the wonderful intensity of her low, musical voice:

'I swear it again! By the blood of my fathers, I will not turn to the right nor the left until my mission be accomplished! I feel the Divine mandate ringing through my brain—' *Vengeance is mine, I will repay!'* And in my ears still throbs the echo of Sinai's thunder, and the awful words, '*I will visit the sins of the fathers upon the children!*''

So absorbed was Helen Radowsky in her own thoughts that she did not become aware of the entrance of the white-capped serving-maid until that person twice repeated:

'A gentleman in the hall to see Miss Radowsky.'

A gentleman, Catherine?'

'Yes, Miss.'

'And did he give his name?'

'No, Miss.'

'What looks he like?'

'Short, stout, full beard, deep voice, aged about thirty,' replied the servant.

'Well sketched, Catherine. Show Mr. Varwitch in.'

The servant retired, and immediately a man answering her description entered the room.

'Ah! Peter Varwitch, my dear friend, I am glad to see you. I was just thinking about you,' said Helen Radowsky, placing a chair for her visitor and sitting down beside him.

'My master dines out to-night,' said Varwitch, 'and I could not resist the opportunity to come over and have a talk with you.'

His voice was very deep, and his utterance deliberate. He was the man who charged Michael Pushkeene with treason at the last Nihilist meeting.

'I am always glad to see you—'

'I wish you were only gladder,' said Varwitch, with an amorous growl and a nervous stroking of his beard.

'Let us rule that subject out to night, Peter. I have given you hope, and that is more than other suitors can say. Were I indifferent you should know it.'

'That is true Helen, but I have made a great sacrifice to secure hope,' he said.

'A great sacrifice!' she repeated.

'Yes! do you not think it is a sacrifice for the gentleman, Peter Varwitch, to take a menial's place in the house of the Prince Gallitzin just to gratify your whims?'

'Truly, it is something of a sacrifice, Peter,' she said, with a winsome smile. 'But the man who wins my love must submit to my tests.'

'Granted; but why should you care to humiliate the man who loves you as I do, by insisting on his remaining in a menial position?'

'Can you not assign a reason for it, Peter?' she asked, with great seriousness.

'I can guess,' he responded.

'And what do you guess in this case?'

'That you want to have a friend in constant contact with General Gallitzin.'

'You have my reason more clearly and fully than I could express it.'

'And how long is this thing to last?'

'Not very long, I hope,' she answered.

'Till he is out of the way?'

'Till I have gained my ends, Peter.'

'What are your ends?'

'To test you first; and then to use that test as a means to destroy him to whose house mine owes its ruin,' she said, with emphasis.

Peter Varwitch stroked his long, brown beard, and still keeping his sharp gray eyes fixed on the fantastic heap of coals, he said:

'I heard it rumored, some days since, that a desperate woman's hand would have put him out of the way before this. The woman is a leader of the Nihilists here—and she has a wrong to avenge. Arrangements were made for her flight, and she actually went to the residence of the prince to enforce her purpose—' Peter Varwitch paused, and after looking into her resolute eyes for some seconds, added: 'But she not only did not carry out her threat, but permitted the prince to take her home in his own sleigh.'

'All of which I believe to be true,' said Helen Radowsky, lightly. Then, in a more serious vein; 'I heard that th' woman changed her mind, at the last moment, and determined upon a destruction more terrible than sudden death; while at the same time she could advance the cause to which she is espoused. All this she will explain at the meeting to-night; and she is certain every man and woman of sense will agree with her.'

'As people always agree with her I am sure they will in this case.' Peter Varwitch looked at her with undisguised admiration, and added, with an altered manner: ' I understood she failed because Vladimeer Ruloff put the prince on his guard.'

'But did he?' she asked, quickly.

'That he did.'

'How do you know?'

'I heard him, plainly as I hear myself now. I was concealed near by, ready to seize the assassin of my master—when the work was done.'

'You heard Vladimeer Ruloff tell the prince who I was?'

'Yes, and who your father was. He confessed that he placed his own life in danger by uttering the warning—and he did; for I had my pistol raised to shoot him,' said Varwitch, throwing off all the third person ambiguity in which he had been indulging.

'I am glad you did not. This matter must be kept to ourselves for the present. Vladimeer the Nihilist has sealed his own fate. Perhaps it is as well, for his destruction was decided on.'

After an embarrassing pause, Varwitch asked:

'Are you yet satisfied that Michael Pushkeene is a traitor?'

'I never had any doubt of it,' she replied.

'And still you try to shield him.'

'To shield him?' she repeated.

'Yes. You have shut off the investigation I proposed.'

'So I did. Pushkeene is at this time an invaluable man. I am setting traps, Peter.'

'Familiar work,' he chuckled.

'I am setting traps,' she repeated. ' And the duty of springing them will devolve on Pushkeene -'

'I pray,' interrupted Varwitch, ' that you may have your traps so constructed as to spring them when Pushkeene is on the inside.'

'The biggest trap, the most tempting trap, is set for himself. It is baited with the beautiful daughter of a countess. The meaner the blood,' she sneered, ' the more

anxious it is to ally itself with the blood of the noble.'

'I have unbounded faith in your ability and caution.'

'Thank you, Peter. Let me return the compliment by saying: I have unbounded faith in your fidelity and devotion.'

'You have Helen?' he asked, eagerly.

'I have.'

'Then why continue testing me? Why not say the word that will make me happy, and permit us to work with double the strength, working, as we can, altogether?'

'Because, Peter, the time has not come. You must continue in patience.'

The white-capped servant came in, with a great preliminary coughing, and announced that dinner was ready. Helen Radowsky asked her visitor to dine with her, but he pleaded another engagement, hinting that it would be a great pleasure to make an appointment for some time ahead; and Helen gratified him.

'I will see you to-night,' she whispered, as he was about to withdraw.

'At the masked ball?'

'Yes, Peter.'

'Very well.'

'And remember, Peter, not a word to a soul of our own secrets.'

CHAPTER X.

PRINCE GORTSCHAKOFF'S BANQUET.

The palaces of St. Petersburg are unsurpassed by those of any other capital on the continent. The residences of many of the nobles are magnificent beyond the dreams of the kings of two centuries ago, and their appointments are quite in keeping with their regal splendor.

It is not to be wondered at that the ignorant peasant, in his dim, damp, smoky hovel, should look up at the noble in his palace as being of superior creation, predestined to use all beneath him for his own aggrandizement. It is not to be marvelled at that the intelligent Russian, eating the black bread of poverty, and crushed down by tyrannical laws, should raise his matted head and demand: ' By what right do these masters rule, when I and my children are famished slaves?' It is useless to shout ' precedent!' and ' power!' Every railroad and telegraph piercing the steppes of Russia daily diffuses freedom's light from the Occidental world; and that light illumines the clouded brain of the patient, down-trodden toiler and sets him to thinking. No law can check thought; and to think is to be impelled to utterance. The powers may issue ukases, multiply knouts, and fill the prisons, while keeping the executioner busy; but it is as impossible for the human will to alter the course of the seasons as to check the growth of liberty and enlightenment, once they have taken root in the human heart. To plow them down is to enrich the soil for a stronger crop.

But this is a digression, though called out, very naturally, by the subject.

Prince Gortschakoff's palace, near the Admiralty, is second only to the palace of the Czar. It is guarded by a detail of imperial troops. It is kept in order by a corps of liveried servants. Its appointments are unsurpassed in their way ; and all is in keeping with the wealth, power and standing of its mighty master.

In the grand banquet hall of this palace the foremost kings of the world have been entertained ; and they felt honored in being the guests of that wonderful man, who, with more than imperial power, and a will superhuman in its force, guided Russia from semi-barbarism to semi-civilization ; increasing her broad domain, and welding, on the ringing anvils of war, her varied races into a homogeneous mass.

The palace of the prince was illuminated to-night till its spires and embattled walls stood out in bold and dazzling relief against the black back ground of sky. The brilliant salons, with their paintings, bronzes, hangings, chandeliers, and carpets, were ablaze with light, and alive with beauty and chivalry.

Here art had set the seasons at defiance ; for though the snow lay six feet deep on the level without, the palms of tropical India and the giant ferns of the Amazon could be seen through the open conservatory, in whose huge tanks rested the broad leaves of the Victoria Regia. Bronze vases of priceless worth and exquisite workmanship were capped with brilliant exotics, that filled the air with a dreamy suggestiveness of balmy nights in sunny lands.

Out of sight, in a gallery that seemed miles away, so delusive and enchanting was the effect, the band of the Imperial Guard was stationed, and the music floated down like a celestial adjunct to the glories of this entrancing terrestrial vision.

Here were two princes of the royal house and a son of England's queen and India's empress. Here were the representatives of every government with which Russia holds intercourse, clad in the resplendent court robes of their respective States ; their breasts covered with jeweled orders that denoted their sovereign's appreciation. The war ships, frozen up at Cronstadt, must have poured into the Gortschakoff palace their officers young and old, for patches of blue and gold met the eye wherever it turned.

Every officer not on duty in the city must have been invited, for the uniform of every regiment in the service could be seen among the guests.

The golden haired daughters of the North, with their blue eyes and calm bearing, were grouped with the dark-eyed daughters of the South, all life and vivacity, as if the splendor of these surroundings were common to them.

The master of this magnificent palace, the host of all these happy guests, received his visitors at the further end of the main salon. He looked as calm and self possessed as if transacting business in his private office, yet he showed that interest in each one that came near as led him to believe his happiness was a matter of much consideration to the great man.

' Has Prince Gallitzin yet arrived ? ' asked General Gortschakoff, addressing Count Kiseleff, who stood near by in conversation with the beautiful Countess Alexandrina.

' He has just entered,' said the count, glancing down the salon to where General Gallitzin stood, a head above the tallest, and strikingly distinguished from that host of handsome men by his splendid bearing and noble cast of face.

' I have not seen him since I was a little girl ; how very handsome he is,' said the countess, her bright gray eyes aglow with admiration, as the prince advanced to pay his respects to his host.

' I feared,' said General Gortschakoff, after he had introduced the prince to his niece, and critically watched the expression of their faces, ' that something had detained you.'

' Yes ; an unexpected message connected with the service. I regret that I have lost a minute of this pleasure,' said the prince, with a courtly bow to his host, and a gallant glance at the beautiful girl by his side.

' He has all the ways of his father.' I can see, they are prepossessed at once,' thought the old diplomat.

He arose from his chair, and motioning to Count Kiseleff, said :

' Your arm my dear Count. I am not feeling strong to-night.'

Count Kiseleff was a born courtier, and so affected to be delighed that General Gortschakoff should ask for his arm, but a pang of jealously shot through his heart, leaving in its track the seeds of bitter hate for the man who was as evidently the great statesman's favorite as he was the admired of his brother officers and the idol of the ladies who had met him.

General Gallitzin promenaded with the Countess Alexandrina, until he became aware that every group in the salons was watching them, and of course making them objects of flattering comment.

'You can see and hear, General,' said the fair countess, 'that your fame has preceded you; and that you have stormed the hearts of Saint Petersburg as effectually as you did the redoubts at Plevna.'

'It is pleasant to think one is not wholly unworthy regard; but I can assure you I would as soon face a battery of guns as the battery of those many beautiful eyes. Let us seek a retired place, where we can sit down and talk undisturbed,' said the general.

The countess led him to a niche in which was an S shaped *tete-a-tete*, and said, as they sat down:

'I am so glad that you have not forgotten me.'

'How could I ?' he asked.

'Oh, very easily. Twelve years is a long time; and boys of thirteen are only a trifle more interesting than girls of seven or eight. You remember where we met ?'

'At Count Ruloff's,' replied the general.

'And the occasion ?'

'The occasion ! Yes, let me recall. I think it was Vladimeer's eleventh or twelfth birthday.'

'Your memory is excellent,' she said, with a bewitching smile. Then she asked, with a sigh in her voice: 'Have you seen the Rulloffs since your return to Saint Petersburg ?'

'I have. I could not think of forsaking old friends, just because the world has. I have always felt that the count was the victim of some base conspiracy.'

'Your heart is quite equal to your memory. I feel just as you do, but have been afraid to say so,' said the countess. 'You must know that it is considered treasonable to say a word in defence of the Ruloffs. I, of course, say nothing, and the consequence is my heart has been for some time full of this kind of treason. You see I am placing myself in your power,' she laughed.

'You can rely on me. But seriously, do you not think something can be done to help the Ruloffs ? No charge has been brought against the countess, nor against her daughter—'

'No, General, nor against Vladimeer, said the young lady with spirit.

'Nor against my life-long friend, Vladimeer,' rejoined the prince.

'I wish I knew what could be done. I have been afraid to speak to any one, though I have thought over very many plans and have written my sympathies to—to Vladimeer,' said the countess,

'I am very glad, my dear Countess, that you suggested this subject. I must confess that one strong inducement for me to take the position I now occupy, was the hope that I might be able to get another hearing for Count Ruloff. I am deeply interested in his family.

'If you would direct me, there is nothing I am not willing to do. But you know how unapproachable my grand-uncle Gortschakoff is.'

'I am aware of that ; but why can we not unite for this purpose ?' asked the prince.

'There is no reason why we should not,' she answered.

'I believe conspirators are always supposed to be plotting evil; let us make an exception by plotting good. What say you ?' the prince extended his hand.

'I agree,' she said, placing her hand in his.

They were in this interesting attitude when Count Kiseleff suddenly made his appearance and took in the situation at a glance. He stamered out an apology and withdrew precipitately.

'There,' said the countess, when they were alone again. 'You have done me a marked service.'

'I ?'

'Yes, you.'

'I am delighted to hear it, but must confess I am not aware of how it was done,' said the perplexed prince.

'Then I must explain,' laughed the countess. 'Count Kiseleff has been pleased to rank himself among my admirers, and to show marked jealously at anything like rivalry. He saw our hands clasped, and putting his own construction on the act, he will keep aloof from me henceforth. He would not dare to enter the lists against Prince Gallitzin.'

'My dear Countess, said the Prince, if you be not mistaken, you lose a troublesome admirer to make me a foe.'

'General Gallitzin is not afraid of such foes,' said the countess, rising and taking his arms.

'Not afraid, perhaps; yet a foe is none the more the disirable that we do not fear him. And then,' he added, archly, 'I do not relish being blamed without good cause.'

'We are united—to aid the Ruloffs. Hark ! the band is playing a march; that means supper. You must continue your escort.'

And the prince conducted her to the banquet hall.

CHAPTER XI.

CONSPIRATORS IN COUNCIL.

'I wish you to congratulate me, said Vladimeer Ruloff, as he sprang into the elevated apartment where his mother and sister were sewing and began to kiss them and wring their hands. 'Congratulate me, for I am at last successful!'

'Successful!' exclaimed both.

'Yes! I have secured the clerkship,'

'With the American merchant?' asked his mother.

'With the American merchant, dear mother. It seems that Mr. Jonathan Cushing met General Gallitzin in America, where they became friends. Yesterday they met in Saint Petersburg for the first time. Mr. Cushing mentioned my name, and spoke of me as an applicant; whereupon, with his usual earnestness and generosity, the general advocated my abilities and fitness for the office of translator and correspondent, and so it comes about that I have carried off the position from twenty competitors. No more sewing for money, sister; no more eating the black bread of poverty. Three hundred roubles a month will enable us to live in comfort and in better quarters. We must get other apartments at once!'

And Vladimeer Ruloff snapped his fingers, waved his fur cap, and danced about like a delighted boy.

'I thank God,' said Madam Ruloff, fervently, 'for this evidence of His goodness. It comes like the gleam of a star through the blackness of a long-clouded sky.

'Now that I am getting used to work,' said Elizabeth, her blue eyes looking larger for their rings of moisture, and her white teeth gleaming like pearls in a setting of rubies—'now that I am getting used to the work, I rather like it. Of course, I am glad for all our sakes, but I am particularly glad for yours, dear brother.'

'For my sake, Elizabeth?'

'Yes, Vladimeer; you will be happier for having something besides our misfortunes to occupy your mind. My work has been a blessing to me in that respect,' replied Elizabeth.

'And,' added Madam Ruloff, 'it will prevent your having so much of the company of that very undesirable young person, Mr. Michael Pushkeene.'

'You are both right. I must confess I am growing weary of Pushkeene. He never could be congenial, but he sympathized with us in our troubles, which is a great deal; and then, he is a man of more ordinary intelligence, though a little mysterious and apparently sly. I have been anxious to drop him ever since I learned that he aspired to the hand of a woman who could not even tolerate him. But let him go,' said Vladimeer, waving his hands. 'I feel now as if the curtain were about to rise and discover an improved situation: the brave,

good father coming in, in the last scene, to bless us and remain with us forever,'

The room grew brighter, and the humble meal to which the three sat down soon after seemed to them more like a banquet than anything they had eaten for a long time. It had been many a day since a smile was seen on the troubled face of Madam Ruloff, but now she beamed on her children, and looked younger and happier than since that day that so crushed her life.

The repast was but just concluded when Ruryk the Cossack, made his appearance with a basket of luscious fruit for Madam Ruloff, and a note for Elizabeth. That note was more precious to the beautiful girl than all the fruit and flowers and precious stones in the world. It had all the effect of the fabled enchanter's wand, for it conveyed her into the presence of the man whom she loved with all the fervor of her pure, gentle heart.

'And you are going out again to-night, Vladimeer?' asked the madam, in a voice shaded with disappointment, as she noted her son's preparations.

'Yes, dear mother; but once I am down at hard word, which will be every day after to-morrow, I will remain with you during all my unemployed hours. I go to-night to keep an engagement made some time ago,' said Vladimeer, standing beside her, cap in hand.

'I have so dreaded, Vladimeer, that a sense of the wrongs we have endured, acting on your strong, impulsive nature, might have led you to seek the companionship of the revolutionary spirits, that, like moles, work blindly and out of sight, sapping the pillars of the government, and never dreaming that if they bring those pillars down they who have wrought the ruin will be killed and buried where they stand. Remember that while it is horrible to suffer under a false accusation, it is trebly horrible to run into a position that makes the accusation merited.'

'I quite agree with you, my mother, nor will I deny that I have associated, in my desperate hours, with the people you spoke of. But you mistake if you think the feeling of discontent and the spirit of revolt is confined to the toilers out of sight. There is not a rank below the throne that is not disaffected. Nihilism, as it is called for the want of a better name, is rife in the army; it permeates the Greek church, from the humblest sacristan up to the head of the order; it clings to the navy—out of sight, to be sure—but it clings like barnacles; it is whispered in the schools, and hinted at in the salons; and every violent attempt at suppression deepens the malignity and spreads the disease, with which even the throne is contaminated. But do not fear for me. I shal be too busy working for my dear ones, and praying for the return of the absent, to care for the form of government, or its rights or wrongs.'

'It makes me happy to hear you say so,' said the madam, taking his arm and walking with him to the door.

Vladimeer descended to the narrow street, and was making his way towards the barrack-like house—where it will be remembered the maskers played a curious game cn New Year's night—when two men came out from the cover of an archway, and one of them addressed him in the unmistakable voice of Michael Pushkeene.

'Ah, my dear Ruloff, I expected you would pass this way and waited. This is my friend, Mr. Neuman, from Moscow,' said Pushkeene, presenting a man who looked enough like himself to be a twin brother.

Mr. Neuman, from Moscow, said something about a great pleasure, and feeling very happy at meeting the son of the distinguished but unfortunate Count Ruloff.

'I presume, from your name, Mr. Neuman, you are a German,' said Vladimeer, resuming his walk by the side of that gentleman.

'No, sir, I feel proud to say I am a Russian. My ancestors, however, like the ancestors of some of the best in the empire, were Germans,' said Neuman.

'By my faith,' laughed Vladimeer, ' if it were a crime to have German blood in one's veins the imperial family of Russia, and for the matter of that, the Royal family of England, and of nine-tenths of our monarchical countries, would be guilty beyond hope of salvation.'

'Yes,' snickered Pushkeene ; ' my mother was a German. But there is a stronger tie than nationality ; the bond that unites freemen against tyranny ; *Mr. Neuman is one of us.*' This information was given with whispered emphasis.

'Is Mr. Newman going with us ?' asked Vladimeer.

'Oh, certainly ! I shall vouch for him, though he could work his way into any meeting from Finlan to the Ukraine,' replied Pushkeene.

'Let us not talk about these matters on the street,' said Newman, cautiously. ' The city is filled with spies.'

'Aye, the land is filled with them,' rejoined Vladimeer.

They reached the barrack-like house, and as on New Year's night, the door swung open as they approached and closed behind them, when they had entered the wide, dim hall. They ascended the cataract of stairs, and in the upper hall were challenged by a tall man disguised in a mask and black gown. The same questions were asked and answered as on a former occasion. They went into the ante-room, and from the honeycomb in the wall from both sides, and the rolling back of the partition, which closed behind them as they entered the apartment, about which sat, or were grouped, very many maskers.

'We have drawn,' said a hoarse-voiced man, coming forward. ' You are too late to take an active part in the proceedings.

'It will be just as improving to listen,' said Vladimeer, taking a chair.

The deep-voiced man, who was none other than Varwitch, went to the head of the table, and wrapping to attract attention said:

'I drew the ace of hearts to-night. The fifty-two will take their places.'

Fifty-two men and women—Varwitch making fifty-two—held up their cards, and sat down before corresponding cards on the table.

Varwitch, as was the custom in assuming the chair of presiding officer, made a speech reviewing public and socialistic affairs since the last meeting, and cautioning the members to greater secrecy.

'I fear,' he said, 'that through the recklessness of friends, spies have been admitted into our camp ; it is so in other places. We should guard against this The man who comes here as a spy takes his life in his hands, and   should ease him of the care of a thing that is dangerous to us.'

A murmur of applause went round the table, and the groups in the back-ground showed their approval.

'I am now ready to receive reports,' said the ace of hearts, sitting down and trying to hide his beard under his mask and inside his gown.

A petite figure rose, and holding up the ten of diamonds, to distinguish herself, said :

'I speak for the committee appointed to investigate certain charges against one Michael Pushkeene.'

It was the low, thrilling voice of Helen Radowsky.

'And what is your report ?' asked Varwitch.

'I report with pleasure that the charges are unfounded. We have found the accused to be a good man, a strong friend and a patroit, in the best sense of that abused word,' said the ten of diamonds.

Michael Pushkeene and his friend Neuman, from Moscow, applauded, while a tall man with red beard, who sat about the middle of the table—he was the ace of hearts the night before—showed disapproval by coughing and muttering incoherently.

'I will state,' said the presiding officer, 'that action in the case of Ghourko's successor has been postponed for the present.'

'I have to state,' said a slender person, speaking in boyish tones and holding up the ace of spades,' that it has been decided to strike at the very fountain head of our wrongs.'

'In what way?' asked Varwitch.

'By killing the Czar!' said the boyish voice, with thrilling emphasis.

'And who has decided this?'

'I have,' replied the youth.

'You!'

'Yes, I. Do you doubt my courage or my power!'

'I doubt neither; but I do doubt the prudence of such an act—at this time,' replied Varwitch.

'It is not with me,' said the youth, 'a question of prudence.'

'Of what then?'

'Of vengeance,' he responded, and his eyes flashed through the black mask, and his white hands were ground in desperation.

'Vengeance" repeated the assembled people, in an awful whisper.

'Aye, vengeance! I had an only brother, a brave soldier and an officer in the service of the Czar. I loved him as I loved my own life—but he is no more,' said the youth, in a cho king voice.

'No more!' gasped the people, like a ghostly echo.

'He is no more,' repeated the youth. 'He was charged with treason, of which he was innocent; tried by a court, convened to convict, that the army might be taught a lesson. He was found guilty and sentenced to death.'

'To death!' like another echo.

'My poor, broken-hearted mother came on here from Odessa, and she and I, yesterday, threw ourselves before the Czar and begged for the life of the condemned man, then in the dungeons of Cronstadt. The Czar spurned us! the Guards drove us away with their swords.'

He clutched at his throat as if strangling.

'And you got no mercy;' asked Helen Radowsky.

'Mercy! This morning my brother was hanged like a dog, on the battlement of Cronstadt, and the news of his death was the last thing my mother heard on earth. I have a right to decide.'

The youth sat down, and a chilling silence of some minutes followed.

Other stories of outrages were told, until the meeting had worked itself up to a demonlike fury, all the stronger that prudence forced them to restrain, and even prevented their finding relief by shouting at the top of their voices, as many wished to do.

When the meeting broke up, the people went out by twos, Pushkeene and his friend Neuman, of Moscow, leaving together.

As Vladimeer rose, half-determined that this would be his last visit, though his feelings were more bitter than ever against the authorities, the tall man with the red beard took his arm and whispered:

'I am Captain Freehoff, let us leave together.'

Vladimeer greeted him like an old friend, and they went out arm in arm.

CHAPTER XII.

THE CONSPIRATORS STRIKE THE FIRST BLOW.

'Well,' said Captain Freehoff, when he and Vladimeer reached the street, and were waling on the unfrequented side, 'what did you think of the meeting?'

'It gave me the horrors,' replied Vladimeer. 'I do not think I will attend again.'

'That is about the conclusion I have reached.' Captain Freeman stopped before reaching the corner of the next street, and drawing Vladimeer into the shadow of a neighboring house, he continued: 'You know that I have ever been the friend of my old commander, Count Ruloff, and his family?'

'I am sure of that, Captain,' replied Vladimeer.

'I am not an alarmist, but I keep my eyes open. If I could point to an actual, manifest danger, I would warn you at once, but I cannot. Without being absolutely certain, however, I feel that you have enemies, and that they are setting a trap for you.'

'Enemies!' repeated Vladimeer.

'Yes, enemies. Do not ask me, for I do not positively know. But beware of Helen Radowsky and Michael Pushkeene.'

The captain wrung Vladimeer's hand, and without waiting for another word, turned and went back in the direction from which they had come.

'This certainly is mysterious,' thought Vladimeer, as he walked homeward, with downhead, 'and yet I have had my fears of Miss Radowsky. She is a demon. Well, well! I shall go to work to-morrow, and while General Gallitzin uses his great power for the return of my father. I will earn enough to keep the dear mother and sister above want; and it may be that I will be able, now and then, through the general, to get a glimpse of Alexandrina. I am sure she is true and will respect me the more for my efforts.'

The tender and ever-delightful subject of the beautiful countess was running through his mind, when he reached the door opened into the high, lean structure of which he lived.

He took out his key, and was about to insert it in the lock, when he became suddenly aware that a man stood on either of the entrance.

Before he could ask what they wanted one of the men stepped forward and asked :

'Are you Vladimeer, the son of Count Ruloff, the exile ?'

'I am."

The other man stepped out, and laying a heavy hand on Vladimeer's shoulders, he said :

'Vladimeer Ruloff, I arrest you in the name of his imperial majesty, Alexis, Czar of all the Russias.'

The words came to Vladimeer with all the force of crushing blows. At length he managed to ask :

'By whose order am I arrested ?'

'By the order of General the Prince Gallitzin of Novgorod, chief of his majesty's secret police,' replied the man.

'There must be a mistake.'

'We make no mistakes We obey orders Come quietly, or we shall use these.' The man drew from his pocket a pair of handcuffs, and shock them before Vladimeer's face.

'I will go with you without resistance, for I have done no wrong ; but first I desire to speak with my mother and sister, who lodge in this house.'

We cannot allow it. Come.'

Can I not send them word ?' pleaded Vladimeer, ' that my absence may be explained ?'

'With your absence we have nothing to do. Your presence is demanded at the Prison of the Exiles. Come.'

Vladimeer cast a glance up at the light buring in the upper stery ; it told him that his mother was up and waiting for him, as was her habit, no matter how late he came home. Then he turned with the feeling that he was suffering from a horrid nightmare, and walked off between the police.

They escorted him across the Troiskoi Bridge, and through the gloomy, vault-like gate that marked the entrance to the prison. The dark, massive walls, pierced by grated windows like port-holes, rose gloomy and gray around a central court, into which tier over tier of black doors opened. It seemed the temple of darkness, and silence, and death. Cold as it was on the streets, here it seemed many degrees colder. A stunted tree, like a distorted skeleton, raised its arms in the centre of the court, and through the embattled coping of the walls the wintry wind howled and groaned like a giant in torture.

One of the men rapped three times with the handcuffs on a low, broad, iron-studded door. There was a rattling of chains and an ominous jarring of bolts inside; then, with a dismal squeak, the black door opened inwards, and a flood of yellow light poured out.

The door swung shut behind them with a dull shud, and Vladimeer found himself in a square room, benches around the wall, and a roaring stove in the centre. On these benches a number of uniformed men were stretched in full length, their muskets being stacked in a corner. On the side, opposite the door, a swarthy, hairy man sat at a desk, with a lard lamp throwing its light on a ponderous book. The book must have been in great danger of escape, for it was chaimed to the desk ; and for its further intimidation a pile of handcuffs glistened near by.

Whom bring you here ?' demanded the swarthy giant, as he jabbed an iron pen into an iron bottle buried like a little black sea in the desk, and prepared to write down the answers in the imprisoned book.

'Vladimeer, son of the exiled Count Ruloff,' replied one of the secret police.

'Vladimeer, son of the exiled Count Ruloff,' repeated the swarthy giant, as he wrote down the words.

'His age ?'

The policeman, not being able to reply, nudged Vladimeer and whispered :

'Answer the other questions yourself.'

'I am twenty-three,' replied Vladimeer.

'Where born ?'

'At Cronstadt.'

'Occupation ?'

'Interpreter and commercial correspondent.'

'By whom employed ?'

'The American house of Mr. Jonathan Cushing.'

'Residence ?'

'Number ten Little Neva Prospekt.'

'Married ?'

'No.'

'Relatives ?'

'Mother and sister.'

'Friends to whom you could apply for proof of character if required ?'

'General the Prince Gallitzin of Novgorod,'replied Vladimeer.

'General Gallitzin !' repeated the police.

·The Prince Gallitzin !' muttered the swarthy secretary, raising his shaggy head and looking at the prisoner for the first time.

'I so said.'

'With what crime are you charged ?'

'That I know not.' replied Vladimeer. ' But I do know that I have been guilty of no wrong.'

'He is charged with treason against our

imperial master, the Czar,' said the detective who had been acting as spokesman.

'Charge—Treason,' replied the secetary, dashing off the word with the rapidity and dexterity of one accustomed to writing it.

'That will do. Search him, then take him to cell 147. The trial, on account of previous cases, cannot take place for three days.'

The secretary closed the book, and sucked the tip of the iron pen with a savage relish.

The policemen, after emptying Vladimeer's pockets, formed on either side, and were about to lead him off, but refusing to move, he asked:

'Can I not communicate with my mother at once ?'

'No,' snapped the secretary.

'Nor with General Gallitzin ?'

'No.'

'When can I ?'

'That I cannot answer. I give and record information, but have neither the power nor the wish to grant favors,' said the savage.

Vladimeer Ruloff was marched off, but he did not hold down his head—that he would not, could not have done if going to his grave.

They led him through many long, dismal dimly lit halls, into which grated doors opened on either hand, and from behind which groans and the rattle of chains could be heard, and the hollow coughing of prisoners in whose lungs Death was drawing up the inevitable warrants of release.

The fall of their feet sounded to Vladimeer like first clods of earth dropping on a lowered coffin.

They stopped at the end of the hall particularly cold and gloomy, where two men sat dozing on a bench.

One of the men had a musket in his hand ; the other carried at his girdle two immense bunches of keys. The man with the keys rubbed his eyes, rose and asked :

'What is it ?'

'Cell 147,' replied the spokesman.

'147.' The man fumbled over the labels attached to the keys, and finding the right one, he slipped it from its hook, waved it like a grim baton, and said :

'This way.'

He inserted the key in the door near by, and with a considerable expenditure of strength, turned it in the lock and pushed in the door, a puff of damp, sickening air rushing out as he did so.

'You must go in there. You will find a bench to lie on."

The policemen pushed Vladimeer in, and the door closed behind him, leaving him in a suffocating atmosphere and a Stygian darkness.

He groped for the bench, and threw him-self along it in full length as the echo of the retreating policemen's laughter died out in the distance.

CHAPTER XIII.

IN THE DUNGEON—IN THE GARRET.

Had all the mental conditions been favorable, Vladimeer Ruloff could have have slept in that damp, mephitic dungeon cell. The air was musty and poisonously impure. There was no draft, and yet the place was hyperborean in temperature. But he did not heed his surroundings. The physical torture was quite overwhelmed and sunk out of sight in the torrent of anguish that surged through brain and heart.

He could not hide from himself that he was a conspirator, banded against the government with other discontented spirits ; nor could he upbraid himself with his conduct, in view of the treatment his family had received at the bands of a merciless tyranny. Yet it was horrible to think that just as his foot was on the threshold of a new life, that promised healthful employment for himself and a competency for his loved ones, that this trap'should be sprung, leaving death or banishment to stare him in the face ; for from the powers that placed him in this dungeon he could expect no mercy.

Through the long black hours, so in keeping with his clouded life, he bewildered—not his own fate—but that of his mother and sister, who would now be left alone in the world.

His loyal heart never once harbored a thought against his friend, General Gallitzin. The prince was not responsible for, did not, could not know of this outrage.

And when he thought of the gallant soldier, hope came, with the promise of release and future security from arrest.

'General Gallitzin,' thought Vladimeer, ' is all powerful with the Czar. He is the idol of Saint Petersburg at this time, and deserves to be. He will hear of my arrest, and come to my relief. I am a fool in despair, and I would not, had I calmly considered my position before.'

Drowning men to catch the straws, and even the lightning that heralds destruction is a relief to one wrapped in darkness. Vladimeer Ruloff's despair gradually vanished, but not so the long Russian night—long enough in the illuminated palaces, but interminable to the hundreds of groaning, coughing victims shut up in the cells, buried alive in this catacomb above ground.

Vladimeer took no note of time. Now and then he heard the guard, pacing the corridor outside, and the bang of the musket butt on the stone floor when the round came to an end.

He was surely dozing, though at first it seemed as if any sleep but that of death were impossible in such a place. He heard a grating in the lock, and started up, just as the door opened, and the flash of a lantern cut, like a bunch of lance blades, through the solid blackness of the cell. The lantern was fastened to the belt of a muffled figure, who stood like a giant silhouette in the opening.

'Are you awake ?' asked the man in the door.

'Awake ! Who could sleep in. such a place ?' asked Vladimeer.

'You'll sleep comfortably enough when you get used to it. Here's your breakfast.'

The man set a loaf of hard, black bread and a brown pitcher, filled with water, on the end of the bench, and was about to withdraw, when Vladimeer called to him.

'Stop my friend, I would speak with you,'

'I have not time. My friends forbid my speaking with prisoners,' replied the man, as he fumbled with the key.

'I am Vladimeer, the son of Count Ruloff, and the friend of your master, General Gallitzin,' s id Vladimeer, speaking hurriedly. 'If you get word to the gen ral that I am here, I can promise you a reward.'

'Why get word to him, when you are here by his order ? Bear your imprisonment with patience.'

The man half closed the door, and was in the act of shutting it, when he stopped, put in his head, and said :

'So you are Vladimeer, the son of Count Ruloff ?'

'I am.'

'It is very curious—might not har pen aga n in a thousand years,' sai l the man, musingly.

'What is curious ?'

'Why, that you should be in this cell. We call it 'the fatal cell,' for never a man that occupied it was declared innocent on trial. This was where your father was confined up to the hour that he was sent to Siberia,'

Vladime r fell back on the bench with a gasp. The door closed ; and the man went on to open other cell doors, and give to their suffering occupants their daily allowance of black bread and water.

While Vladimeer lay in his cell, his mother with increasing fear and anxiety, sat by the window in the upper story, straining he: eyes down the narrow street, in the hope of catching a glimpse of her son, and bending her head at every gust of wind that shook the crisp snow from the roof in expectation of catching the footfall—as familiar as his voice.

The lard lamp burned lower, and threatened soon to lea e her in darkness, if not replenished. She left it in the window, and went back to a little room where Elizabeth lay, but not asleep.

'Vladimeer has not yet returned, my, daughter,' said Madam Ruloff, with a half suppressed sob.

'I know it, my mother. I have not slept, but have listened all through the night. Come, lie down. I fear no danger to him. Doubt not but he will return by daylight with some good excuse,' said Elizabeth, with well-assumed cheerfulness.

'But he never stayed out so late before. I may be unduly nervous, Elizabeth. I hope I am.'

'I feel very sure you are, dear mother. Come lie down, for the night is cold, and you must be suffering,' urged Elizabeth.

As if she had never heard her daughter's words, Madame Ruloff continued :

'It was just such a night, one year ago, that your father left to dine with a friend. He came not back that night, and it was days before we learned his fate.'

'True, darling mother ; but General Gallitzin, was not then at the head of the secret police,' rejoined Elizabeth.

'And if he were, his powe n ight be futile before the edict of the Czar. Was not your father as rich, as honored, as trusted, before his arrest as is General Gallitzin now ?'

'True, my mother ; but he occupied a different place.'

'Place, honor, wealth, or service, count not in the eyes of our masters, The breath of the meanest spy in the realm is powerful to tarnish the brightest reputation below the throne. Oh ! she wailed, with hands clasped, as she fell on her knees before the bed, 'God's face is averted from Russia. and ruin crouches in every home, and the black wings of death beat the air above every house ! Better be an ignorant peasant, in a more favoured land, than to bask in the royal favor of a land so uncertain as this ! The only security here is in the grave ! The daring of the Russian soldier, the indifference to life of the people, is due to the living death we are forced to endure ! Oh ! my son ! my son ! my Vladimeer ! if harm has come to you this night my heart will break ! I can no longer endure this torture ! Better that I could curse Russia and its ruler—and die !'

'Do not give way, dear mother !' sobbed Elizabeth, drawing her mother's head nearer, and kissing her. 'I will dress and go out. I may learn something from the police. I could go to Michael Pushkeene's; perhaps he could tell me something about

Vladimeer. But I see no cause for your great anxiety.'

Elizabeth was about to rise, but her mother held her back.

' No, my child, stay you here. Hark ! the bells are striking six. It is morning. I wil go out, and return before breakfast.'

Madame Ruloff threw on her hood and mantle—relics of better days—and before Elizabeth could protest again she w s gone.

It was unutterably cold, wretched and dreary in the streets. The lamps winked drowsily, as if quite exhausted by their efforts to keep alight so long. The fatigued policemen, with their collars turned up huddled in the shelter of protecting doorways, and mechanically stamped their heavy feet, as if to make sure they had not turned to lumps of ice. In covered alleys the famished dogs and ragged beggers crouched together for mutual warmth, and shivered and whined as the wind, in very spitefulness, dashed handsful of cutting snow into their lean faces, and then went howling like a delighted night demon through the chimney tops.

A few peddlers, of frozen milk and frozen fish, crept stiffly along with their burdens. The horses of the gens-d'armes at street corners seemed quite shrunken and humpbacked from the excessive cold, and their riders looked frozen into torpor and an utter indifference to their duties.

Frightened, yet urged on by the stimulus of the, to her, all important mission Madam Ruloff walked with a rapidity that seemed marvelous in contrast with the groping movements of other pedestrians. until she came to the dingy, squat house with the sign above it, ' Michael Pushkeene, Pawnbroker.'

In answer to her knocking a little window like a lid to a sightless eye, opened under the eves, and a night-caped head was pushed cautiously out, while an asthmatic voice demanded :

' Who's down there, at this hour ?'

' I—Madame Ruloff. Is your son in ?'

' No. Wait ; I will come down.'

The head was withdrawn, and the eyelid dropped. In a few minutes the pawn-shop door opened, and old Michael Pushkeene, lo king like a ghoul in an ill-fitting, second-hand shroud, stood, candle in hand, before her.

' Come in ! Come in !' he chattered. ' It is fearfully cold, and I am fearfully delicate.'

Stepping into the pawn-shop, Madam Ruloff asked :

' Was your son home last night ?'

'N-n-no,' stammered the old man. ' But

I don't feel uneasy. He often remains out all night.'

' He has been of late much with my son. I thought that he might tell me why Vladimeer did not come home.'

' I don't think Michael could do that, even if he was here. When a man is missing now his friends need not be long in doubt is to what has become of him,' wheezed the old man.

' What do you mean ?'

' I mean, madam, that if a man is expected home and dosen't come, it is apt to be that the Czar's officers have taken charge of him.'

The old man set the candle on the counter, and rubbed his yellow, talon-like hands. And in his attempt to smile he made a ghastly exhibition of his long, yellow teeth.

' Have you any idea where I could find your son ?' asked the madam, taking a step toward the door.

' Not the slightest, Madam Ruloff. But if Michael knew you wanted him he would fly. He is deeply attached to your family, and never wearies in talking about your beautiful daughter—'

Had the maiden waited to listen, the garrulous old man would have kept on indefinitely ; but the moment he mentioned his son's attachment she turned and left, with a bow and a glance several degrees more freezing than the keen atmosphere.

She decided to get breakfast, and then to find General Gallitzin, and invoke his aid. She knew, but gave no thought to the fact, that the house of every recently arrested prisoner was watched, and that while any pers n might leave unchallenged, those entering was subject to arrest. She was about to ascend to her lodgings when two men—the same two that had arrested her son—stepped out from the shadows, and one of them said :

' This house is marked, madam. You are our prisoner. Make no outcry.

CHAPTER XIV.

HELEN RADOWSKY RECEIVES A REPORT AND MAKES ANOTHER MOVE.

The house in which Helen Radowsky lived, with her servant, belonged to the government, and was one of a number of the same kind of structures occupied by teachers and musicians in the employ of the court. It might be said to be in the shadow of one of the royal residence, and she was in daily intercourse with the children of the royal family. A strange situation, truly, for a woman who hated Russia as she did ; but it was by no means an exception. Nihilism had warmed its way even closer to the throne ; and many of the most trusted recipients of imperial favour were secretly working for its overthrow.

The afternoon following the arrest of Vladimeer Ruloff, Helen Radowsky entered her house, the professional duties of the day ended, and prepared to renew that work, that was the ruling motive of her life.

She was about to pass the cozy little-sitting-room, when the white-caped servant whispered :

' A gentleman awaits Miss Radowsky.'

' Who ?'

' Mr. Michael Pushkeene.'

' How long has he been here ?'

' An hour.'

Helen Radowsky entered the sitting-room, and Michael Pushkeene rose to meet her.

' Well Doctor, what news ?' asked Helen, after she had submitted her hand to his clammy grasp.

' Good news !' glorious news !' replied Pushkeene.

Laying aside her cloak and hood, and so bringing to view her rosy face and flashing eyes, she asked, as she sat down :

'What is this glorious news?'

' Vladimeer is out of the way,' chuckled Pushkeene.

' Out of the way ?' she repeated.

' Yes ; seized last night, and now awaiting trial, in the Prison of the Exiles.'

' That is quick work.'

' Yes ; but why delay, when it had to be done ?'

' There is no reason, Michael. But how did it come about ?'

' I will tell you.' Pushkeene drew nearer, and spreading out his tallowy palm, as if the words he was about to utter were quite legible to him thereon, he went on to tell how he introduced Braski, a detective, to Vladimeer, passing him off as a friend Neuman, of Moscow ; how they went together to the Nihilist meeting, and how he—Pushkeene—there secreted certain treasonable papers in Vladimeer's pockets ; how Braski—who was a Nihilist at heart— entered into his plans, promising not to give information about the meeting only as it affected their victim ; and finally he gave the particulars of Vladimeer's arrest.

' That was wonderfully well done ; but the work is not yet completed,' she said deliberately.

' Oh, I am aware of that, but you will say it is well under way ?'

' Perhaps so. After the conviction of Vladimeer Ruloff this Braski must be put out of the way.'

' Out of the way ?' exclaimed Pushkeene.

' Certainly; a useless tool may be a dangerous weapon ; to prevent that danger it must be destroyed. But tell me, have you seen Madame Ruloff ?'

' I just came from there. Got in by a letter from the Captain of the Little Neva Division. Madam Ruloff is arrested—'

' Madam Ruloff arrested !'

' Yes ; she went out to seek her son, and was seized on her return.'

' I am sorry for that, but it cannot be helped. It is one of the sad necessities of my plan,' said Helen Radowsky, with something like a sigh.

' I saw the beautiful Elizabeth,' continued Pushkeene. 'The gens-d'armes are stationed about the house and won't let her leave. She is in great tribulation.'

' And you,' said Helen, with an arch smile, ' did all in your power to make her happy.'

' Yes, and I am sorry I undertook it.'

' Sorry ?'

' Aye, sorry. I never dreamt she had so much scorn and temper. Had a Baltic iceberg suddenly turned into a moving volcano, emitting fire and brimstone, I could not have been more astonished. She blamed me ; she scorned me ; she ordered me, indignantly, to leave and never again to show my face in her presence.'

' So you left,' laughed Helen Radowsky.

' What else could I do ?' he whined.

' Absolutely nothing. But tell me Doctor Pushkeene, will you now leave the field clear to your rival, the Prince Gallitzin of Novgorod ?' she laughed again, and laid her white hand on his arm, and looked with an indescribable, mocking, maddening expression into his face.

' I'll kill him first !' hissed Pushkeene.

' You mean you will continue to obey me ?'

' Yes.' he said, desperately.

' Then you must see your friend Braski— or Neuman of Moscow—and tell him it is necessary to start the rumor that Prince Gallitzin is disaffected, and that he is in correspondence with Nihilists, and that he is using his high position to overthrow the government.

' But can that be proven ?'

' You must ask me no questions, nor attempt to see through my plans. Obey me implicitly in the future, as you have in the past, and I promise you, you shall have the beautiful Elizabeth to yourself.'

' Command me ! Command me !' he exclaimed, leaping impulsively from his chair.

Helen Radowsky stroked her brow thoughtfully, and after a time drew a paper from her pocket and began turning it over and over.

' Doctor.'

'Miss Radowsky.'

'You say you know well the valet of Prince Gortschakoff ?'

'Very well.'

'Intimately ?'

'We are like brothers.'

'And you think he is at heart a Nihilist ?'

'I am sure of it.'

'If he could leave this letter on his master's table, within the next forty-eight hours, it would be a great advantage to you and me.'

She handed him the sealed paper, addressed 'to General Gortschakoff,' and marked 'private and confidential.

'I shall attend to this at once,' said Pushkeene, taking the paper.

'Without doubt ?'

'Without the shadow of a doubt.'

'Very well. Let us hear from you again to-morrow.

She arose, and Michael Pushkeene, looking upon this as a desire to terminate the audience, rose also and took his departure.

For a man who had been so successful, Michael Pushkeene did not feel elated; indeed, the reception given him by Elizabeth Ruloff was depressing and unsatisfactory in the greatest degree ; in addition to which he was convinced that he, as well as his friend Braski, was but a tool in the hands of this remarkable woman.

'She wants to put Braski out of the way, when she has got all the good out of him. 'Useless tools,' she says, ' may de dangerous weapons.' She may soon come to look on Michael Pushkeene as a dangerous weapon, and then—'This thought came with such force as to bring him to a dead halt in front of a drinking shop. ' I would rather have the demon against me than this same Helen Radowsky. But she's mortal ; if she can beat him in cunning, let her, She has warned me, and I will keep my eyes open.'

This conclusion did not banish the sickening feeling of dread that took its place in Michael Pushkeene's heart, never again to leave it for any length of time.

'It is cold. I have been working very hard and need a stimulant,' this he muttered, by way of excuse for the step he was contemplating.

He walked into the shop, and entering one of the little curtained stalls that lined the room, he ordered some brandy.

The liquor was brought and drank, and a cigar lit ; after which Michael Pushkeene reasoned hi self into the belief that his recent uneasiness had been purely physical, and that the brandy had quite relieved him. He drew the curtain aside, and was in the act of raising, when, like an unexpected stroke of fortune, the valet of Prince Gortschakoff entered.

Pushkeene saluted him, gave him a seat at the other side of the little table, that nearly filled the stall, and having ascertained that the servant of the great man had a weakness for an expensive article of Hungarian brandy ,he ordered a half bottle and more cigars, with which they were soon as comfortable and more confidential than the Czar and the prince in their magnificent palaces.

The valet felt that much of his master's greatness was reflected on him ; and he sustained the burden with a great affectation of diginity, and a bearing quiet gouty and statesman-like for one so young. He used the pronoun ' We' with great freedom, just as if he were in partnership with the Czar and his master, and had serious thoughts of assuming all the burdens of State, without the aid of other ornamental incumberances.

Knowing his man, and every atom of the very common earth he was created from, Michael Pushkeene humored his quest with flattery and moistened him with brandy, and smoked incense at him from cigars unusually expensive for him, but rather common weeds to the valet, who always snuffed the very best smoke—second-hand, to be sure, but not to be despised for that.

The result of this meeting was that Pushkeene carried his point, the valet agreeing to leave the letter, the next morning, on his master's desk,

Having finished the brandy, the friends went out in great good humor ; and Ruryk and Cossack left an adjoining stall and followed them to the street.

CHAPTER XV.

GENERAL GALLITZIN LEARNS THE NEWS.

Rumour likes to fill her trumpet with a great name and sound it through all lands; particularly is that the case where the name of a hero is coupled with that of a fitting heroine, and the keynote is love.

After the reception of General Gortschakoff's all Saint Petersburg—from the drinking-shops where the valets met to the most aristocratic salons—rang with praises of General Gallitzin's manly beauty, and there was a universal approval of his rumored betrothal to the Countess Alexandrina. A more fitting marriage, it was universally conceded, could not be made, On the one side were fame, fortune, family, and a great future ; on the other side were youth, beauty, high social position, and Prince Gortschakoff's niece.

General Gallitzin was congratulated on

every hand, to his great annoyance. As there was no betrothal, and could not be, much as others might desire it, he did not hesitate to deny the rumor, in his well-bred way.

But the people looked on the denial as an excusable equivocation; the betrothal was just as certain—in the mind of the public—as if the high contracting parties had affixed their aristocratic signatures to the marriage paper; and the patriarch of the capital had given his priestly blessing.

Of all the men who heard this rumor, Count Kiseleff was the one who stoutely denied it. And so much feeling did he manifest that his friends on the imperial staff and the officers of the guards never ceased joking him about his failure, while the ruder and more thoughtless plainly told him that the young general had ' put his nose out of joint.' Physiologically it may be impossible to put any nose out of joint—short of an alligator's; but figuratively, we all know, it is a thing of very common occurrence.

Count Kiseleff was annoyed; Count Kiseleff was angered and jealous; and this because Count Kiseleff was as desperately in love as it was possible for a man of his shallow, malignant nature to be. In short, Count Kiseleff hated the man whom every one else admired, and he set about finding the weak part of his armor, with the deliberate intent of assailing him, should opportunity promises success.

General Gallitzin had just returned to his office after an interview with Prince Gortschakoff, in which interview he had argued, with characteristic earnestness, for a rehearing in the case of the exiled Count Ruloff. He had every reason to believe his request would be granted, and was congratulating himself on the delightful surprise he would be able to give Madam Ruloff and Elizabeth, when Paul, his valet, came to the door and said:

' May it please your excellency, Count Kiseleff, aid to his imperial majesty the Czar, is in waiting and requests an audience.'

' Admit him at once,' replied the prince,

He rose from his chair to meet his visitor, muttering as he did so:

' It is not a personal matter that brings Kiseleff here; he has treated me very coldly of late.'

The count entered, walking very straight, and looking as cold and dignified as it was possible for a stumpy, sanguine man to look.

Prince Gallitzin was about to extend his hand, with soldierly heartiness, when the count bowed, and with a preliminary cough, and the manner of a stage herald, delivered himself after this fashion:

' General, Prince Wladislas Gallitzin of Novrogod, I am commanded by his imperial majesty, our master, to convey you to his greetings –'

The prince bowed and smiled.

' To convey to you his greetings, and to order that you meet him to-morrow, in council with Prince Gortschakoff, in the royal council-room of the Winter Palace, at the hour of noon.'

' To obey the commands of his imperial majesty, my master, must ever be my greatest pleasure, replied the prince.

Count Kiseleff turned like a soldier at his post, and was about to march away, when the prince, with much good feeling, said :

' It is necessary that Count Kiseleff should at once withdraw ?'

' It is not necessary, but it is my pleasure,' replied the count, with the same inflexible bearing.

' Under such circumstances, I can offer no objection ; but I was on the point of asking that you remain and take a soldier's dinner with me. We shall be alone, and there is much that I would say to you.'

' I regret that I cannot, to-day, avail myself of the honor conveyed in your invitation. Should it remain open, it will afford me the greatest pleasure to be the guest of the hero of the Balkans.'

Count Kiseleff bowed from his hips up, took his trailing dress-sword in his left hand, and made his exit with unflagging rigidity and wonderful dignity.

Alone again ; and the prince dropped into a chair, and clapping his hands, gave way to a fit of laughter that was even boyish in its enjoyable exuberance.

By my faith, Kiseleff is jealous ! Oh ! it is as plain as the sun in the desert at midday. Poor, foolish fellow ! though I stand not in his way, the fair Alexandrina would no more smile upon him than she would on his valet. He is but little of the courtier, or he would better disguise his feelings. And it strikes me, that as a gentleman, it would be more proper to behave quite like one. But we all have our faults with our virtues.'

Having arrived at this philosophical conclusion, the prince took up his pen and was about to go on with his writing when the tall figure of Ruryk the Cossack appeared in the door, hat in hand, and straight as a ramrod.

Ruryk's face was usually stolid, and there was a dress-parade look about his eyes ; now his cheeks were flushed, and his grey eyes flashed in a way that at once attracted his master's attention.

' What is the matter, Ruryk ?' asked the prince.

' I have been scouting in the camp of the enemy, General, and have important information to report,' said Ruryk, with a military salute and three forward steps.

It was so common for the soldier to use military terms and figures in speaking of every-day events that the general was not surprised at this speech ; but he certainly was astonished at what followed.

With soldierly brevity Ruryk told of the conversation he had overheard between Pushkeene, whom he did not know, and Prince Gortschakoff's valet, with whom he was acquainted.

' They abused you, sir, and called you a Nihilist, and said it would be proved.'

The general laughed at this, and told Ruryk to proceed.

' And the man told the valet that Madam Ruloff and her son Vladimeer were arrested, and are now in the Prison of the Exiles.'

The effect of these words was to bring the prince to his feet and drive the color from his cheeks. He made his orderly repeat what he had said, which he did with the amendment, ' And the man said that you signed the order for the arrest of Vladimeer, son of Count Ruloff.'

At this the Prince fairly gasped. So voluminous were the reports of the papers brought before him that he found it impossible to read them through, and, for a knowledge of their contents, had to depend on the statements of his clerical subordinates. It was possible that he had signed such a paper, but, at the same time, highly improbable. The matter must be looked into immediately. He ordered Ruryk to get out his sleigh at once and prepare to accompany him.

In a few minutes the three horses, attached abreast to the vehicle, were dashing down the streets of the city at such a furious rate that pedestrians stopped and watched them out of sight, fully convinced they were running away.

They galloped into the narrow street, and reined in suddenly before the high, thin house in which were the Ruloff lodgings. As the prince leaped out he saw a cordon of gens-d'armes surrounding the place.

Unminding them, he was about to enter when two men emerged from the door, and laying their hands on his shoulder, demanded :

' Whom want you to see ?'

' How dare you ask, or stop me ? Dogs ! let me pass !'

He dashed them aside, and was about to spring up the stairs, when a man on the steps raised his musket and called to him to ' Halt !' At the same time the two men again seized him, and said :

' In the name of his imperial majesty, Alexis, Czar of all the Russias, you are our prisoner !'

Unhooking his fur cloak and throwing it to Ruryk, who stood close behind, with his sword half drawn from the scabbard, the prince shouted :

' Fools ! know you not who I am ?'

' A general of artillery,' said one of the detectives.

' I am Prince Gallitzin, head of his majesty's secret police and your master ! Back from my path !' His sword flew out, and the frightened men started back.

Halting on the stairs, the prince called back to Ruryk :

' Place those two men under arrest. Call to the gens-d'armes to conduct them to prison, and report to me in the morning.'

' With the greatest of pleasure, your excellency,' replied Ruryk.

And before the prince had reached the apartment under the roof, the detectives were on the way to prison, under guard.

CHAPTER XVI.

GENERAL GALLITZIN MOVES WITH ENERGY.

A faint ' enter' came back in reply to the prince's knock on the door leading into the apartment.

He hastened in, and found the room fireless and cheerless, with Elizabeth, pale as death, lying on a lounge under the window.

' Elizabeth, my darling my life !'

The prince was on his knees beside her, and his strong arms folded her to his breast.

So far the heroic girl had endured her mental torture and physical suffering without complaint ; but now that love and sympathy were near, she broke down, and the overwrought feelings sought relief in a flood of tears.

' Poor child ! Poor darling ! Could I have known of this, how short would have been your sufferings !' said the prince, in a choking voice.

' I care not for myself. But my mother and brother are in the dungeon of the Exiles. Save them ! Ah, save them, Wladislas !' she cried, raising her hands appealingly.

' I will save them !' he said, hoarsely. Then kissing her, he rose to his feet, and his eyes flashed as he continued :

' God's curse must come to the land where such things are possible ! And this is Russia, the land of my fathers—the land for which I drew my sword and risked my life ! Better—ten thousand times better—that she were overrun by the Moslem than that she should subject her people to torture to save a life that can only exist through tyranny.'

' Do not speak so, Wladislas ; you may be the next victim,' said Elizabeth, pleadingly.

' There are times when it is a relief to give tongue to thoughts that have grown too large for restraint. But come, Elizabeth. You must go at once to a hotel, and have a doctor's care. I will leave a soldier in charge here. Then to the Prison of the Exiles ; and before many hours the Countess Ruloff and her son sh·ll be free !'

With a strength born of hope, Elizabeth Ruloff rose, and put on her mantle and hood first placing in a satchel some necessary articles of apparel, which the prince said he would send for.

They descended to the street, where Ruryk the Cossack stood like a statue, watching the crowd attracted by the not unusual matter of an arrest.

' Ruryk l'

' Yes, General.' Ruryk touched his hat.

' Take charge of Madam Ruloff's apartments. I will send a man to relieve you in two hours.'

Ruryk saluted, wheeled and marched up the stairs, as he would have marched to the cannon's mouth had the same lips issued the order.

' To the Hotel America,' said General Gallitzin, as he took his place in the sleigh beside Elizabeth Ruloff.

The gens-d'armes came to a salute, and the horses dashed off with the impetuosity with which they had come.

' In the hotel to which I take you,' said the prince, folding the fur robes about her shoulders, ' lives Mr. Jonathan Cushing and his family, the merchant who agreed to employ Vladimeer. I met the family in America, and found them to be delightful people. You can depend on a warm welcome, for they know of your troubles.'

' Could you not,' asked Elizabeth, ' first take me to my mother and brother ?'

' Gladly, if anything were to be gained by it. But why fatigue yourself, when it will be my great pleasure soon to bring them to you ?'

Elizabeth consented to be guided by him, and went on to the hotel at which lived the Cushings.

The prince not overestimated the merits of the warm-hearted Americans. Mrs. Cushing met the beautiful girl as if she had been her own child ; and Mrs. Cushing's daughter, Belle, as she heard the story of Elizabeth's sufferings, wept and gave vent, by turns, to expressions against Russia that would have sent her to Siberia for life had she been a Russian and some spy was near to report her words.

' Poor child ! she must have a doctor at once. I wonder she has lived under her sufferings,' said good Mrs. Cushing; and in a medicinal way she administered to Elizabeth a glass of warm wine, and assured the prince that herself and daughter should devote their whole time to their guest and patient.

' To the Prison of the Exiles,' said the prince, as he leaped again into the sleigh.

Away speed the foaming horses ; and those who recognized the prince as he dashed by, reasoned that he was on business of unusual importance connected with his department. Through the arched gate, that seemed like the entrance to a grim, gigantic mausoleum, and the prince sprang from the sleigh before it had well s'opped, and hurried into the receiving-room.

There, at the table, with the pile of glistening handcuffs on one side and the chained book before him, sat the swarthy secretary, erasing with red ink the names of a batch of prisoners that had been sentenced that day.

The man looked up, and recognizing in the general an officer and a noble, he rose and stood with his hand to his bushy head.

' I am General Gallitzin, chief of her majesty's secret police.'

At the mention of that name the guards seized their arms and came to a salute, and every man in the room rose to his feet.

' You have in this prison the Countess Ruloff and her son Vladimeer, arrested without my knowledge or consent,' continued the prince.

The clerk referred to the book and said :

' The arrest of Vladimeer Ruloff was made on your written order. Madame Ruloff was arrested under the rule in such cases.'

' Under the rule,' repeated the excited prince. ' Where is the order of commitment ?'

' Here,' said the swarthy clerk, handing him the paper in question.

The prince glanced at it, recognized his own hurried signature, and then tore the paper into fragments and crushed it under his heel.

' I wish to see Madam Ruloff and her son at once.' he said, peremptorily.

The swarthy clerk motioned to a man whose broad girdle was weighted with bunches of ponderous keys, and said :

' Conduct 147 and 213 to the reception room immediately.'

The man with the keys vanished, with a rattling noise, and another man, standing in humble attitude before the prince, said :

' If your excellency will follow me, I will show you the reception room.'

This reception room, a cold, cheerless apartment with a stone floor, and a border of wooden benches surround ing the wall, was near by.

The prince paced the floor nervously, till a door, opposite to that by which he had entered, opened, and Madam Ruloff and her son, who had just met, came in hand in hand.

At the sight of General Gallitzin Madam Ruloff uttered a cry of joy, and would have fallen had he not caught her and carried her to a seat.

Short as the period of his imprisonment was, Vladimeer Ruloff looked pale, haggard and aged, as if he had been deprived of his liberty for years. The light, after long hours of darkness, so affected his eyes that he could scarcely see, and had to grope his way to his mother's side.

'Elizabeth is safe, with my friend, the Cushings, at the Hotel America. I only learned of this outrage an hour or so ago,' explained the prince, when Madam Ruloff had revived sufficiently to see and hear him.

'It would have been a mercy to have killed us, instead of taking us to those vile dungeons,' said the madam, shuddering at the thought of her sufferings.

The governor of the prison came in, and to him General Gallitzin said .

'These people are my friends ; they were committed under an error. I am going to take them from here.'

'It would please me to oblige General the Prince Gallitzin,' said the governor, obsequiously ; 'but while many have the power to imprison, but one has the right to free.'

'Who is that ?' demanded the prince.

'The Czar, your excellency.'

'I will take the responsibility of correcting my own error. Madam Ruloff and her son leave with me,' said the prince, rising and giving Madam Ruloff his arm.

'Against that I protest,' said the governor.

'You protest !'

The prince walked forward the door, Vladimeer following.

'I protest, your excellency, and must call in the police,' persisted the governor, at the same time clapping his hands thrice.

A score of armed men rushed in, and the governor, pointing to Madam Ruloff and her son cried out :

'Those two prisoners are about to leave without orders. Seize them !'

The police started forward to execute this order, but came to a sudden halt, as the prince shouted, with the ring of a bugle in his martial voice :

'Seize those people at your peril ! Back to your quarters, men ! Back, *I command you !*'

The men shrank back, and General Gall.tzin advanced again.

CHAPTER XVII.

FREE BUT NOT SAFE.

'Again, in the name of my master, the Czar, I protest against freeing those prisoners, untried and unpardoned,' said the governor of the prison, walking backward, as the general advanced, with Madam Ruloff on his arm.

'And again I order you from my path ! if I have violated the regulations, you know the remedy. I am now acting on my own responsibility, confident that my conduct will meet the approval of the Czar when I have brought it to his notice, as I shall do at once,' said the prince.

'Then why not go to the Czar first,' asked the governor, 'and so do things regularly ?'

'First, because I wish to release a sick woman, who may survive if freed at once ; and, in the second place, I exercise a right in visiting any and every prison in the realm, and in correcting the errors of my subordinates, for which I am responsible.'

The governor, seeing that further objection was useless, and perhaps satisfied that he had done all the law and his position required of him, fell back, still muttering, and saw the prince placing the Countess Ruloff and her son in his sleigh and driving off.

'By my faith ! said the prince, with a grim laugh, ' I little thought, when I assumed my duties in the hope that I might stand as a mediator between the Czar and the swarming discontents, that I would be using my position in such a short time for the ruin of those I love best.'

'But you have remedied the evil, said Vladimeer, whose eyes now became accustomed to the moonlight glare on the dazzling snow, and whose spirits rose every instant as he inhaled, like refreshing draughts, God's free, pure air, which was denied to the prisoners in that horrible dungeon.

'I fear,' sighed the madam, ' that this is by no means the end of trouble.'

'I feel very sure,' said the prince, positively, ' that it is the worst of it.'

'And you feel very sure,' she asked, ' that harm may not come to yourself from this act ?'

'I see nothing to fear,' he said, lightly adding as the horses slackened their speed ; ' Here we are at the hotel America. Here you will find Elizabeth, and here you must all make your home for the present. I shall see that the old lodgings are guarded.'

He helped Madam Ruloff, from the sleigh, and Vladimeer and he half carried her into the hotel, where Mrs. Cushing and her daughter greeted them with true American warmth.

The meeting between Elizabeth and her

mother and brother could not have been
more touching had they been parted for
years. Mrs. Cushing and Belle did not attempt to keep back their tears ; and General
Gallitzin went to the window and looked out,
using his handkerchief the while as if he
had suddenly caught a violent cold.

After a few minutes the prince came back
from the window, and kissing Elizabeth, he
took Madam Ruloft's hand and said :

' I have much to attend to, and must be
going. Here you will be safe for the present ; and I can speak from a happy experience when I tell you you are with friends.'

' That they are !' said Mrs. Cushing.

' And to make them safer,' joined in the
generous, enthusiastic daughter, ' I am going
to hang the flag of my country over the entrance to these apartments, and if any of
your police or soldiers attempts to pass it,
he must do it at his peril.'

' I can promise,' laughed the prince, ' that
there will be no need to invoke the protection of your flag ; though, were it necessary
no national emblem other than that of Russia is so powerful in St. Petersburg.'

Promising to call early on the morrow,
General Gallitzin left the Cushing apartments, Vladimeer following him into the
hall.

' Now my dear Vladimeer,' said the general, draw him to one side, and speaking in a
low tone, ' I want you to tell me, frankly, all
you know about this matter.'

Briefly, and without any effort to shield
himself, Vladimeer told of his connection
with the Nihilists, how he came to join them,
and all the events of the night preceding
his arrest. But he mentioned no names.

' There are two people—fellow-Nihilists of
yours—at the bottom of this matter,' said
the prince, when Vladimeer had concluded.

' Who are they ?' asked the astonished
Vladimeer.

' Michael Pushkeene and this woman Helen
Radowsky,' replied the prince.

' But why should they persecute me ?'

' They persecute you, Vladimeer, the better to strike me. You remember that woman came to my house to assassinate me, and
you warned me ?'

' Yes ! and you should have punished her,'
said Vladimeer.

' I think not. I propose to try other
methods. I understand the baseless cause
for her hatred. Her father tried to assassinate mine. and my father pled sucessfully
for the would-be-murderer's life. The son
cannot be less magnamious with the daughter. As to that presumptuous wretch Pushkeene, he is nearing the end of his own rope
and my patience. Now, Vladimeer, do not,
as you value your safety and the happiness

of your mother and sister, leave the place
without consulting me.'

' I will not.'

' And, Vladimeer, tell Mr. Cushing fully
and frankly about your trouble. The Americans are a cool, shrewd, far-seeing people.
Full of courage and generosity. This man
is a good specimen of what I consider the
very finest people in the world,'

With this understanding the friends shook
hands. And once more General Gallitzin
was being whirled away in the sleigh.

Despite her freedom and kind reception received at the hands of Mrs. Cushing,
and her daughter, Madam Ruloff was so
prostrated by the shock consequent to her
arrest, and her subsequent sufferings, that she
had to go to bed, and a doctor was called
in.

Vladimeer sat in the sumptuous private
parlor, the ladies being in attendance on his
mother, and he mused over his position and
tried to see, through the future, to the end
of his troubles.

As he sat there the door opened, and a
tall man with a smooth face and keen eyes
entered.

' What, you, Mr. Ruloff ?' said the new-
comer, shaking his hand. ' I am right glad
to see you. I wondered why you had not reported for duty at the warehouse ; but as I
came along I heard of your arrest, and also
of your extraordinary release. It was a bold
act and a righteous one, though I fear it may
prove to be a rash one to your friend General Gallitzin.'

This was Mr. Cushing, The American
merchant.

Vladimeer spoke of the manner of his arrest and release, and asked :

' But why do you think it may work injury
to General Gallitzin ?'

' I have just come from change, where the
event was being discussed in whispers by
frightened groups. Those who dare to speak
their minds— and they are mighty few, I regret to say—applaud the general ; but the
most ardent admirer of the act is convinced
that the general will find himself in trouble.
Your Czar is very jealous of his prerogatives,'
said Mr. Cushing, with a dry smile.

' But, should not the general know this at
once ?'

' He will know it as soon as if I started
after him and said what I have to you. He
is a bold, magnificent fellow. He should be
an American. But while regretting his coming trouble- -do you think you are safe ?,

' I do not,' replied Vladimeer.

' Nor do I ; but I think I can help you ; at
any rate I can try,' said Mr. Cushing shaking Vladimeer's hand.

' And I, Mr. Cushing, thank you from my

heart for the intention. But if the general gets in trouble, through aiding me, I cannot forsake him.'

'That is manly in sentiment, but it wont work in practice,' said the matter of-fact American. 'If by hanging on here you could help General Gallitzin, I'd say do it and face the music; but you can't. Why throw life and freedom away for a useless sentiment? You must leave Saint Petersburg, and at once. I will fix it,' said Mr Cushing, slapping his knee with the emphasis of a man who has just reached a strong, feasible conclusion.

CHAPTER XVIII.

THE PROCLAMATION.

Helen Radowsky was too cunning to make her own house a headquarters for the discontents, whom she had led and managed; nor was their need that she should, when more than one half the roofs in the city sheltered the heads of Nihilists and places of rendezvous were open, to the initated, on every hand. Indeed the very publicity of some of these places and the high character of the people resorting there, were their greatest protection against the prying eyes of the Czar's spies. She stood before the fire in her sitting-room, dressed to go out, and patting her little foot impatiently on the red hearthstone.

The door opened behind her, and turning, she stood face to face with Varwitch.

'Did you think, I was never coming ?' he asked, retaining her hand, and looking intently into her bright, mysterious eyes.

'I supposed you had good cause for delay; but there is so much to do and such a short time to do it in, and I cannot help feeling impatient,' said Helen Radowsky, beaming and pouting with well affected pleasure on Varwitch.

'I did what you ordered. Should a search of the prince's apartments be made to-morrow, documentary evidence of his anti-monarchical feelings will be found in abundance,' said Varwitch.

'And in his own handwriting ?' she asked.

'So much like his own handwriting that I defy all the experts in Russia to tell the difference.'

'Good !' she exclaimed. 'I knew you could do it. Ah ! you are an invaluable man.'

'And an unrewarded one,' he growled.

'Patience, patience, my dear Varwitch.' She laid her hand upon his arm and gazed into the fire in an abstracted way, then looking up, as if the thought had just flashed upon her, she continued :

'We must go to our publication office at once.'

'What for ? he asked.

'You know Vladimeer Ruloff and his mother were released by General Gallitzin, without authority of the Czar.'

'Yes. All Saint Petersburg is ringing with it,'

'You also know that nine-tenths of the students in the city are Nihilists ?'

'It is so thought.'

'And it is true. Now, Varwitch, within twenty-four hours this proclamation must be in print, mailed to the chief officers of the government, and posted in all the public places in the city.'

Helen Radowsky drew from her pocket a folded paper, and opening it handed it to Varwitch, and asked :

'Can you read that ?'

'No; it is written in characters of our own invention,' he responded, returning the paper.

'You are a very learned man, dear Varwitch. You are right as to the characters; but the document is further protected by being in the Manx language, which outside of a little island in the Irish sea, is unknown to the world. I spent a summer there before my father died.' She then read as follows :

'To THE FREEMEN OF ALL THE RUSSIAS ! —We, the students of St. Petersburg, do send this proclamation, and send this greeting :

' We organize to disorganize.

' We must destroy the palaces and prisons of the autocrat and tyrant before we can even consider plans for the temple of Liberty.

' Every means that adds to our strength is justifiable.

' The army is coming to our side.

' The Navy is disaffected.

' The Czarwitz— eldest son of Alexander— sides with us.

' The chief of the Czar's secret police is discussed with his position.

' The tyrant arrested Vladimeer Ruloff, son of our friend, the exiled Count Ruloff, and confined him in the dungeon of the exiles. The tyrants arrested Madam Ruloff, and our hearts became heavy. But, joy to us ! and all honor to Wladislas the Prince Gallitzin of Novgorod, who freed our friends in defiance of his imperial (?) master.

' Patience yet awhile.

' No more cavalcades to Siberia.

' No more impressment.

' No more grinding taxes.

' No more desolate homes.

' No more nobles.

' No more tyrants.

' In the name of Russian Patriots and freemen, we greet you,

'THE STUDENTS OF SAINT PATERSBURG!'
'What do you think of that?' she asked, replacing the paper to her pocket.

'It is characteristic,' answered Varwitch, 'But what is the object—to rouse the people?'

'No,' she laughed; to rouse the tyrant. This proclamation will force the removal of Prince Gallitzin at once. His arrest will follow. Already Gortschakoff, is in possession of papers pointing out the prince's treason. He will be arrested if he does not fly. Flight would confirm suspicion. But he is a bold man, and conscious of his innocence; he will bravely meet his accusers—and perish!' she said, sinking her intense voice to a whisper.

'If you were not beautiful as an angel,' said Varwitch, shuddering as he watched her, 'I would say you were the most cold blooded and insatiate demon that ever appeared in the guise of humanity.'

'To brood over a wrong that religion is powerless to console, is to become a demon or a maniac. But come; let us to the printing office.'

They went out, and as they walked along the well-lit streets many recognized them as the major domo of Prince Gallitzin's household and the pretty teacher to the children of the Czar's heir.

They entered a restaurant, before which policemen lounged, and in which many army officers sat about the little white tables, eating drinking, and chattering. A waiter, in obedience to Varwitch's request, conducted them to a private room in the back part of the building and left them, without asking their order.

They did not sit down, but opening another door, passed through and ascended a dimly lit stairs. They went up flight after flight, and came to the end of the stairs and a door, with a circular aperture in it, at the same time. Varwitch knocked, and like an echo from the other side, a knock was heard in reply.

The drop that covered the aperture was pushed back, and Varwitch sent a message through, in a whisper of great hoarseness.

The door opened, and a man in a knit jacket turned the key behind them, and after much winding through dark passages, and a great deal of knocking and mysterious whispering they were conducted into an apartment filled with all the appurtenances of a printing office.

At a table, with his coat off, for the room was hot and close, sat Michael Pushkeene, reading proof, and looking very much like an elderly printer's devil in a congenial swelter.

At sight of Helen Radowsky, Pushkeene sprang up, grasped their hands, declared he he was overpowered with joy at meeting them and gave evidence of the fact by dancing about like a particulary lively monkey.

'Have you the proclamation?' he asked, finishing his antics and resuming his chair.

'I have. Let me read it to you. Take your pen and make a copy,' said Helen Radowsky.

Pushkeene obeyed her, making a transcript of the proclamation.

A man with a green shade over his eyes came up, and greeted the new arrivals. Helen Radowsky drew him to one side and whispered:

'Preserve the copy in Pushkeene's handwriting.'

The man with the green shade puckered up his lips, as if about to whistle, and nodded intelligently.

'And,' she said, raising her voice, so that Pushkeene could hear, 'the proclamation must be printed at once, and ready for posting before daylight.'

'It shall be done,' said the man with the shade.

'And copies must be mailed to those addresses,' she said, handing him the list.

'Is that all?'

'That is all,' she said, turning to leave.

Michael Pushkeene put on his hat and overcoat and accompanied Helen Radowsky and Varwitch to the street.

'I am going,' he said, 'to call on my friends the Ruloffs, and congratulate them on their freedom.'

'Where are they?' asked Helen Radowsky.

'At the hotel America, I understand,'

'I am afraid,' she laughed, 'that your friend Vladimeer will not long enjoy his liberty. If he is not in prison again before ten hours, I mistake the spirit and power of the authorities. Good night.'

Pushkeene had no thought of leaving so soon; but looking on her 'good night' as a dismissal, he wisely and immediately took his departure.

At the door of her own house Helen Radowsky dismissed Varwitch, just as abruptly; and that gentleman went off, mad with love, and the feeling that he was only welcome so long as he could be of use; and he wondered if this would continue till she cast him off permanently—like a worthless garment.

Helen Radowsky went to her own room, and was in the act of writing, when the servant announced:

'A gentleman to see you.'

'Did he give you his card?'

'No, Miss.'

'Nor his name?'

'No. He is very handsome, and says he

will only detain you a few minutes,' replied the servant.

Surveying herself in the glass, with an expression of self-satisfaction, Helen Radowsky sent the servant to say she would see her visitor directly; then she secreted the jewel-hilted dagger in her girdle, and went down.

She trembled at seeing a tall figure standing before the fire. Coughing to attract his attention, great was her amazement at finding herself face to face with the man to whose ruin all her energies were bent.

'Prince Gallitzin!' she gasped.

'Yes; you did not expect to see me?' he said, in low, musical tones, that thrilled her, while she grew nervous, under the glorious eyes.

'I did not, nor can I imagine the reason for this—this honor,' she replied, with an effort at self-possession

'I will not detain you long. I came on a matter of the greatest importance to you and me—'

He hesitated, and Helen Radowsky motioned for him to proceed.

'The cause of your violent antipathy to me is as groundless as your manner of showing it is dangerous to yourself. Of the truth of this I can convince you, if your prejudice is not too strong to be influenced by your better judgement. But I came not to speak of myself; the fact that my knowledge of your acts and associates has not led to your arrest, is a warrant that my feelings for you are kindly, at least—'

'Your excellency is magnanimous,' she said, with a little satirical laugh.

'I claim no such credit, Miss Radowsky; but I must confess, I am at a loss to know why you should persecute the Ruloffs, who have never done you a wrong.'

'I persecute the Ruloffs!' she exclaimed.

'Pray do not deny what I have the strongest proofs of. My object is not to upbraid nor to intimidate, but to ask that you rest satisfied with what you have done. I assure you it will be the only way to retain your own safety.'

'I thought you were not going to threaten,' she sneered; adding: 'I have no desire to injure the Ruloffs; and in saying that I was the cause of their being sent to prison, you give me credit for a power second only to that that released them.'

'I have no desire to argue with you, Miss Radowsky. You know, in your own heart, if I am right. I know, in my own heart, I would not do you an injustice. Again I beg that you desist from your efforts against the Ruloffs, and save me the labor of protecting them at your expense. Against myself, if you will not be changed, continue the heritage of causeless hate; the purity of my mo-

tives and the fairness of my acts must ever be my defense.'

He bowed in his courtly way; and Helen Radowsky tried to reply, but the words stuck in her throat. When she had regained the command of her tongue, the door had closed behind the prince, and she heard the musical jingle of bells as his sleigh drove off.

'My God! My God! why did I permit myself to see him again!' she cried, her clinched hands upraised, and a pleading, hunted look in her dark eyes.

She threw herself on a lounge, and closing her eyes, covered her face with her handkerchief, but she could not shut out from her mind or sight the splendid, sodierly form, nor the tender, brave eyes and Apollo-like features of the prince. His musical voice, still rang in her ears, and she swayed herself as if to its rhythm.

'Oh my father! my father!' she wailed. 'Can no less noble sacrifice avenge thy many wrongs!'

She lay there till the fire burned low, and the cold from without began to creep in, but no cold could chill the fever of her whirling brain.

CHAPTER XIX.

PRINCE GORTSCHAKOFF ASTONISHED AND ANGERED.

At the hour of ten the following morning General Gallitzin went to the Gortschakoff palace, to see the old statesman, before going at noon to the Winter Palace.

Having announced his arrival he was amusing himself by looking over the pictures in the salon in which he was waiting, when to his delight and surprise, the Countess Alexandrina entered.

'I am glad, and yet sorry, to see you,' she said, retaining his hand, and leading him to a deep window, where they could converse unobserved.

'Sorry?' he repeated, with a questioning smile.

'Perhaps that is not the right word; but I have been very anxious for you and Vladimeer,' she said.

'Vladimeer is free again; and I stand before you healthy in body and untroubled in mind,' rejoiced the prince.

'True, dear General, and your conduct made my heart leap with joy. But, alas! I fear it is all to be undone.'

'Undone!' he exclaimed.

'Yes! I sent a message to Vladimeer telling him to get into concealment for the present. I do not hesitate to tell you that our separation has but strengthened our attachment, and forced us to claudestine communication.'

'That is ever the case. But why should you advise Vladimeer to hide ?'

'Because, from the mutterings of my uncle I am satisfied Vladimeer will be arrested again this day ; and I am equally well satisfied that your action will be reversed by the Czar, and result, perhaps, in the loss of your position.'

'For the position I care nothing; but should the dissapproval be as pointed as you think I will resign every office, and quit Russia for ever.' he said deci ively,

'No, No !' she cried. 'It must not come to that. My uncle likes you ; and seems determined that you and I shall be married. I have not dared to undeceive him. But it is fortunate that you and I fully understand each other.'

'Very fortunate my dear Countess. Yet, General Gortschakoff, must know the truth sooner or later ; and, for myself, I intend to undeceive him at once. He has much power, but even the Czar cannot control the affections of his own family, much less of his subjects—'

'Hush ! here comes Count Kiseleff, whispered the Countess.

The count must have seen them ; but except a deepening of the color on his florid cheeks and a more rigid carriage of the head, he gave no indication of the fact.

'There is one man that will rejoice at your misfortunes,' said the countess, nodding after the retreating courtier, and adding : But little good it will do him. Ah! he little imagines that the despised son of an exile is his rival.'

'Prince Gortschakoff, awaits General Gallitzin.'

'You will hear from me again to-day, God grant success,' whispered the countess.

The prince pressed her hand, smiled encouragingly, and followed the messenger.

During his long military and diplomatic career, General Gortschakoff, had gained a complete mastery of his feelings ; and so great was his control of face and voice that it was simply impossible to get any clew from them that would lead to an idea of his actual thoughts. Had he sent for Prince Gallitzin to compliment him on some act that particularly met his approval, his manner could not have been more pleasant, nor his greeting more cordial.

Nodding for the aid to withdraw, he made some common place remark about the weather, thought the ice would be broken up in the Gulf of Finland in a month, and rejoiced that the days were getting so much longer. On all these subjects the prince was of the same mind, though he could not help admiring the apparent indifference of the man to the subject, that was uppermost in both their minds.

At length, General Gortschakoff, with the manner of a man just recalling a question of no particular importance, asked :

'Do you find the duties of your office onerous ?'

'They keep me busy, and it seems almost impossible to become familiar with the delicate intricacies of the place.' replied General Gallitzin.

'Young soldiers fresh from the field usually find civil positions irksome. I know it was so with your grandfather after we returned from the French campaign ; and your father never liked the position in Poland. But it is the part of a good soldier to obey orders—'

'I agree with you, General.'

'And I must confess the orders are not always of an agreeable nature.'

'Decidely not, in my case. But while orders must be obeyed, it is mortifying to think that, in one's zeal, an injury is done to the innocent—'

'True,' said the old diplomat ; but I hope you have had no such experience.'

'I regret to say I have.' General Gallitzin saw that he must open the subject himself, and so determined to plunge into it at once.

'It is simply impossible for me to examine critically all the papers brought for my signature, and I find I cannot trust the judgement of my subordinates.'

'Then you should replace them with men that can be trusted,' said General Gortschakoff, with emphasis.

'True, but that does not destroy responsibility for past errors. Here is a case in point ; I signed, without knowing what it was, an order for the arrest of Vladimeer, son of the exiled General Ruloff, and it was executed. Subsequently, the Countess Ruloff was arrested, under the rules, for attempting to enter her own house, There was no charge against her, and that charge against her son was false. The mother and son were placed in the vilest cell in the Prison of the Exiles. The moment I heard of their arrest I hastened to the prison and released them.'

'The act did great credit—very great credit – to your heart,' said General Gortschakoff, stroking his brows, against the grain, with a thumb and finger. 'But it is to be regreted that you assumed the power, of freeing prisoners, which, up to this time, has been the jealous prerogative of the throne. The guilt or innocence of prisoners can only be determined by a proper trial before a regularly constituted tribunal. Your error must be remedied.'

'Remedied, your excellency? Why that is

just what I have done? I could not wait to explain to the Czar the manner in which these people were arrested through my error. To leave them in that wretched dungeon would be inhuman. So I released them on my own responsibility. If I have erred, the blame and the punishment, are mine, not theirs.'

'You think this Vladimeer Ruloft innocent, eh?' asked General Gortschakoff, toying with a bundle of papers on the desk before him.

'Of this charge—most emphatically.'

'I regret that you did not look into it more carefully. I have here evidence—indisputable evidence—furnished by the detective Braski, and others, that Vladimeer Ruloff is a conspirator, a Nihilist, and a Socialist. The young man is said to have fine abilities, but this only makes him the more dangerous. I can see no reason why we should make an exception in his case. The safety of the country is the first consideration.'

'If the country can only be saved by continued inhumanity, I shudder for its existence.'

' If the idle and discontented aim at the life of the land, they must bear the consequenc . And we, who are patriots, should stand ready to remove our dearest friends to achieve this end. Neither rank nor fame can be an excuse for treason. And more, if found in a member of our own family, that member should be at once given over to justice,' said Prince Gortschakoff, speaking in a higher pitch, and with an icy glitter in his eyes.

'Your rule is, no doubt, wise; but, if enforced, it would break up one half the families in Russia, and make us two classes —prisoners and jailers. But to return to Vladimeer Ruloff, You know his family is impoverished—once they were the richest and most honored in Russia. He was dismissed without cause or notice from a petty professorship in the school of mines. He was idle for some time, and, consequently, discontented, and with no reason to love the powers that broke up his family and parted them. On the day following his arrest he was to have taken a position with the American merchant, Mr. Johnathan Cushing, that promised him the means to support his mother and sister. If he is permitted to go on, I will pledge my honor that he offends not in the future.'

'Your generosity may get you into trouble. Is it quiet becoming or prudent in one holding the confidential and important position that you do, to associate with the family of a man convicted of treason?' asked General Gortschakoff.

'The fact that I have done so and will continue to do so must be my answer as to the becomingness and prudence. The Ruloffs

and Gallitzins were ever friends, and the Gallitzins are not distinguished for forsaking friends in misfortune,' said the prince hotly.

'And to maintain the family reputation you associate with those people?' said General Gortschakoff, with the shadow of a sneer.

'Yes, your excellency,' replied the prince, rising, with flushed face and flashing eyes. 'To maintain the honor of the Gallitzins, who have been brave in war and true in love l'

'What has love to do with it?'

'Much, your excellency, Elizabeth, daughter of the exile Count Ruloff, has blessed me her pure love, and gladdened my life by consenting to be my wife.'

'What!' exclaimed the old man, his excitement getting the better of him. 'Do you dare tell me this?'

'I dare do anything that becomes a man?'

'And you think it becomes a man to lead me to believe that you are paying your addresses to my niece, when you are betrothed to—to—'

'To the first lady in Russia, your excellency. As to the Countess Alexandrina, her heart is bestowed on a member of the same family.'

'Prince Gallitzin, you are working your own ruin! Reconsider before it is to late.'

'I have considered my acts, In anticipation of discharge, I here resign to you the office obtained through your favor.' The prince advanced and laid his resignation on the table.

CHAPTER XX.

THE RESIGNATION,

What, sir! Do you dare come into my presence prepared to set me at defiance with this resignation?' demanded General Gortschakoff, his grey eyes flashing and his long hands trembling with excitement.

'On my honor as a noble of Russia, I disclaim any disrespect to General Gortschakoff as a man, or as the second officer of the empire,' said Prince Gallitzin, restraining his indignation at this outburst. 'But I claim the right to resign a position I never sought, when my acts meet the disapproval of the appointing power! My sword, my fortune, my life, are at the service of my country; but my affections are my own, so far as they are under my control. I think your excellency understands me.'

The prince bowed and steps back as if about to withdraw.

'Hold l' cried General Gortschakoff. 'Hold l this, the last audience you may ever have with me, is not at an end. Do not think I am disappointed that the daughter of my nephew is not to form an alliance with the house of Gallitzin ! But I am disappointed, that the son of my friend should have consorted with such people.'

The old man rolled a bundle of papers in his hands as he spoke, and in conclusion struck them forcibly on the table.

' I protest that your office does not warrant this freedom to insult me, and through me the remnant of the house of Ruloff, that as yet is not in your prisons, nor condemned by your tribunals ! Must I stand under your palace roof and hear, without retort, your unwarranted attacks on the family of that lady who is soon to become my wife ? The swords of my ancestors would leap against me from their scabbards if I permitted it. One year ago I . left the great, free land of the West to fight for Russia. Now,' continued the prince, dejectedly, ' there is peace with the Moslem, and I am ready to leave the graves of my fathers and the land of my birth behind me forever.'

' Ha, ha ! You have been preparing for this, eh ?' half shouted the old man.

' No ; I said I was ready.'

' To go whither ?'

' To the free land of the West.'

' Nay, Wladislas, Prince Gallitzin, you are ready to go to the slave land, the exile laud, the prison land of the East,' exclaimed General Gortschakoff, all his diplomatic self-control scattered to the winds.

' As ready, and with as much against me, no doubt, as many who have gone there. But the man, be a base-born or noble, who says that Wladislas Gallitzin was ever, by word or act, faithless to Russia and our Czar —whom may Heaven protect—lies !' said the prince, proudly,

' I did not say you had been so charged.' General Gortschakoff opened the bundle that he had been toying with, and said : ' Glance at those papers, and tell me whose writing is on them.'

' It—it—looks like mine,' replied the prince.

' Is it not yours ?' asked Gortschakoff, laying his hand so as to prevent the reading.

' That I cannot tell without knowing the contents.'

' These papers were sent to me—how, it matters not, at this time. Men skilled in handwritting declare they are yours, and the evidence they contain against you is strong enough to warrant your arrest—to forfeit your life.'

' Your excellency jests,' said the prince, with a complacent smile.

' I am not given to jest. My duty is to hand it over at once to the law you have outraged, but my respect for the dead blinds me for the time. I will make an effort to save you.'

' To save me !'

' Aye ; to save you. I will retain those papers, and other evidence against you, for thirty-six hours ; this will give you time to get outside of the empire, and to save your life. I council you to leave here at once, and depart from Russia forever. Do not add madness to treason, by remaining,' said the general, tapping his bell.

' Treason !' exclaimed the prince.

' Your excellency,' said an aid, entering, in response to the bell.

' My interview with Prince Gallitzin is through. Order my sleigh. I am due at the palace at noon,' said General Gortschakoff to the aid.

Prince Gallitzin could not remain after this. Like one in a horrid dream he turned and left the palace ; and as he entered his waiting sleigh, he saw Count Kiseleff standing near by with a fiendish sneer on his florid face.

' To the Winter Palace?' asked the driver; he knew that his master had intended going there at noon.

' No ; to the Hotel America,' replied the prince.

As the prince was about to ascend to Mr. Cushing's apartments, he met Michael Pushkeene coming down, with a smile on his face that showed he was pleased with himself, if not with the world. Seeing the prince, he stopped, raised his hat, and said :

' Pardon me, General Gallitzin, but I am sure you are a friend of my friends—the Ruloffs.'

The prince replied with a haughty look that made the little wretch very cold and uneasy.

' I have been calling on the countess and her daughter ; they are not in a condition to receive visitors, and I feel I am not exceeding the liberty warranted by my interest in Miss Elizabeth when I protest against any intrusion at this ti—'

Before Pushkeene could finish the sentence the prince had seized him by the collar and pitched him, with the greatest ease, to the landing below.

' Curse you ! I'll get even !' Enjoy your freedom ; it won't be for long ! I'll get even !' shouted Pushkeene, who would have gone on shouting and shaking his fists in the direction the prince had taken had not Vladimeer Ruloff appeared unexpectedly behind him, and by a well-directed kick precipitated him into the street.

Madam Ruloff had not yet recovered from her shock, but she was able to sit up in an American easy-chair in the parlor, where

Elizabeth was ready to anticipate her every want.

'Oh, Wladislas!' cried Elizabeth, meeting her lover, and taking both his hands. 'I am so happy to see you! We feared that the rumors might be true!'

'The rumors?' he repeated, after stooping and kissing her.

'Yes,' she said, choaking back a sob, 'that you were arrested for liberating my mother and brother. Even Mr. Cushing thinks you are both in danger.'

At that moment Vladimeer and Mrs. Cushing entered the room, and gave a hearty greeting to the prince.

'By the great Washington!' said Mr. Cushing, with more excitement than his wife and daughter ever saw him manifest before, 'I wish you and young Ruloff were out of this country; and if you would save your necks you must get out, for there is a black storm gathering about you, and it will burst before you know where you are.'

'I came,' said the prince, 'to advise Vladimeer to fly at once—'

'That,' joined in Mr. Cushing, 'is what I have advised. I have just been out and made preparations for his flight. He must leave before another day dawns, and he must conceal himself at once. And you, my dear Prince, should not allow your pride to stand in the way of your safety. It is conceded by all right thinking men that you are the victim of a conspiracy; but it is not the custom of your judges to seek causes. It is to sentence, not to secure justice, that your courts are organized.'

'Alas! that is too true!' sighed Madam Ruloff.

'But it is a shame,' said Mr. Cushing, 'that the people submit to it! They wouldn't if they were Americans!'

'Vladimeer should save himself. As for me,' said the prince with lo:ty firmness, 'I would not fly from a real danger. Why should I notice the rumors with which the air is filled? Why should I, against whom no wrong can be alleged, fly from the laws of the land, which but yesterday I bled to uphold? No! I will stay and face the accusers! But I am certain not even treachery can bring aught against me.'

'That's brave!' said Mr. Cushing, admiringly; but it isn't discretion.'

Vladimeer was just on the point of adding that he could not think of saving himself while danger threatened his friend, when he was prevented by the entrance of a closely veiled lady.

Hastily discoverring her face, the Countess Alexandrina kissed Madam Ruloff and her daughter; then throwing her arms about Vladimeer, she cried:

'Fly! fly! Within one hour the gens-d'-arms will be searching for you. A sleigh awaits you near the Troiskoi Bridge! Use my name! Here is a disguise! There is not a second to lose!'

'Save yourself, my son! my son! For our sakes, go!' wailed Madam Ruloff.

'Come with me,' Mr. Cushing drew Vladimeer into another room, and in a few minutes a stout, heavily-bearded man came with the brave American; and after he had taken a hurried farewell to his friends, Vladimeer, thus disguised, left the room.

'And now,' continued the young countess, 'let me beg you, General Gallitzin, to follow the example Vladimeer has set. The walls of Saint Petersburg are covered with Nihilists proclamations applauding your recent acts, and speaking of you as a friend.'

'What care I, when the story is false?'

'Was not the story false that sent my father to Siberia? Oh, Wladislas! as you love me, be advised,' cried Elizabeth, taking his hand and covering it with her tears.

'Nor have I told you the worst,' said the Countess Alexandrina, flushed with excitement and indignation. 'Your palace has just been searched, under the direction of Count Kiseleff, and papers—incendiary papers in your own handwriting—have been found!'

'A forgery!' shouted the prince.

'Aye, a forgery, but none the less dangerous for that. Your servant Varwitch has been a spy on you. He it is that showed where the papers could be found.'

'And where is he now?' asked the prince.

'Varwitch, with his companion, one Helen Radowsky, has gone with General Gortsckakoff to the Winter Palace; there they will tell their stories to the Czar.'

'And what care I for their lies?'

'Fear and danger, real or imagined, has made the Czar suspicious of his own children. He is ripe to credit treason to any one and eager to punish. He will believe these people; and you know what the result will be.'

'I concede your earnestness, and the truth of what you say. But Wladislas Gallitzin faces the danger, even though it leads to the scaffold! I will go to my own palace and there await the result of this excitement.'

Prince Gallitzin took an affecting leave of Elizabeth and the others, then went down to his sleigh as calmly as if he were bent on a journey of pleasure.

'To my palace,' he said to the driver; and was whirled away as if in flight.

CHAPTER XXI.

BEFORE THE CZAR.

The rosy color had fled from Helen Radowsky's face, and there was a wild, troubled look in her dark eyes, and a masculine set to her lips, as she listened to Varwitch relating the success of the conspiracy he had advanced under her guidance.

'The papers are in the hands of Count Kiseleff—in Gortschakoff's hands by this time, and the next sleep of Prince Gallitzin will be taken in the darkest, deepest dungeon of the Prison of the Exiles,' said Varwitch, in conclusion.

'He cannot escape arrest,' she said, as if thinking aloud, rather than asking a question.

'Impossible! Nay, he cannot escape death. In view of his rank and gallant services, they may give him the choice of being shot or being hanged. As a soldier, he will of course elect to be shot. You have done your work well, Helen—admirably well. You have a genius for such work.'

'Yes, Varwitch!' she exclaimed, with a chilling laugh. 'I have a genius and the best of tools ready in my hands. But come; you say we are ordered to the Winter Palace.'

'Yes, and it may be that we are forced to stand in the very presence of the Czar, and answer his questions,' said Varwitch, with the manner of a man not at all pleased with the prospect.

'For that I care not. Alexander is but a man, and neither a good nor a great one.'

True, Helen, but all the more dangerous for that. Ah! here comes Pushkeene; he is to accompany us,' said Varwitch, coming back from the window, just as a knock was heard on the door.

'The puppy will soon be powerless to bark or fawn.' The sneer with which this was said was in striking contrast with Helen Radowsky's manner when Pushkeene entered the room, and proved her to be a consummate actress. 'I am glad to see you, Doctor, very glad to see you! What is that without —a sleigh?'

'Yes, Miss Radowsky, Count Kiseleff placed his own sleigh and driver at our disposal,' said the elated Pushkeene. 'Oh, it will be grand for us to enter the great square of the palace in state and have the guards present arms. When my father hears of it his old eyes will weep for joy, and his heart will flutter with delight!

'Little hearts, like little leaves, are easily fluttered. Have you seen the Ruloffs?' asked Helen Radowsky.

'I left them an hour ago; and as I came away I met a sergeant and a squad of gens-

d'armes, going to the Hotel America, for Vladimeer,' replied Pushkeene. He thought it prudent not to detail the particulars of his exit from the hotel.

'And did the fair Elizabeth smile on you?'

'Oh,' rejoined Pushkeene, 'her mother and two American *women* were present, so of course she had to dissemble her love. But she will soon be completely under my protection; I have planned for that. Now let us be off. Hey! but the people who play our game and wear masks, throughout the land, would be amazed to see us going to a royal sleigh to consult with the Czar of all the Russias.'

Varwitch led the way, grinding his teeth, for he was a Nihilist at heart; and Helen Radowsky, refusing Pushkeene's proffered hand, made no attempt to hide the expression of loathing that his words brought to her face.

'Drive around the palace. Show us off. Take us where as many soldiers as possible must present arms. I will pay you for it,' said Pushkeene, who, in order to be more conspicuous, had taken a seat before the driver.

Refusing to be tempted into a violation of orders, though he did not return the rouble Pushkeene had slipped into his palm, the driver went directly to the entrance near the Hermitage, where Count Kiseleff was waiting to conduct them to the audience chamber.

'Follow me,' said the count, with the manner of a man who despised his tools in this dirty work.

As they followed him in single file, Braski, who had figured in these pages as Mr. Neuman, of Moscow, fell in behind and accompanied them to the presence of General Gortschakoff.

The old man was in the same room, and sitting in the same attitude and by the same table, as on the night when Prince Gallitzin of Novgorod received from his hand the high evidences of his imperial master's approbation.

'Which of these people is Peter Varwitch?' asked General Gortschakoff, looking from a memorandum in his hand to the people whom Kiseleff had brought in.

'I am, may it please your excellency,' said the owner of that name, coughing and bowing.

'How long have you been in the service of Prince Gallitzin of Novgorod?'

'Nearly one year.'

'You know his habits?'

'Thoroughly, your excellency.'

'His companions?'

'Yes, excellency.'

'And his handwriting?'

'As well as my own, your excellency.'

'Is that the statement you swore to?'

General Gortschakoff handed him a paper; and after glancing at it intently, as if to be very, very sure of the truth of every statement he made, Varwitch handed the paper back, with a profound bow, and said:

'That was written by me; and to its truth I have sworn.'

'Why did you not inform the authorities, when you discovered that your master was consorting with Nihilists and making his palace the fountain from which emanated the incendiary publications that flood the nation?'

'I was a servant, your excellency, and my master among the most powerful men of Russia. Who would believe the son of a serf against the son of the Gallitzins of Novgorod?' replied Varwitch,

General Gortschakoff raised his shaggy brows, as if he saw the truth of this reasoning, but he did not say so. He turned to Helen Radowsky and told her to tell what she knew.

What she knew was through her lover, Varwitch, who long since had communicated to her the facts to which he had sworn. Prince Gallitzin had visited *her*, but being an honorable woman, she had not encouraged him. On one occasion, when she went to his palace to see Varwitch, the Prince had driven her home in his sleigh, and, at parting, had given her a dagger with which to defend herself. Here it was.

She laid the weapon on the table, and General Gortschakoff picked it up and examined it with much curiosity.

Your name is Radowsky?' he asked, suddenly.

'Yes, your excellency,' she answered.

'Family from near Warsaw?'

'Yes, excellency.'

'Father released and fled to England?'

'Yes, excellency,'

'I thought as much. This is very remarkable. The dagger I hold in my hand is the one with which your father attempted the life of General Gallitzin—father of the prince—who was then governor of your province. Your father would have been executed, but General Gallitzin, who was a most magnanimous man, plead for his life, and saved it. Afterwards he worked for years to have your father pardoned, and he succeeded. I even think he sent the very money, by a strange hand, that helped to establish your father in his new home. But I forgot: Pushkeene and Braski, let me hear your statements.'

General Gortschakoff turned to the men named, and so did not see the deathly pallor that came over the young woman's face as, with a trembling hand, she again concealed the fatal weapon in her breast.

Pushkeene and Braski told their damning falsehoods with all the glibness of experts and the gloating of ghouls. They had seen the prince a dozen times with Vladimeer Ruloff, who was the head of a Nihilist organization. They had seen the friends going in and coming out of the secret meetings of the discontented students. But why repeat after them the hideous and poisoning falsehoods?

'His majesty desires to see the witnesses against Prince Gallitzin,' said Count Kiseleff, entering while Pushkeene was in the midst of an interminable narration condemnatory of the prince and highly laudatory of himself.

General Gortschakoff rose with more difficulty, and a sigh escaped his lips as he led the way into the smaller reception chamber where the Czar was impatiently waiting.

'In the presence of the Czar! This is but the first step of my advancement. Oh, if my father could only see this!' thought Pushkeene, as, with trembling limbs and downcast eyes he neared the august presence.

'Kneel,' whispered Count Kiseleff.

The four conspirators knelt before the Czar, who sat on a chair and watched them suspiciously.

'These are the people, your majesty, who have brought to your notice the conspiracy and treason of Wladislas Gallitzin, Prince of Novgorod, and general in the imperial artillery,' said General Gortschakoff, speaking as if he hoped for replies that would show there had been a great mistake as to the conduct of Prince Gallitzin. The Czar questioned each in turn.

The three men spoke first, with as much strength if not so fully as before; but when it came to Helen Radowsky's turn, she stammered, clutched at her throat as if strangling, and then fell unconscious at the imperial feet.

She was carried out by the attendants, and the three men were sent away with Count Kiseleff.

'A most serious charge strongly sustained,' said General Gortschakoff, when he was alone with the Czar.

'If this be true,' replied the Czar, raising his hands, 'whom can I trust? whom can I trust?'

CHAPTER XXII.

HEMMED IN.

Reaching his palace, Prince Gallitzin hastened to the room where he had heretofore transacted public business, and throwing himself into a chair, summoned Ruryk the Cossack.

The orderly at once responded, and, as he stood before his master, there was a fierce gleam in his eyes and an ashy hue on his bronzed cheeks.

'Ruryk!'

'Present, General,' replied Ruryk, with the inevitable salute.

'Who has been here since I left?'

'Thieves and robbers under the efficient leadership of his diminutive excellency, Count Kiseleff,' responded Ruryk.

'What was done?'

'They came with a warrant to search the palace; had it been otherwise I would have spitted a half dozen with my sword; as it was, I was forced to see the vultures going through your private apartments and looking through your papers,' said the indignant Cossack.

'Who told Kiseleft where my papers were?'

'Who but the traitor and spy, Varwitch! A man who once licked your hand like a starved cur, and who now snaps at your heels like the whelp that he is!'

'I fear he is a spy,' mused the prince.

'Worse than a spy. I have seen him writing and working with pens and paper, about which dangerous weapons, thank Heaven, I know but just enough to print my name. Varwitch, it is said, could imitate even the writing of your master, the Czar.'

'I doubt it not, Ruryk. And where is Varwitch now?'

'Gone, General. He was too cunning and cowardly to remain. By Saint Peter I will come even with him, or I wear not a sword!'

'You must keep calm, Ruryk; I am in the meshes of a plot, and only the greatest coolness and firmness on the part of myself and friends can keep me from ruin,' said the prince, dejectedly.

'From ruin, my master?'

'Aye, Ruryk; from ruin.'

The Cossack stepped back, and closing the door softly, again advanced and said, in a low, earnest tone:

'Ruin can never come to the house of Gallitzin.'

'It has come to houses as great Ruryk.'

'There are none so great under the throne. Hear me, my master, nor believe that it is my rash Cossack's blood that prompts my words.' Ruryk hesitated, and the prince nodded for him to continue.

'From the barrick of the private to the throne itself, all Saint Petersburg is debating the loyalty of Prince Gallitzin of Navgorod. The doubt is only in the eyes of the envious—and noble.'

'That I believe,' said the prince.

'That I am sure of,' continued Ruryk. 'The men in the ranks are all your friends, and the ten thousand Cossacks now in the imperial city are ready to a man to die for you.'

'I thank them, but want no such sacrifice.'

'Nay, my master, hear me out,' said Ruryk, dropping on one knee and bowing his head as if in prayer. 'The Gallitzins of Novgorod have ever been Cossack chiefs, ere Sobieski of Poland and Catherine the Muscovite united to enslave Little Russia, then ruled by the Attaman, Bogdan Gallitzin, the successor of the renowned Mazeppa. The Gallitzins have led the Cossack lancers to victory; and when there is no Gallitzin to lead them, the lances will rest, and the valor of our race will be an old man's story to please the doubting young. Yield not to tyranny at the prompting of treachery. Fly faom here at cnce, and raise the banner of revolt! This, rather than wear the chains of a condemned exile! The soldiers await your signal! And the sound of the Gallitzin bugle, a hundred thousand lancers will respond with gladsome shouts, from Bothnia to the Azov—'

'Hush, Ruryk, you must not talk in this way,' interposed the prince; but he could not check the fiery language of the indignant and impetuous Cossack.

'I am not saying, my master, what nine tenths of the soldiers in the city are thinking, if not saying, at this time.'

Ruryk sprang to his feet, and raising his arm, he demanded, as if addressing a throng:

'Is the hero of the Belkans to be treated like a dog, at the instigation of spies! Are we, who followed him through the hell of Plevna, and under his lead descended to the very gates of Constantinople, to stand like terror-stricken children, while our idol is torn from us? Not so I for, by the blood of all the Cossack dead, we are still men! and though willing to endure individual wrong, we shall strike back at him who aims a blow at the last represensative of our Attamans— our kings!'

'You mistake, Ruryk; nothing is to be gained by revolt. The authorities have not yet laid a hand on me. If they should do so, rest assured they have what to them is good and sufficient reason. Fear not that I shall not come out right. I will face the conspirators and prove my innocence. To fly from here, and even to openly revolt against a wrong, is to acknowledge to the world that I am, or have been, guilty of a dishonor. Believe this, Ruryk, and so tell all my friends. Russia must be saved by our patience and self-denial, as she was by our swoids. My foes are the foes of my country. Hark! Was that a bugle?' asked the prince.

Ruryk stepped to the window and replied:

'Yes, General; the bugle of Freehoff's Cossack battallion, sounding a halt.'

'Before my palace?'

'They are surrounding the palace, General. See,' said Ruryk, pointing to the street.

The prince looked out and saw the horsemen forming a cordon about the building.

'A guard of honor,' said the prince, with a sad smile.

'True, your excellency, for from Captain Freehoff down, there, is not a man holding a lance below there who would not lay down his life for you if need be. But see, General a lady has descended from a sleigh—a veiled ady, and she has been halted.'

The prince looked in the direction pointed out by Ruryk, and saw the Countess Alexandrina, veiled as when she visited the Hotel America.

Hastily penciling a few words on a slip of paper, he bade Ruryk take it at once to Captain Freehoff, who was then expostulating with the lady.

Ruryk hurried down, and the captain read the words :

'The lady is the Countess Alexandrina—niece of General Gortschakoff :

GALLITZIN.'

The countess was admitted, and, under Ruryk's guidance, was at once conducted into the presence of the prince.

'I hastened hither,' said the countess, 'hoping to get to you before the soldiers reached the palace. But though I did not succeed, it may not be too late for me to utter again my warning—to fly!'

'I have not yet been informed of my misdeed,' replied the prince ; 'and as to the Cossacks, until their presence is explained I must consider them a body-guard, more honorary than essential.'

'I heard the order given; they are not to restrain you, but to watch your movements,' said the countess.

'A distinction without a difference,' he laughed, adding, in his calm way : 'I hope Vladimeer got away.'

'I do not believe that he has even left the city. I have a sleigh and the best horses at his service; and Mr. Cushing had even more perfect arrangements, but he availed himself of neither.'

'Yet he left in disguise.'

'True ? but you know how impulsive he is. Should he be caught there can be but one end.'

'Exile ?'

'No, General,' she gasped, 'death !'

'Well, there are worse things than death,' said the prince, thoughtfully ; then asking with some earnestness : 'But do you not forget, my dear Countess, that you are exposing yourself to the very dangers from which you would save Vladimeer and me ?'

'I think not of myself,' she answered, sadly.

'Then we must consider for you. You know how, at this time, suspicion attaches without cause. I question if even your uncle would interfere in your behalf if he thought you did not favor his every act.'

'I have not tried to conceal my feelings from him ; and I propose to be more candid in the future than in the past. If there were fewer dumb mouths there would be less muttered treason. I wish I were a man !' she said, almost fiercely.

'General, his excellency Count Kiseleff desires an audience,' said Ruryk, appearing in military attitude at the door.

'Will you not enter another room until the count leaves ?' asked the prince.

'No! I desire him to see me hear. I will look at him, and make him feel more than ever what utter contempt I have for him 'she responded.

'Conduct the count hither,' said the prince.

The count, in full uniform, and looking more elated and consequental than usual, advanced into the centre of the room and began his speech before he became aware of the lady's presence.

'Wladislas, Prince Gallitzin of Novgorod, I am ordered by my imperial master, Alexander, Czar of all the Russias, to direct that you move not outside the limits of your palace without further orders.'

'It is always my pleasure to obey the orders of my master,' said the prince, with a courteous bow.

'Say to your imperial master,' said the countess, coming forward and piercing the aid with her eyes, 'that I, the niece of the great chancellor, pledge my life for Gallitzin of Novgorod.'

CHAPTER XXIII.

STRANGE VISITORS.

When Count Kiseleff saw the Countess Alexandrina and heard her words, he was so overwhelmed with confusion and jealousy, that he quite forgot what else he had to say. He coughed, stammered, walked backward, and trippling on his trailing sword, he stumbled out of the room with a tremendous clatter and not a particle of dignity.

'There,' said the countess, as the aid disappeared, 'I think Count Kiseleff will not be in doubt as to my feelings—from this time on.'

'Surely not ; but he will have more rea
son than ever for his animosity toward me
We do not hear nor fear the howling of th
wolf when the lion is roaring. I do not giv
Kiseleff a thought.'

'Nor do you give your own safety
thought.'

'I think of it continually, for life is dea
to me, for Elizabeth's sake. I cannot say
it in the way my friends propose. That i
settled,' he said calmly, but with unmistak
able firmness.

'As a noble you are right. I have been
speaking as a woman, not as one who would
shrink from martyrdom. With the Ruloffs
and Gallitzin of Novgorod I cast my lot.
From this day on, we shall be more than
friends.'

The beautiful girl threw her arms about
him, kissed him on both cheeks, and then,
with the veil drawn over her face, she ran
down to the sleigh and was driven off.

Alone again, the prince set about preparing his house for his expected departure.
Ruryk and his valet, Paul, helped him with
his papers, and received instructions as to
what they should do in the event of their
master's arrest.

They were still working at midnight, when
Captain Freehoff knocked at the office door.

'A messenger from General Gortschakoff,'
said the captain when Ruryk admitted him.

'Conduct the messenger here at once,' replied the prince.

In response, Captain Freehoff led in a
stout, heavily bearded man, dressed in a
mixture of peasant and clerical garb.

'What! does General Gortschakoff in-
trust such a man as you with a message to
me?' demanded the prince, while the messenger stood bowing and waving his sheepskin cap.

'It is but a note, excellency: here it is.
It was handed me by an aid; and he gave
me two roubles to carry it here.' The man
handed the note, and looked furtively up as
the prince read.

(PRIVATE.)

GENERAL :—Should you remain in Saint
Petersburg, his majesty will be forced to
bring you to trial. The consequences you
can imagine. I have represented to him
your youth, noble descent and brilliant services, all of which he conceded; and I
begged that you might be permitted to leave
Saint Petersburg, within the ext twenty-
four hours, undisturbed. To this he agreed.
Captain Freehoff has been privately instruc-
ted to permit you to pass his guards. Should
you need other aid, it will be furnished by
communicating the fact to Count Kiseleff,
through Captain Freehoff. A neglect to
vail yourself of this most gracious, and I
may add scarcely warranted permission, will
be looked upon as a defiance of the author-
ties, and a corroboration of the charges now
made against you. Arrest, trial and conviction must inevitably follow. If not for
yourself, for the memory of your ancestors,
think of this,   GORTSCHAKOFF.

'Who was the aid that gave you this
note?' asked the prince, folding the paper
and placing it in a portfolio.

'Count Kiseleff, may it please your excellency.'

'Where is he now?'

'He awaits my return and your answer,
at the entrance to the Prospekt,' replied the
man, shading his eyes and bowing.

'Say to the aid that Wladislas, Prince
Gallitzin of Novgorod, refuses to be insulted.'

'That is all, excellency.'

'That is more than enough. Here are
five roubles for bearing my answer back.'

The man kissed the coin, and bowing and
muttering again, with that cringing servility
that marks the ex-serf, he withdrew, and was
conducted to the street by Captain Freehoff.

In the shadow of the great portico the
messenger stopped. Suddenly his stooped
shoulders straightened, the head was raised
proudly erect, a youthful fire came to the
eyes, and the voice changed from harsh dis-
cord to music as he took the captain's hand
and exclaimed :

'He did not suspect me !'

'No; by my faith, Vladimeer, the disguise
is perfect, and your acting wonderful,' said
the captain, who, though a soldier, was yet
as the reader will remember, the ace of
hearts at the first Nihilist meeting we have
recorded.

'That note purports to come from Gortschakoff. It asks General Gallitzin to fly—'

'Good advice,' interrupted the captain.

'It is not so intended ; at all events it is
wasted. The note was written, to my knowledge, by Varwitch. at the solicitation of
Kiseleff. If the general got through your
line—and I presume you would not see him?'

'My eyesight is not good to night,' laughed the captain.

'If he got through your line, it would be
to run into the lines of the gens-d'armes,
now watching every avenue.'

'You amaze me !'

'It is the truth, Captain. But I must be
going. When and where can I see you
again ?'

'I guard here until relieved to-morrow at
noon.'

'Who relieves you ?'

'After that hour Prince Gallitzin will be
in the dungeon of the Exiles. Come to my
quarters after dark.'

With this understanding, Vladimeer Ruloff suddenly became a stiff, clumsy man, past middle age; his shoulders stooped, his neck shortened, and he shambled off, a veritable serf, with his big sheepskin cap pulled over his face. As he went down the middle of the wide street a sleigh sped past, and reined in.

'Hello! you, sirrah!' said Kiseleff, from the back street.

'I am getting back, excellency; and faithfully have I performed my duty,' said Vladimeer, advancing and bowing, with his eyes on the ground.

'What answer?'

'The answer is, 'Wladislas, Prince Gallitzin, refuses to be insulted?''

The count repeated the message and bit his lip.

'Excellency, your servant lies not; those were his words, and accompanied they were with much anger of manner.'

'And the note—he t e it up?'

'Of course, excellency; for he was in truth angered.'

'So be it; so be it.'

Kiseleft drew up the robes, and was about to settle back in the sleigh, when he stopped and surveyed his messenger for some seconds.

'Where come you from?' he asked.

'I am, or was, till my wife died, a poor school teacher at Kief,' replied Vladimeer.

'And what brought you to Saint Petersburg?'

'To see my son, a corporal in Freehoff's lancers, and to get employment, that I may drag out my remaining years in usefulness and comfort.'

'You can read and write, and hold your tongue?'

'Excellent well, excellency.'

And Vladimeer cringed and scraped and bowed, and reached out as if he would seize the aristocratic hand and press it to his bearded lips.

'Here, call at this address to-morrow morning before ten. If on further inquiry I find you deserving, I may do something for you.'

Kiseleff tossed him a card, and as the sleigh dashed off he mused:

'I want a man who knows something and who is unknown here; this boor may answer my purpose.'

Vladimeer picked up the card, and for an instant straightened up and held it aloft, with an exultant glow in his eyes and a defiant wave of his arm.

'I shall follow you, nor lay aside this good disguise till I have probed to the bottom of the villainy that has cursed my life. Ah! the peasant's garb and the peasant's ignorance are a mighty armor when suspicion turns against the nobles.'

He lapsed again into his slouching manner, and reaching the sidewalk he went along with great rapidity, but never was he tempted into the use of any gesture, step, or look that was not perfectly consistent with the character he had assumed.

He peered into the restaurants and public houses as he hurried on, and came to a halt before an establishment brilliant in its illumination and in the crowds of officers and civil dignitaries within.

He entered, and taking a seat in a shadowy corner, where he could hear the groups talking in loud tones without being himself observed, he ordered a plate of black soup, and pretending to be cooling it with the spoon and his breath, as is the habit of the peasant, but his ears were open to every word.

'Too bad, said one. 'I would never have thought it of the handsome, gallant Gallitzin. I saw him leading the charge at Plevna, and—'

'Oh,' interrupted another, 'it is a case of love. He became blinded by the arrows of the gentle god and forgot himself.'

'Love?' repeated the officer who was going to tell about the charge at Plevna.

'Yes. It is said that the general has loved since his boyhood the beautiful Elizabeth, daughter of the exiled Count Ruloff. He could not associate with the sister without meeting Vladimeer, and being impressed by that reckless but talented young gentleman's Nihilistic notions. It is too bad.''

'Where is Vladimeer Ruloff now?' asked an artillery officer, puffing a line of smoke directly at the peasant near by, and following it with his eyes.

'He was captured, released by Gallitzin without authority, and is now fleeing the country. See: here is a reward of ten thousand roubles offered for his capture. It is impossible that he can escape.'

The speaker drew the proclamation in question from his pocket and read it through. It was principally filled with a description of that fugitive, which, despite some inaccuracies, was highly complimentary to his manly beauty and fine accomplishments.

'I knew Vladimeer Ruloff,' said a lieutenant of engineers. 'We were classmates; and I must say his flight disappoints me. I never thought he could fly a friend in distress. I could not think that he would save himself and leave his sick mother and beautiful sister in the hands of the gend'armes.'

'What? Have they been again arrested?' asked the artillery man.

'Yes,' replied the engineer. 'Two hours

ago, against the protest of Mr. Crshing and all the Americans in the city, they were taken to the hospital of the Prison of the Exiles.'

CHAPTER XXIV.

HELEN RADOWSKY WOULD PAUSE, BUT CAN-NOT.

'Why, Michael, Michael, my boy, what is this?' asked old Pushkeene, peering through his big, iron-rimmed spectacles at his son, who sat at the opposite side of the supper table, in the little room over the pawnshop.

Not knowing what it was, the son seized the newspaper which his father held toward him, and read, among many paragraphs of a similar nature:

'Madam Ruloff and her daughter are in the hospital, Prison of the Exiles. The daughter, against whom there is as yet no charge, elected to accompany her mother. It is believed in official circles that Vladimeer Ruloff will be caught before twenty-four hours.'

'Did you know that?' asked the old man.

'I knew the mother was going to be arrested again, replied Michael, 'but I didn't think the daughter would be so foolish. But perhaps Elizabeth could not help it. She had no home nor friends. What else could she do?'

'Why, aint you her best friend?

'I am, father; but she will not marry till her troubles are past, and I do not see where I could care for her.'

'Why, aint there your mother's room back there, neat and trim as when she died? Tell her she can have that; and, Michael, if she was to accept our hospitality, I wouldn't stop at hiring a servant—a medium-sized servant,' said the old man, his sallow face shining with the oil of generosity.

'I could get her here, I am pretty sure,' said Michael Pushkeene, looking contemplatively at the sooty ceiling. Then bringing his eyes down to his father's face, he added : 'She'd pretend not to like it at first.'

'Would she, indeed?' grunted the old man, comparing mentally his home with the gloomy Prison of the Exiles.

'Yes. The Countess Elizabeth Ruloff is of a romantic turn, and great as is her love for me, she would naturally contrast our humble but happy abode, not with where she is now, but with the stately halls of her ancestors.'

'And that's what you call romance, eh?'

'That's one phase of it, father. But get a woman to dust the room up a bit and make it cheery. I think we'll have the Countess Elizabeth here before long,' said Michael Pushkeene, rising, and putting on his cap an l great-coat.

'Don't run any risks for her; remember, my son, the good name of a merchant is better than the tarnished name of a noble. Oh, things are getting leveled very finely indeed, very finely.' And chuckling with pleasure at this thought, the old man went down to the pawnshop, and the young man went out of the house, as was his invariable rule, after supper.

Michael Pushkeene's mission was to find Varwitch and Helen Radowsky, but, as he went on, his thoughts were certainly not of a friendly nor trusting character.

'I can see through her,' he reasoned. 'I can see she is making a tool of that love-blind Varwitch, and she thinks she is making a tool of me. Ha, ha! She is going to hand me over to the authorities just as soon as I cease to be useful to her. Funny that we should both be playing the same game; very funny indeed. She is moved by a spirit of revenge that must soon be gratified and exhausted ; I am moved by a spirit of ambition that is sleepless and undying. I can use my knowledge, which, in this case, is truly power, to ingratiate myself with the Czar. I can strike a blow at Nihilism that will ring through the empire and shatter the organization. Peasants have been ennobled and poor men given princely estates for less service to the nation. Oh, I see my way up, up, up ! For my sake the beautiful Elizabeth will be again received in the society she once adorned ; and it may be that Michael Pushkeene will have as proud a title to give her as that I helped tear from the crest of her father. Did not the ignorant, peasant-born Catharine become an empress ? Why should the coronet of a count be beyond the reach of the cultured Pushkeene?'

Why, indeed ! The ambitious young man saw no insuperable reason, nor is it our duty as a faithful chronicler of these stirring events, to interpose an objection. From Fortune's magic wheel greater improbabilities have been evolved, and less competent men have rushed, rocket-like, from lower depths to far more giddy elevations.

As has been said, Helen Radowsky had many places where she could meet her fellow-conspirators besides her own home. Indeed it was a part of the tactics of the Nihilists to meet in places apparently the most public ; certainly the best calculated to avert suspicion ; and they changed about so often that only the initiated, and only such of those as were constant attendants, could tell where the next meeting would be. Like sharp stones at the bottom of a stream, they most agitated the water when in sight.

On the Little Neva, which is one of the

city's arteries, there are a number of cave-like wine vaults, resorted to in summer for their coolness and in winter for their heat, not to mention the fluids dealt out to parties that for a trifle can control, for the evening, a little side vault, of which there are many, all damp, close, and with a graveyard smell that the city sextons declare to be very pleasant and home-like.

To one of these vaults Michael Pushkeene went, unconscious that a stout peasant with a slouching gait, and wearing a sheep-skin cap, was keeping up with his hurried strides.

In the front of the vault was a bar, before which idle sailors and broad-shouldered porters were drinking.

'Any of my friends here?' asked Push-keene, addressing a man behind the bar, and at the same time winking and turning up the corner of his mouth, in a way intended to be quite agreeable and confidential, but the effect of which was positively ghoulish.

'Back in the very furthest back vault,' whispered the man retailing the wine; and he, too, winked and turned up the corner of his mouth, and made a sound of sucking his teeth. Michael Pushkeene lit a cigar and sauntered back in the direction of a gaslight that in the gloom seemed miles away. After turning and twisting among great hogsheads, rows of inverted bottles, and side vaults—like cells set in the walls of a subterranean prison—Pushkeene came to what looked like the end of the passage. Here he kicked with his boot against the wall, and in response the deep, hoarse voice of Varwitch, sounded as if it came up from the bottom of a very deep well, was heard demanding:

'Who is there?'

'I, Michael Pushkeene.'

Pushkeene, felt very certain he heard the same hoarse voice growling 'the devil!' by way of comment, but not being a sensitive soul, the ejaculation did not offend him.

There was a grating sound; the door, by a powerful push, was slid into the wall, and a branch vault, twenty feet deep by ten in width was revealed.

As Pushkeene entered, the door closed behind him, and a murmur, that might be in welcome or disapproval, ran from lip to lip of the score of people seated about a table that occupied the centre of the vault.

There were decanters and glasses on the table, and one-third of the assembly was composed of women—harsh-featured and strong-minded, unless, indeed, Helen Radowsky, who occupied the post of honor, might be considered an exception to the first peculiarity.

'Ah, Pushkeene, you are just in time to have the decanters filled up. Your credit is good here,' laughed one of the men.

'Give the order, and I'll stand it,' said Pushkeene, with a fine affectation of gallantry and liberality.

The wine was brought in, and the glasses filled. Helen Radowsky was evidently stopped in the middle of a matter of importance that she was communicating to the assembly, for when quiet was again restored she took up the thread of her opinion and began speaking in those low, intense tones that struck against the side of the vault and came back in chilling echoes.

'Yes; it does seem hard that Prince Gallitzin should be sacrificed; he is so brave, so noble, so handsome, everything calculated to win the admiration of men and the love of women, that it is natural to shrink from contemplating the ruin hanging over and about him to crush him. But his death—his death will be a blow that will ring through Russia, and shake the throne, as if the volcano on which it rests would break out; and it may—it may.'

'I must confess,' said an old man, who looked like a veteran conspirator, and spoke in a cautious, piping voice, 'that I cannot see just how things are moving. There must be trea on in our ranks, else how comes it that Vladimeer Ruloff is a fugitive? I cannot see through it, unless there are traitors in our ranks. In the days of Nicholas, the faithful had but few traitors; we made short work of t em, I can tell you.'

'He was impetuous,' said Varwitch. 'I think he was m re dangerous to us than he was to the authorities. But I was going to say, that as we have made it a part of our plan to implicate the nobles, would it not be well to set a trap for his fussy excellency, Count Kiseleff?'

The suggestion was greeted with a shout of laughter and the rapping of glasses on the pine t ble.

'It can't be done,' said Pushkeene. 'The man is too sharp.'

'You think so, Michael!'

'I do, Varwitch.'

'Well, you are more innocent than I have thought. I could to-morrow, and without manufacturing evidence, convict Count Kiseleff of a crime that w uld send him to Si-beria for life. I know he hopes to send me there when he has finished using me, but I propose to keep of service to him.'

'As you did to General Gallitzin.'

'No, Pushkeene, nor as you did to Vladimeer Ruloff, but of genuine service,' sneered Varwitch, while Helen Radowsky's beaming eyes showed that she enjoyed the chance of a conflict between her tool and her lover. 'By Saint Peter,' he continued, as he filled up his glass, 'I will initiate him, and have him seized by the gens-d'arms, whom I will start on the tiral of some one else.'

'Better, far better,' said the veteran conspirator, 'that we stick to our legitimate purpose. Agitation, agitation, agitation; with now and then the destruction of a monster by a cool, strong hand. Know you n t that Ghourko is recalled ?'

Helen Radowsky said she was aware of the fact, and a keen-eyed woman of thirty by her side, said spitefully :

'Let him come back ; let im return, and true as my name is Vera, there will speedily be a vacancy in his office.'

After an hour's talking in this way, Helen Radowsky proposed that 'the sociable' should adjourn for the night, which was agreed to, with the amendment that all the wine—with a doubtful view to economy— should first be drank.

The announcement could be heard on the cppposite side of the door ; for as soon as it was made the old peasant, who had been crouching with his ear pressed to the boards, rose a d hobbled away. He stood on the street when the party came out ; and while he did not ask for alms he wav d his sheepskin cap obsequiously, and made such other overtures as led Helen Radowsky to believe he would not object to a gratuity, for she dropped a coin into his palm before going off between Varwitch and Pushkeene. They went to Helen Radowsky's house, and on the way her lover, by hints t at were rude and even coarse, tried to get rid of Pushkeene ; but that amb tious young gentleman had a skin over his feelings that was quite impervious to any verb l attack.

'If,' he said, when they reached the house, 'you let me have a few minutes private conversation with Miss Radowsky I will leave you at once.'

Without waiting for Varwitch's consent, Helen Radowsky drew Pushkeene to one side and asked :

'What is it ?'

'I want you to help me to release Elizabeth Rul ff, whispered Pushkeene.

'She is free to leave the prison.'

'I know ; but I want to have her under my charge. My father will prepare apartments for her ; and this will give me the longed-for opportunity to show my love.'

'In short, you want me to help you kidnap this beautiful girl ?'

'That is not the word ; she loves me.'

'Then you can have no trouble in getting her con ent to come under your protection,' said Helen Radowsky.

'I have looked into the matter from all sides, Helen, and I have come to the conclusion that you *must* help me.'

'Must !' she exclaimed.

'Aye, *must !* that was the word I used,' he said, with a snaky glitter in his little black eyes.

'And if I refuse? she asked, shrugging her shoulders and elevating her eye brows pettishly.

'You cannot refuse this,' he persisted.

'To refuse would be to make you my bitter foe, eh, Michael ?'

'Draw your own conclusions ; but answer ; Will you help me ?'

Helen stroked her low, broad forehead thoughtfully for some seconds, then looked up with a sweet smile and said :

'Yes, Doctor, I will help you ; direct me, and I will help you.'

CHAPTER XXV.

THE IMPENDING SWORD FALLS.

Prince Gallitzin remained up all night finishing his report to the government and setting in order his own private affairs.

'Ruryk, who refused to leave him, declaring he felt as if he never wanted to go to bed again, said, after breakfast :

'I am afraid, General, the wretches will seize you to-day.'

'And if they should, Ruryk, what matters it to one who is innocent ?' asked the prince, looking with a sad smile into the troubled eyes of his faithful follower.

'By my faith, master ! it seems to be of no moment to you ; but for many hours I have been thinking of myself,' said Ruryk.

'Of yourself ?'

'Yes ; what is to become of me, should death or the prison claim you ?'

There were tears in the Cossack's voice, and his long, brown hands twitched nervously.

'Have you not followed me into the harvest fields of death Ruryk ?'

'Aye, General ; many a time.'

'And had I fallen, would you not have rejoined your regiment, and fought on as gallantly as if I led ?'

'No, General ! no ! Had you fallen as we crossed the Danube, the waves of that river would have closed above my head. Had you fallen at Plevna, there would have been no Ruryk to bear you back. Had you gone down in the passes of the Balkans, the Moslem's fire would have freed my Cossack soul, and I would have followed you to Heaven's gates, certain of admission if in your train !' The Cossack raised his hands, and eyes and voice were now filled with tears. 'Master, the moment you ● not free I shall become a prisoner !'

'No, no, my faithful Ruryk ; remain free to uphold the good name of the house of

Gallitzin,' said the prince, now deeply affected by this evidence of devotion.

'Ah! if you too would will to remain free, a hundred thousand Cossacks would die before harm could befall you. But you choose to submit—'

'To obey is ever the first duty of a soldier.'

'True, my master; but the Cossacks say: "Obedience, where the heart does no approve, is cowardice!" My father died while bearing your wounded father from a Circassian battle-field. The Cossack was true to his Attaman, but gave no thought to his emperor. Blood is stronger than water, and the traditions of centuries are dearer than the ukases of to-day—'

A cough at the door interrupted the fiery Cossack. Captain Freehoff stood in the entrance with his hand to his hat.

'A message for me, Captain?' asked the prince.

'A message, General, from our imperial master the Czar,' replied the captain.

'What is it?'

'I am ordered to conduct you at once to the Winter Palace, where his majesty awaits to give you audience.'

'To obey the Czar is ever a pleasure. Wait; I will join you shortly.'

Prince Gallitzin retired, and soon came back dressed in the resplendent uniform of a general of artillery.

In the meantime Ruryk had ordered out the general's horse, and his own, and stood holding their bridles before the palace.

The prince vaulted into the saddle. Ruryk mounted and took an orderly's position to the rear. The Cossack trumpet rang out, the Cossack lances were upraised, and like a body-guard they followed the prince to the Winter Palace. On the way the soldiers on guard, or standing in groups on the street, came to a salute. Citizens stopped and raised their hats to the young hero; and, unmindful of the chilling blast, windows were thrown open by fair hands, and handkerchiefs were waved in salutation.

The Czar was in the small audience chamber, with a few attendants, and his great chancellor, Gortschakoff, when the prince entered, and advancing directly to the emperor's chair, bowed, and dropped on one knee.

The sad, troubled face of the 'Autocrat of all the Russias' was paler and more troubled than usual this morning; but as his bluish-gray eyes looked at the young soldier at his feet an expression of undisguised admiration lit them up with an unusual glow. He said, with a touch of feeling in his voice:

'Wladislas, Prince Gallitzin of Novgorod, rise, for we would speak with you touching acts that to us are inexplicable, save on the ground of mental aberration.'

Prince Gallitzin rose, and General Gortschakoff nodded approval of the royal words.

'If my acts have not met the approval of your majesty,' said the prince, ' it is generous to attribute them to mental aberration; but as a noble and a soldier, I disclaim any desire to be freed from the responsibility of my acts. Whatever I have done has been deliberately done. This I say, strong in the consciousness that I have done naught to warrant the disapproval of your majesty, naught that I would undo, naught that would not become a noble and a soldier of the empire.'

'What! General Gallitzin, do you dare to intimate that we have summoned you into our presence without good. cause?' said the Czar, a shade of haughty anger in his voice.

'May Heaven forbid that my heart should harbor such a thought against your majesty,' the prince hastened to say. Adding: 'I but speak from my own knowledge of my own acts. For one day I have been imprisoned in my own palace; and now I stand accused without a charge; assailed without seeing my assailants.'

The Czar turned to General Gortschakoff, and said peremptorily:

'Explain the charges against General Gallitzan, and name his accusers.'

'The principal evidence, your majesty, is in the handwriting of the prince, obtained through one of his servants named Peter Varwitch, and corroborated by one Helen Radowsky, a teacher of languages in the imperial family,' said General Gortschakoff.

'What say you to those papers? asked the Czar.

'I have not seen them,' replied the prince, ' but if they contain one word that is treasonable, by any interpretation, or that would compromise me as a soldier and a noble, I pronounce them forgeries, and declare myself to be the victim of a conspiracy.'

'Conspiracy,' said the Czar, bitterly, 'is the plea of all the accused.' Then turning again to the old chancellor, he said:

'Question him touching the Ruloff matter.'

'To the truth of that, your majesty, Prince Gallitzin has confessed.'

'Confessed!' repeated the Czar.

'Nay, pardon me, your majes'y, not confessed; for that word would imply regret for a criminal act. Certain that I have done no wrong, I could make no confession.'

'Prince Gallitzin takes a fine diplomatic exception to the meaning of words,' said General Gortschakoff, with a cold smile. 'It may be that I have not used the proper term. Acknowledged may be better than *confessed.* Prince Gallitzin *acknowledged* to me that he liberated from the Prison of the Exiles, and against the protests of the governor, Madam Ruloff and her Nihilist son Vladimeer.'

'Both of whom were imprisoned through my own error,' responded the prince. 'I could not permit them to remain in a dungeon, to which my own mistake confined them.'

'Prince Gallitzin was appointed a chief of our secret police, but impatient of honors, he constitutes himself a judge, and assumes as a right the royal preorgative,' said the Czar, with unmistakable anger.

'If I have erred,' said the prince, proudly, 'I, not the innocent Ruloffs, should suffer.'

'I will say to your majesty, as an offset to the innocence of the Ruloffs, that Prince Gallitzin—who has been pleading for the pardon of the exiled coun'—*acknowledged* to me that he was still a frequent visitor to the disgraced family; nay, more, that he was betrothed to Elizabeth, sister of Vladimeer the Nihilist, for whose head it has pleased your majesty to offer ten thousand roubles.'

In response to the Czar's angered, questioning look, Prince Gallitzin, calmly, though his cheeks were blazing and his eyes on fire, said:

'If this be a charge, I plead guilty. It is true that I visited the Ruloffs; true that Elizabeth Ruloff—against whom neither slander nor conspiracy has yet dared to utter a word or raise a hand—is to be betrothed. For this I have no excuse to offer. It may be well to remind your majesty that the houses of Ruloff and Gallitzin have mixed their life currents on the battle-field, through the centuries of struggle that built up the throne which your majesty adorns, and whom may Heaven protect. And at the altar, too, have those currents been united. The exiled count was my friend. His daughter was the idol of my boyhood, and the pride of my maturer years. On my return from the war I found the countess and her children poor and friendless. Policy might have prompted me to keep aloof; but the Gallitzins of Novgorod spurn policy when it runs counter to the promptings of their hearts. Yes, I freed the mother and brother of my betrothed wife. I have explained my conduct, and stand ready to bear the royal displeasure, should that act be disapproved.'

'It is disapproved,' said the Czar, stamping thrice on the floor. 'It is disapproved and condemned as a treasonable utterance that confirms the other charges.'

The prince bowed and stepped back, at the same instant a captain and file of men from the imperial guard entered the chamber.

'Hand your sword to Count Kiseleff,' said the Czar.

The prince turned pale, but obeyed.

Then, addressing the officer of the guard, the Czar continued:

'General Gallitzin is a prisoner. Conduct him at once to the Prison of the Exiles, and counsel the governor to guard him closely.'

The officer bowed. The guard formed about the prince, and on foot they took him from the imperial palace to the dungeon of horrors.

CHAPTER XXVI.

A SAD MEETING AND A SADDER PARTING.

Madam Ruloff lay on a cot in the prison hospital, and by her side sat Elizabeth, holding the sick woman's hand and looking out of the low window at the court-yard, in which the snow was melting under the spring sun, and through which soldiers and prison officials were coming and going.

Madam Ruloff was sleeping, but the pained expression of her face, and the spasmodic working of her hands showed that, even in sleep, she had not left her troubles behind, but was living over again the sufferings that shadowed her life.

There were other cots in the room, all occupied by women, many of them noble by right of birth, and all of them prisoners, charged with the one crime of treason.

From her position Elizabeth could look up and across the court-yard, and see, like a giant pepperbox, the wall with its little, black iron-grated openings, through which light was admitted at times, into the gloomy cells. Here and there she saw a bleached face, with glassy eyes upturned to the far-off blue, and a bony hand clinging to the rusty bars.

All this she saw, and all the horror it implied she felt; but the appalling scene did not monopolize her thoughts. Where was Vladimeer? How did the prince combat the enemies who were hemming him in.

As if in answer to her question, suddenly there appeared before her eyes the form of the prince surrounded by soldiers. At first she could not credit the evidence of her senses. It was a realastic waking vision. She saw him stand and calmly survey the prison walls. He turned and their eyes met.

It was no vision, but a gladsome reality. Surpressing the cry that rose to her lips, she ran to the door, opened it, and before a hand could be interposed to stop her, and flew into the court-yard.

'Wladislas! Wladislas!' she cried, breaking through the line of astonished soldiers, and throwing her arms about him.

'Elizabeth! my own Elizabeth!' whispered the prince, pushing the loosened golden hair from her beautiful pale face and kissing her.

'Come, come with me, and see where my mother lies sick unto death; a sight of you will bring back the light to her eyes and warm the sluggish blood in her veins?' sobbed Elizabeth.

'I cannot go now, dear one,' said the prince, turning away his face to hide his emotion. 'Soon I hope to see her. Soon, I trust all will be well.'

At this moment the officer in command of the guard came out of the reception room, and raising his hat to the prince, said:

'The governor of the prison is ready to assign you quarters.'

'Go, Elizabeth. May heaven protect you!' The prince kissed her again and took a step as if he should leave her.

'Tell me! tell me!' she cried, 'are you too, a prisoner?'

'Alas! yes. But it will not be for long, he answered.

She staggered back, with her hands clasped to her forehead, and would have fallen had not the prince caught her.

Recovering, she turned with a fierce energy to the officer of the guard and said; with tragic impetuosity:

'Know you this man is that you are daring to imprison?'

'General Gallitzin.' replied the officer, saluting. 'But think not, my lady, that I am doing one thing, in connection with this matter, that does not cut me to the heart like a sword thrust.'

'Then how comes he here?'

'By order of the Czar, my lady.'

'By order of the Czar!' she repeated slowly. Then with the intensity of Medea before making her awful sacrifice, she raised her white arms to the drooping sun and cried out: 'And this is the way Russia rewards patriotism and valor! And by sacrifices like this Alexander hopes to cling to his rocking throne! Oh, men of Russia, soldiers of the Imperial Guard, there is one greater than the Czar! One who now looks down at the first Gallitzin of Novgorod a prisoner—by order of the Czar. Soldiers, look up at the pale faces in those barred windows. They are your countrymen; your brothers, consigned to this living grave by a score of base tyrants! Denied God's free air, which even the dogs in the streets have in abundance, and dying! dying! dying!!—By order of the Czar!'

The soldiers bit their lips and a wild light shone on their bronzed faces. The priestess

had given expression to thoughts which the bravest would not dare to utter.

'The governor awaits the prisoner,' said the swarthy, hairy secretary, holding the door open with one hand, and glaring like a savage beast at the prince and Elizabeth Ruloff.

The prince folded his arms about her again and straining her to his breast, he whispered:

'To God, to my darling, to Russia, I am faithful unto death.'

With an expression of heroic resolve on her face, she stood in the court and watched till the prison door closed behind the prince and the soldiers. Then she returned to the hospital, and knelt beside the cot on which her mother still slept. She clasped her hands, and her lips were set with a firmness that no words could strengthen. Her eyes were closed to earthly sights, that she might the better look unobstructed into the Eternal presence. Not a whisper, not a sigh escaped her, and yet to the hearer of prayers her supplications were more audible than the musical thunder of all earth's organs.

Helen Radowsky saw the guards marching with the prince in their midst, and keeping out of sight—for she dreaded the eyes of the man she had ruined—she followed the escort to the prison.

She stood in the arched entrance and saw the prince towering like Saul above his fellows and looking more than ever like a demi-god. Her heart smote her, and she could have rushed in and thrown herself at his feet, and begged for pardon and mercy. A feeling inconsistent with, but stronger to a fiery nature like hers, than revenge, possessed her. She could have placed his foot upon her neck, at that moment, and died happy if he crushed her. She loved him! Loved him! and the truth flashed on her like the light of a terrible revelation.

'I will confess all! He must not die! I can save him, for is not this my work?'

Under the impulse she would have run in at once, had not the unexpected appearance of Elizabeth Ruloff checked her, as if an icy cold hand had seized her heart-strings and held her back.

'How beautiful she is! How like an angel, with her blue eyes, yellow hair, and snowy skin! She is in his arms: his lips are pressed to hers. He loves her! he loves Elizabeth Ruloff! Hark! that is his voice. How like music in its low, sad cadences. What! Is she calling down imprecations on the Czar! Bravely said! Noble words! Ah! the hot iron of tyranny has burned into her heart and lit there the fire of liberty that can never die! See; they are parting. He is whispering his love!' Helen Radowsky took a step forward, stopped and fell back with a groan, as the prison door closed.

She recovered and watched Elizabeth Ruloff going back, watched her till she disappeared.

'Why should I hate that beautiful girl?' she asked herself; and to herself made answer : ' Because I am a fiend and she is an angel. Because my heart is fil ed with the boiling lava of revenge and malice, and hers is pure as snow. Because—I hate her because she loves—because *he* loves her! Oh ! if I could have kept my vow and destroyed without ever looking on him ! Oh ! if I had never been born, or been born without this heritage of hate ! It is too late to stop now, Too late ; too late ! Ruin, inevitable ruin, impends over all who come in contact with me—Ah ! who was that ? What, you Puskkeene ! Why play the dog by coming on me unawares ?' She asked, stopping and glancing at Michael Pushkeene till he turned a paler yellow with fear.

' I have followed you and called to you, but you seemed so absorbed in yourself,' whined Pu hkeene, ' that the only way I could attract your attention was by laying my hand on your arm.'

' And why should you want to speak to me here– here on the street ?' she demanded, drawing her dress aside with a gesture of indescribable contempt.

' I saw you and wanted to congratulate you on your splendid success. Gallitzin is in prison, and he won't come out again till the day he walks between two files of lances to execution. Oh, your present game is ever so much better than striking him down with a dagger. Of course, you will wear a gala dress the day the handsome hero of the Balkans kneels on his coffin. He won't have his eyes blindfolded. He will insist on looking into the barrels of the rifles. Are you ready ? Aim ! Fire !'

Pushkeene threw up his arms, staggered, closed his eyes, and by other expressive pantomine showed how the prince would act when the fatal moment came.

' You are a monster !' she hissed.

'What ! A monster for admiring your work, come, now, Miss Radowsky, if I am a monster for going into ecstacy over this masterpiece, what must the artist be that conceived and executed it ?'

' A demon !' she replied.

' By Saint Peter, that sounds true, though I doubt if demons would feel complimented if they heard the comparison. Why, Helen, my father thinks you are the most wonderful woman that ever lived, and he knows but little of your doings. If your own father knows—in his disembodied state—what you have done to avenge him on the house of Gallitzin, he must turn over in his coffin in a paroxysm of joy,' said Pushkeene, with a ghoulish leer.

She gasped, as if trying to speak; but unable to make a reply, held down her head and effected indifference to her companion till she came in front of her own house.

' Well,' she said, with much of her old manner, ' I suppose Doctor Pushkeene, will continue to honor me no further. I thank you for your gallant escort. Here I am safe.'

She made as if to go into the house, but he stepped before her and whispered :

' When will you be ready to help me ?'

' To help you ?' she repeated.

' Yes—to help me to the guardianship of the beautiful Elizabeth.'

' I am ready now.'

' Now ?'

' Yes ; but you must give me a plan, she said.

' My plan is this : She is still free to leave the prison. Varwitch can imitate Vladimeer Ruloff's writing as easily as he did Prince Gallitzin's—indeed, I have seen him do it to perfection. Get Varwitch to write a note in Vladimeer's hand, which I will have conveyed to Elizabeth. Let it say he is still in the city, and ask for a meeting at this address. Pushkeene gave her one of his father's cards, and added : ' Nothing must be said about me or my father—that would be ruinous. When she comes there, veiled and alone, I will take the responsibility of managing the rest. What say you ?'

Helen Radowsky hesitated, and looked up at the snow thawing on the roof.

' I will think about it,' she said.

' I want an answer now. I am not a child to be treated in this way,' he said, angrily. ' Will you do it or not ?'

' Yes, I will do it,' she said, with decision.

' Ah ! now you are youself again. I will see you to night.' And Michael Pushkeene raised his hat, twirled his cane, and walked off with the light, brisk step of a successful man.

CHAPTER XXVII.

VLADIMEER SECURES AN APPOINTMENT.

' It was his own fault. I assure you he alone is to blame, and whatever he may suffer he will deserve. The Countess may shake her head and bite her lips, yet what I say is true, said Count Kiseleff, addressing the Countess Alexandrina, who stood with him in the main salon of her uncle's palace.

' You differ from nine-tenths of the people in Saint Petersburg,' she said.

' Perhaps I do ; but, to tell you the truth,

I have never gone into ecstacies over Prince Gallitzin.'

'No '

'Others have, but I can see nothing that he has done that any one else might not have done if in his shoes,' said the Count lightly.

'In his shoes!' she repeated, with a curl of the lip. ' It is impossible for you to imagine yourself so fortunately situated ?' This with a little laugh that the count r.ghtly construed to be satirical. She continued : 'I am told the prince was ordered by the Czar to hand you his sword ?'

'You were rightly informed. He surrended his sword to me,' said the Count, with an air of pride that he would not have assumed had he any conception of the honor it would have been to the soldier who forced the surrender of that sword in battle.

'Pardon me, Count Kiseleff—Prince Gallitzin did not *surrender* his sword. He yielded it at the bidding of the man in whose service he had worn it with such honor, and you took it, as Ruryk the Cossack, or any other orderly, might have taken his master's bridle or cloak. Though I must confess that there is an honor reflected on the man who holds the weapon of such a soldier for an instant.'

'I cannot debate with the Countess Alexandrina,' said Kiseleff, loftily. ' Some day I trust you may know me better, and respect me more.'

As he turned to leave, the countess, who at heart despised him, and saw she might be able to use him to defeat himself, called to him.

'Pardon me, Count Kiseleff. It is the privilege of our sex—or rather, a characteristic that exhibits itself by privilege, to speak without due thought. Let us at least be friends, seeing that there is nothing to be gained by being foes.'

Scarlet with excitment and joy at this unexpected expression from the lips of the woman he worshiped, the count turned back, dropped on one knee, and taking her proffered hand, pressed it reverently, if not passionately, to his lips.

'I thank you for those words,' he whispered.

He rose and would have remained to say more, great as had been his haste before had not a page entered with a message that called the countess away.

Feeling very much happier and consequently like a very much better man, Count Kiseleff went down to where his orderly was holding his horse. He was in the act of mounting, when the old peasant with the sheepskin cap and matted hair and beard approached him with gestures so abject and

a bend so obsequious, that he could not have got lower without getting down on all fours at the nobleman's feet.

'Ah, you again !'

'Yes, excellency ! I, your servant, your slave ; I kiss your feet,' whined the peasant.

'You took my note to the governor of the Prison of the Exiles ?' asked the count.

'Yes, excellency, I took it and he engaged me ; and I come to thank you,' said the cringing peasant.

'He let you look into the hospital ?'

'Yes, excellency. Oh, I saw the hospital; strong is the prison attached thereto, and mighty is the Czar.'

'You saw the Countess Ruloff and her daughter ?'

'Oh, yes excellency, I saw them. Sad is the mother, and beautiful as the moonlight on an ice field is the daughter.'

'I do not care to hear you drivelling. You are sure you would know the daughter again ?'

'Anywhere, excellency, anywhere ; and after the lapse of many years.'

'The secretary of the prison will know when the lady Elizabeth goes out, for she is free ; he has instructions to let you follow her—'

'Yes, excellency, yes.'

'Hear me out, dog. You are to follow her, and mind that you do so faithfully, and let me know where she goes, what she does, and, if possible, what she says.'

As he said this Count Kiseleff tossed the peasant a coin, mounted his horse, and rode away with the dignity of a man who felt no little pride in having been appointed that day assistant-chief of the secret police, under the tyrant Ghourko.

Our readers having already learned to look, under the admirable disguise and acting of this peasant, for Vladimeer Ruloff.

Watching the count out of sight, Vladimeer hobbled down to a wine vault on the Little Neva, and going back to one of the side vaults he found Captain Freehoff and Ruryk awaiting him.

'What news ?' asked the captain, after Ruryk had closed the door, and, as a further precaution, stood with his back against it.

'Good news ; glorious news,' replied Vladimeer.

'Then my master is free !' cried Ruryk.

'Not yet, Ruryk, not yet ; but he will be, as certainly as you stand against that door.'

Vladimeer then narrated his interview with Kiseleff, as an introduction to his saying that he had been to the prison.

'I saw my mother, but she was too weak to bear the shock, so I kept on acting, though I thought my heart would burst, so intense was my desire to throw my arms about her and kiss her wasted face. I made myself known to my sister.'

'And how did she bear it?' asked Captain Freehoff.

'Like the heroine that she is. To-night I go on duty as an extra watch. I am to have charge of the cell in which the prince is confined, and Kiseleff desires me to get him to speak, and if possible, to induce him to violate the prison discipline.'

'And what can be the object for that?'

'That was the question I asked myself, Captain, and this is the answer I have given myself. If the prince is reported against, by the meanest attendant—and Heaven alone knows how unutterably cruel and mean they all are—he will be sent to the dark, damp cells far under ground, where the count, no doubt, hopes he will die before the trial comes off.'

'But, whispered Ruryk, bending forward in his earnestness,' you can release him at once!'

'Not immediately, Ruryk, for he would not leave. We must wait till he is condemned to death, as he soon will be—'

'Condemned to death!' cried the Captain.

'Yes, that is the programme. We must have all the arrangements for flight ready. In this Mr. Cushing, the American, to whom I have made myself known, will help me. But those are details that can be entered into hereafter.'

'You are playing a desperate game,' said the captain.

'True for I am a desperate man.'

Vladimeer rose, and with a suddenness that was positively startling to the others, he took on the character of the old peasant, which he had dropped for the moment. It was particularly alarming to Ruryk's superstitious nature.

'Here, Ruryk, here is Count Kiseleff's last gratuity; order some wine.'

'Heaven forbid that I should touch his gold,' said Ruryk, drawing back.

'Nay,' laughed Vladimeer, 'it is now my gold, and was originally the Czar's in proof of which it still bears an impress of his head.'

Reconsidering his resolution, Ruryk took the coin and went for the wine.

After all had drank, Ruryk, now back in Freehoff's company, bade Vladimeer and the captain good night, and went to his quarters.

'Well, Captain,' said Vladimeer, when they sat opposite, with the door closed, ' which is the worst, the treason of Nihilism, or the tyranny of the Autocrat?'

'Between the infidelity of the one and the iron hand of the other there lies no choice. For one I wish Russia were a thousand leagues behind me, and my face turned to the West,' said the captain, despondently.

'Nibilism is the outgrowth of a want; we can hardly blame a people who were yesterday slaves for trying to gain the favor of past masters by becoming sycophants. Russia is in a horrible state to-day, but could we reverse the order of things, and make masters of the crawling herd, Russia would be a hell. Oh, for a leader! Oh, for another Joshua to lead us through this desert! A Washington to guide us with great patience up to liberty?'

Vladimeer and the captain—leaving the wine untasted—talked until midnight was pealed from the hundred steeples of Saint Petersburg; then they left the vault, each taking a separate way.

CHAPTER XXVIII.

PREPARING FOR THE TRIAL.

It could not have been chance on the part of the governor of the prison that led him to assign Prince Gallitzin to the fated cell which even the heartless officials grew to look on as the grave of hope.

'From this cell,' said the turnkey, 'Count Ruloff went to the mines of Siberia. Here Vladimeer the Nihilists was confined. He, if living, is the only man that ever left here for freedom.'

'I thank you for your comforting information, my friend,' said the prince. 'Now, if you will see that I have fresh air and pure water I will not trouble you.'

The man went off, muttering that fresh air and pure water were not down in the list of articles furnished to prisoners. And the prince, weary in body, and at heart, and confused in mind, lay down upon the hard bench, with his cloak under his head.

Assured of his own innocence, he felt no sense of degradation in his humiliating position; but looking back on his services and sacrifices, his noble soul rose in revolt against the ingratitude of crowned monarchs.

The lengthened day died out, as he could see by the Stygian darkness that took the place of the cold gray light in the cell.

At times he dozed, but never for an instant did he sleep; for through the long, black hours he heard every step of the guards, the clanging of musket-butts in the stone passages, and the groaning and coughing of the slowly dying victims in adjoining cells.

Another day came, and a similar night followed, and Prince Gallitzin, whose active life had been spent among men, began to feel that oppressive sense of loneliness that makes solitary confinement so horrible, even the full glare of the sun.

He repeated aloud a few stanzas of a poem learned in early childhood, but the strange sound of his own voice startled him, it seemed so out of place in this abode of darkness, solitude and silence.

He was dozing again, as a weary soldier dozes on a wintry picket post, when he heard the great key clanging in the lock, and saw the ponderous door swing open.

'Have you brought me water?' asked the prince.

'Aye, water and wine,' replied the watchman, partly closing the door behind him.

'I want not the wine, though I thank you. In the prison, as in the army, he can only do his duty who obey orders. The prison rules forbid wine,' said the prince.

'The prison rules forbid many things that are right. The will of the Czar would place me in one of those cells if I did not stoop to deceit to help myself and friends.' This was whispered by the man, who had now advanced and taken the cold hand of the prince.

'Who—who are you?' asked the prince, recalling the voice, but unable to believe that its real owner was in truth before him.

'Your friend unto death—Vladimeer Ruloff,' replied that young gentleman.

Only the fine self possession and complete mastery of his own feelings prevented the prince from giving a shout of mingled fear and joy. As it was, he folded his arms about Vladimeer, and kissed his cheek as if he had been a brother.

Briefly but clearly Vladimeer explained the manner in which he had vaulted, as it were, into his present menial but most desirable position; adding in conclusion:

'The whole credit is due to the Countess Alexandrina, whose plan I am carrying out.'

'But you will be detected!' said the prince.

'That I do not fear. My disguise is perfect, and I am fortunately able to act out my character. In this position I remain until after the trial.'

'Until after the trial?' repeated the prince.

'Yes. You do not know it begins tomorrow.

'I have not been informed about it.

'It begins to morrow, and the conspirators, Helen Radowsky, Varwitch, Pushkeene, and Count Kieseleff, have their condemnatory evidence so arranged that your escape is impossible—'

'You think so?'

'Yes, to my sorrow; and I but repeat the belief of your thousands of friends and admirers, and all who firmly believe in your innocence.'

'And the sentence—have you heard it rumored what that will be?' asked the prince commposedly.

'Death?' whispered Vladimeer.

'I have looked into the death-angel's face before, without blanching.'

'There will be no need to do it now. Retaining my position. I can make your escape from the prison certain. Ruryk and Captain Freehoff, with Mr. Cushing, will be ready to aid. The ice is flowing out of the Neva; and within a week steamers and ships will be loading and unloading at Saint Petersburg. We can get you on board, and away, before you are missed from the prison.'

'And your mother and Elizabeth?'

'They are embraced in the plan. Hist! here comes the guard. Wringing the prince's hand, Vladimeer laid a parcel containing wine and a few nutritious articles of food on the bench and hurried out, locking the door after him.

'Late on your rounds,' said the sergeant of the guard, halting his men near the prince's cell and addressing Vladimeer.

'I'm new to the business; it's my first night,' chuckled Vladimeer, now back in his peasant character, 'but when I've got used to it, I'll be active, as younger men, I warrant you. In my village I once acted, for a whole week, as balliff to the Stanavoi, and he paid me two roubles, and said I did well.'

'Ha, ha, ha, laughed the sergeant, and his men—as in duty bound—laughed with him.

'Your village training will be of little use to you here. They should put you to making fires and carrying out ashes, old man.'

'The fire-making would be truly more congenial, while the weather continues cold; but I am a good servant, and obey my master, doing faithfully the work he sets before me,' said Vladimeer.

'And who is your master?'

'His excellency Count Kiseleff, aid to his imperial majesty the Czar, and second chief of the secret police. Fools call him the Czar's spy, but he is a good man and true, I'll warrant,'

Vladimeer hobbled off on his round of the cells, and the sergeant and his men went away with an increased respect for the protege of Count Kieseleff.

After making the rounds, Vladimeer went down to a great barrack-like room, along the sides of which were tiers of bunks, in which slept the turnkeys and watchmen. He could go to sleep, as the others not on duty had, if he desired, or he could wander about the interior court-yard, but could not go outside the prison without the consent of the governor, which was never given at night. Uninviting as the gloomy court-yard was, he went out, smoking a short pipe, and began walking close to the building, with his hand rubbing against the stones. He kept on his way, without being observed, till he came directly under the hospital window that indicated the whereabouts of his mother and sister. Here he found a string hanging out, and pulling it gently three times, an answering signal came back.

Writing a few words on a slip of paper—on which he told his sister that he had seen the prince and that he was well—Vladimeer fastened it to the string and it was drawn up.

Soon the string came back with another note attached; this Vladimeer took, and continuing his walk about the court, went back to the room, and read by the light of a dim lamp suspended from the ceiling:

'Mother is no better. I have told her that you are here, and her anxiety for your safety is telling against her. She invokes you to fly while there is yet time, and with her I join in imloring you to leave.'

'Hello, old man! reading a love letter, eh?' asked a burly turnkey, looking out from the bunk.

'No,' growled Vladimeer, 'it's a bank note for a hundred roubles. I never light my pipe with anything smaller.' And so saying he twisted up the note, stood on tiptoe and lit it at the lamp, and before his pipe was going to his satisfaction, the last bit of the tell-tale paper was consumed.

Early the next morning, by request of Count Kiseleff, Vladimeer, under the name of Lushkine, was permitted to go into the city, and he at once, reported to his benefactor.'

'Well, old man, have you seen and talked with the prisoner?' asked Kiseleff.

'That have I, excellency,' said Vladimeer bowed and cringed and swayed his arms till his sheepskin cap swept the floor.

'What said he?'

'Much excellency—very much.'

'You dog! tell me exactly what did he say.'

'He wished for writing paper that he might send, by me, a note to the lady Elizabeth Ruloff; but I could not provide it,' whined Vladimeer.

'But you should have given him the paper,' said Kiseleff angrily.

'I feared the governor, excellency.'

'Here is the letter; the count drew from his pocket a paper in the handwriting of Prince Gallitzin. 'You see it is addressed to Elizabeth Ruloff?'

'Yes, excellency, yes.'

'Keep this letter, and mention not to a soul that you have it till I call for it.'

'And, when will that be, excellency?' ask-

ed Vladimeer, bowing and concealing the letter in his breast.

'Perhaps to-morrow for then the trial will be under way. You will be called on as a witness; and on the stand you must produce this letter saying it was given you by Prince Gallitzin, who promised you a great reward if you handed it unobserved to the name in the address. Do you comprehend?'

'Clearly, excellency, clearly.'

'Do this well, and I will reward you with a better place.'

'I will deserve it. I kiss the ground on which your excellency stands. Long may you live, and long live the Czar.'

'Here, is a coin. Go drink my healthy, then back to your post. Do you hear me?' Kiseleff tossed the peasant a coin, and strode away, with an expression of lordly contempt on his florid face.

Vladimeer picked up the coin, and hobbled off, croaking his thanks and vowing his fidelity, with many cringing bows.

CHAPTER XXIX.

THE TRIAL BEGINS.

Trials for political offences in Russia, and particularly in Saint Petersburg, were of daily occurence, and consequently attracted but little attention from any but the friends of the victims. But for once this indifference gave way to a deep general interest, which might be said to excite the people of the city, irrespective of rank, as the time for Prince Gallitzin's trial approached.

In public, where the Czar's spies might overhear and report, comments were made with caution; and the most warmly-disposed toward the young prince could only express hope that a conspiracy would be proven on the trial.

In private, however, the officers in friendly groups at their clubs, the sailors bending the sails to the liberated warships at Cronstadt, the merchants, with intimate friends, or in the privacy of their own families—yea, the very maids of honor to her imperial majesty the empress, spoke of Prince Gallitzin's arrest as an outrage that would react on the government, and prophecied that an adverse sentence would create a revolution that all the power of the government would be too weak to stem.

It was the policy of the authorities to treat the accused, whether noble or plebeian, the same before and after trial, but the courts before which offenders were arraigned differed with the rank and standing of the prisoner.

The highest military court in the empire

was convened in one of those magnificent halls which so distinguish the great Admiralty Building.

The fair spring day was calculated to bring out the great crowds that poured from every quarter into the streets between the Admiralty and the Prison of the Exiles. But it was not the beautiful weather that kept them standing with anxious faces, and speaking in frightened whispers, for the hours between sunrise and ten in the forenoon. Throughout the whole distance nearly ten miles—regiments of mounted Cossacks and long lines of foot soldiers were drawn up, with here and there a light battery, to intimidate the people; for Kiseleff had spread the rumor, and it reached the ears of the Czar, that the Nihilists would make an attempt to rescue the prince. Between these lines of soldiers mounted aids flew up and down, showing themselves oft to the finest advantage, but having nothing else to do that the people could see.

At ten o'clock a single gun was heard to boom in the direction of the Prison of the Exiles, and as the reverberation went rolling along the streets the sea of faces was turned in anxious expectation toward the point from which the prisoner was to come.

Away in the distance the bright sun flashed on a forest of moving lances. Freehoff's Cossacks came between the lines at a trot, escorting a plain, open carriage, in which sat Prince Gallitzin, pale, but proudly erect.

A hoarse murmur, like the angry sound that often makes prelude to the tornado, ran along the crowd, and a savage light flashed from the angry eyes. Even the grim soldiers, many of whom had followed the young hero in battle, coughed to hide their emotion, or drew their braided sleeves across their eyes.

Apparently as unconscious of the battery of eyes as if he were riding through a desert waste, the prince looked neither to the right nor to the left, until the escort halted before the granite steps of the Admiralty,

Here an officer appeared, and opening the carriage door, touched his hat and said :

' Prince Gallitzin will descend.'

The prince sprang lightly out, and immediately he was surrounded by a body of gens-d'armes, with fixed bayonets.

' Forward !' commanded the officer, and with the prisoner in their midst, the soldiers moved up the steps and proceeded to the great hall, where the greatest civil dignitaries and the first soldiers of the empire—all in their resplendent uniforms—were waiting for the accused.

The tickets of admission were at a premium, and the place was packed by men and women determined to see the trial through to the end.

If matters of greater interest did not concern us, it might be profitable to describe the forms and ceremonies—as hollow and meaningless as they were glittering and impressive—that opened the proceedings.

The chief of the bureau of military justice acted as judge and president of the court. Twelve officers from the same tyrannical establishment, " convened to convict," took the place of jurors—or rather the position jurors would fill, if such a tribunal were allowed in Russia.

There was a small army of clerks, criers and guards, all in uniform, and all apparently fascinated by the tall, pale young man sitting alone in the centre of the court.

The presiding officer coughed behind his hand till he grew purple in the face, but his real object was to hide his own nervousness and attract attention.

A chilling stillness suddenly fell upon the assembly ; even the clerks stopped writing that the scratching of their pens might not be heard.

There is no silence so profound as that solemn hush of a human gathering in the presence of death, or when the fate of a fellow-mortal is to be decided. Each person present heard his own heart beat, and felt very certain the sound must be distinctly audible to those near by—every person but the calmly heroic man most deeply concerned in the object of the court.

'The secretary of the board convened to try Wladislas, Prince Gallitzin of Novgorod, a general of artillery in the service of our imperial master the Czar, and late chief of the bureau of secret police, will read the charges against the accused,' said the presiding officer, trying to cough down a whole pond of frogs that would come into his throat.

An officer arose, and adjusting his eyeglasses, began to read through what seemed an interminable lot of manuscript. There were twelve charges, and under each charge there were as many specifications. All these charges pointed to treason against the Czar ; an unwarranted assumption of the royal prerogative ; infidelity to sacred trusts, and an association with, and open sympathy for, the traitors known as Nihilists.

When the reading was finished, and the secretary sat down, wiping his spectacles - as if the protracted exercise had thrown them into a violent perspiration—the presiding officer said :

'General Gallitzin, you have heard the charges and specifications against you. Rise and make answer before this court of your countrymen, met to inquire into their truth, and do justice to you, as well as to our imperial master the .Czar.'

The prince rose, and after the manner of Russian nobles making oath, he laid his hand upon his heart, and in a clear, ringing voice that, without being loud or defiant, could be heard distinctly in the farthest corner of the room, he said :

' On my honor as a noble and a soldier I solemnly declare that I am innocent of all the charges and specifications I have heard read, excepting that one which says I released the Countess Ruloff and her son, Vladimeer ; for this act my reason was good at the time ; and failing to make you see it as I did, I stand ready to bear all the consequences of what, at most, is an error of judgment, and in which only prejudice can see a crime.'

The prince bowed ; and the presiding officer said :

' The secretary will record the answer.' Then to the prince :

" General Gallitzin, it is your right to select a member of the bureau of military justice to aid you in your defence.

' I waive my right,' replied the prince, ' and will conduct my own defence.'

As he looked about the court before resuming his seat, he saw near by Helen Radowsky, his traitorous servant Varwitch, and the sallow face of Michael Pushkeene. After an hour of tedious preliminaries the first witness was called.

' Peter Varwitch will take the stand,' shouted the chief crier, distinguished by holding a white pole, on the top of which was a gilt double-headed eagle,

' Courage, Varwitch. Be cool, and do not say to much,' whispered Helen Radowsky, as Varwitch pushed his way nervously through the crowd in the direction of the witness-box.

This was sensible advice, but Helen Radowsky did not look as if she could follow it when her turn came. Her face, usually plump and rosy, was now pale and haggard ; her dark eyes had given place to a expression half fierce, half hunted. There was that desperate set to the thin lips which the most daring assume in the presence of certain death, or in the carrying out of a purpose against which all the better nature is in revolt.

Conspicuous as Varwitch suddenly became, he did not succeed in drawing to himself the battery of eyes fastened on the prince. But not one looked at him with such a fixed fascination as Helen Radowsky.

The calm dignity of his bearing, the heroic expression of his matchless face, the musical ring of his voice, the glory of his splendid record, the unmistakable evidences of high descent, and the indescribable magnetism that seemed to emanate from the man, thrilled and influenced every fibre of her being.

This man, whose life she sought, whose ruin she compassed, whose fame she was about to blast, impressed her as a being divine, and by contrast she felt herself to be a fiend.

She was seized, as Varwitch began his damning evidence, with an impulse to rush into the centre of the court and, throwing herself at the prince's feet, to proclaim his innocence and her own guilt.

To restrain this impulse she set her teeth and clung with a desperate tenacity to the brass rail on which she leant.

The deep, hoarse voice of Varwitch struck her like the beating of a muffled drum in a funeral procession. She heard him telling the infamous falsehoods—swearing away that noble life that he might be rewarded by her hand. She had brought him under her spell, schooled him to her work of vengeance, and for what ? That she might destroy the man she now worshiped.

CHAPTER XXX.

IN CONSULTATION.

The first day's trial was over, and only two witnesses—Varwitch and Pushkeene—had been examined.

To avoid exciting the public, the prince was not taken back to the Prison of the Exiles, but assigned quarters and placed under guard in the Admiralty Building.

So far as the evidence was known abroad, there seemed to be a general and, it may be added, a saddening impression that it must result fatally to the prisoner.

Varwitch found himself, for the first time, to be the most notorious man in the city ; and, as he passed along the streets, he heard men who did not know him speaking of him as another Judas, who had betrayed his master for less than thirty pieces of silver. Ah ! those people did not know the reward for which Varwitch had sold his soul.

At one time Peter Varwitch was a schoolar and a gentleman, but he felt that he could never lay claim to the latter title again. The prince would certainly be convicted, and, perhaps, executed, providing that his evidence was accepted ; but Varwitch felt that he could not remain in Russia. As soon as the trial was over he would marry Helen Radowsky and fly to a foreign land. He was on his way to her house, and though hitherto not addicted to excessive drinking, he stepped into a half dozen places and drank raw brandy each time. He felt better and stronger and braver for this. The liquor put a new life into him, and blinded him to the utter loss of his own self-respect.

'Hallo, Varvitch! Going to see Helen?' Varvitch heard Michael Pushkeene's voice, and felt Michael Pushkeene's arm drawn through his.

'Yes,' he growled, and made as if he would cast off his fellow-conspirator, for he had a feeling of horror for him. He forgot his own perjury in the thought of Pushkeene's crimes. He imagined his own wickedness to be dwarfed in comparison with that of the oily, snaky man who did so much to swear away the young nobleman's life.

'I, too, am going to see Helen, so let us go together.' Sticking to his side like a leech, Pushkeene continued: 'Ah, Peter Varvitch, you are a great man, a very great man. Every man, women, and child in Saint Petersburg is saying so to-night. When the prince cross-questioned you, and asked if you were not skillful in imitating the writing of others you denied it boldly. And what a grand hit you made when he asked you if you were not in sympathy with the Nihilists. 'Like master like man, you replied. 'How could I be the servant of General Gallitzin without being influenced by his views?' Ah, Varvitch, you drove the nail home and clinched it. My testimony was as a spring zephyr compared to a tropical tornado.', And Pushkeene laughed, and shook his black head, and tightly closed his eyes as if he found the greatest possible enjoyment in his own conclusions.

'You lied worse than I did! You lied without a cause. I had a good reason for what I said. Varvitch tottered and his voice became sepulchral in his earnestness.

'No, no, Varvitch; you obeyed Helen Radowsky because she promised to become your wife; I obeyed her because she promised to help me to secure the woman I love. Yesterday I expected, by means of the letter you wrote for me in the hand of Vladimeer, to have met the beautiful Elizabeth at the humble abode of my sire; but she came not —she gladdened not my eyes,' said Pushkeene, with affected sentimentality.

'You are a presumptuous dog; a low-born cur of a mongrel breed, and barking in the company of bloodhounds will not improve you. You'll be either muzzled by your friends or hanged by the law; and that very soon,' grunted Varvitch, freeing himself from Pushkeene and springing up the steps of Helen Radowsky's little house.

'My mistress is very weary and sick to-night,' said the white-capped servant, half opening the door and recognizing the visitors.

'I *must* see her,' said Varvitch. 'Tell her it is a matter of great importance to her and to me. Go, Catharine, and tell her this.'

'And say,' called out Pushkeene, 'that I, too, am here to see her ladyship.'

The servant withdrew; and coming back in a few minutes, conducted the visitors into the little sitting-room.

There was no fire on the hearth, and the lamp, left by the girl on the mantel, looked as if it thought seriously of going out.

The two men sat and watched each other, but neither felt like speaking; indeed each felt that the other was an intruder, and that, in addition, they hated each other cordially.

Dressed in white, excepting a scarlet wrap wound round her head and falling over her shoulders—like fresh blood on a shroud— Helen Radowsky walked in slowly, and going to the mantel, rested thereon one of her white, perfectly-modeled arms, and surveyed her visitors in silence.

Pushkeene was the first to speak.

'I come from Count Kiseleff. He asks to see you to-night in relation to the testimony you are to give to-morrow.'

'Tell Count Kiseleff I cannot see him to-night, for I am sick and weary; this may prevent my giving in any testimony,' she replied, in a low pained voice.

'Oh, that will never do. You must be on hand if you have to be carried. You have planned the whole affair. Our testimony,' Pushkeene waved his hand toward Varvitch 'will kill the prince. Your testimony will drive the last nail into his coffin.'

Helen Radowsky gasped at this, and clung to the mantle to keep from falling. Suddenly she recovered self-command, and with much of her old manner, said:

'I hope to be at the court. I will see the count early in the morning. I wish to rest to-night. You will now please to excuse me, Doctor Pushkeene; I desire to have a few words in private with Mr. Varvitch.'

After this there was nothing left for Pushkeene but to leave, but before taking his departure he whispered:

'Our plan did not work with Elizabeth Ruloff. I want you to help me again.'

'Very well. I will see you to-morrow. Good night.'

The moment the door closed behind Pushkeene Helen Radowsky sat down on a chair, facing Varvitch, and in her low, intense voice, said:

'For our own safety, we must get rid of that man at once!'

'At once?' rejoined Varvitch.

'At once. We have no further use for him. Every hour we delay places our own lives in jeopardy.'

'You think he contemplates betraying us?'

'I am sure of it.'

'Very well: I will care for him,' growled Varwitch, savagely. So far his manner indicated that he had been drinking; but on the instant he became his dogged self, and asked: 'Do you mean that you may not testify again the prince?'

She looked at him for some seconds before replying, then answered with averted face:

'I feel as if I would rather die.'

'What!' he roared. 'After you have worked the case up to this point, to glut your insatiate vengeance, do you mean you are becoming frightened?'

I fear I have done a terrible injustice to Prince Gallitzin,' she replied, 'and I shrink from pressing him further.'

'Helen Radowsky, are you insane?' he demanded.

'No, but I have been.

'It is too late to reason so now! I have become a perjurer, a forger, a traitor, and have just pledged myself to become a murderer—at your bidding—whatever I am, I became to show the intense fidelity of my mad love for you!' Varwitch rose to his feet, and threw back his lion like beard and hair, while his eyes blazed with excitement. 'There can be no regrets, no retracing now! You must carry out the programme to the end! This you must do in sheer self-defence, if you feel that your vengeance is appeased!'

'In self-defence, Varwitch?'

'Aye, in self-defence. Break a link in the chain of evidence we have forged against the Prince Gallitzin, and do you know what the result will be?'

'What?'

'The prince will be declared a victim of a hellish conspiracy, and you and I, your tool, and all who have been associated with us, will be hanged like dogs. Nay more; Nihilism will receive a death-blow; and from that broken chain the tyrant will fashion manacles for the people. Gallitzin of Novgorod is a noble of the nobles, an intense adherent of the Czar, and a foe to liberty and progress. What his father did for unhappy Poland—your land, Helen—the land where wrongs were heaped upon your house —he would do for the freemen of Russia. His death will kindle the fires of liberty and spread disaffection, as did the charge against Count Ruloff. To save him by neglect or confession is to crush our cause, and send you and me to ignominious graves! Oh, Helen, Helen! By the love I bear you— by the acts blindly done to show it—do not falter in this the hour when strength is needed! Say you will be true! Pledge me that will not consign to the gallows the man who has given his manhood—yea, his very soul, to your service!' He droped on his knees before her, and taking her white, passive hand, he pressed it passionately to his bearded lips, and looked wistfully into her face:

'Rise, Varwitch, rise!' she cried. 'I have gone too far to turn back; have been too long steadfast in my purpose to falter. I will appear and I will testify.

CHAPTER XXXI.

THE TRIAL CONTINUES AND VLADIMEER IS CALLED.

Vladimeer, still secure in the perfection of his disguise, met Ruryk the Cossack early on the morning of the second day's trial; their rendezvous being the little wine vault before referred to.

The faithful Cossack was in very low spirits and seemed to blame his master for not having raised the standard of revolt as he had urged.

'I know the Cossacks, and have spoken with hundreds,' said Ruryk, 'and there is not one in the city, nor do I believe there is one in the empire, that would not sacrifice his life to rescue the prince. It is too late now; too late. But I shall share his fate.'

'How do you mean, Ruryk?' asked Vladimeer, deeply touched by the soldier's devotion.

'I am to be called as a witness; but why I cannot imagine. I intend telling the judge and court what I think of the empire from the Czar down.'

'Then you will be arrested.

'I want to be.'

'And tried.'

'Yes.'

'And executed.'

'I have sworn not to survive my master,' said Ruryk.

'If die you must, better lose your life trying to free him. The students of the city are organizing for the purpose, and twenty thousand civilians are ready to join us. More than that number of troops, I am informed, are ready to come over. We propose—should the prince be sentenced to death – to attack the palace the night before the day set for the execution, and seizing the royal family, hold them till a free pardon be granted to the prince and to all—'

'By Saint Peter!' exclaimed the Cossack, that is a grand scheme. Your excellency can command me, and all Captain Freehoff's men, to the death.'

They left the vault, and taking different

directions, went to the Admiralty Building.

For squares around the streets were blocked with citizens and soldiers, and the great hall was even more crowded than on the previous day.

As the clock in the tower, near by, struck ten, the criers began shouting for order, and by the time the last stroke died out in a resonant murmur the pained hush had again come on the people.

Helen Radowsky, Varwitch and Pushkeene sat in a little group not far from Count Kiseleff, whose florid face wore a look of triumph and self-satisfaction.

'Call Elizabeth Ruloff,' said the presiding officer.

The name was called three times, and the crowd swayed in its anxiety to get a look at the witness.

Elizabeth Ruloff—to the amazement of court and spectators—was accompanied, to near the witness chair, by her friend, the beautiful and audacious Countess Alexandrina, the niece of the great Gortschakoff. As if to show her utter defiance and contempt for her surroundings, the countess kissed Elizabeth, and whispered, as so to be heard by hundreds, 'Courage, my sister, courage!' Then she sat down beside Prince Gallitzin and shook his hand with a sympathetic heartiness that brought tears to the eyes of many in the assembly.

Elizabeth Ruloff was plainly attired in a black dress, wholly devoid of ornament; but this fact only served to bring out more distinctly the exquisite symmetry of her willowy form and to rivet all eyes on the faultless beauty of her face. The lustrous, golden hair—in the plain Greek style that only becomes a Grecian face—covered her Junolike head, like the halo with which the old masters delighted to cover the heads of their favorite saints.

'Merciful Heaven!' whispered Helen Radowsky, 'that woman is not of the earth—she is an angel! An angel of light and beauty, and purity!'

She drew her chair nearer, and, with her fingers interlocked, bent forward to catch every intonation of the low, musical voice; to watch every shade of expression and wave of color playing like cloud shadows over the face.

She—Elizabeth Ruloff—had known the prisoner, Prince Gallitzin, from her earliest years. As children they were betrothed, for their fathers were friends. As she grew to womanhood she saw less of the prince. He travelled in foreign lands, and only returned when the war broke out with Turkey. Her father, Count Ruloff, had been falsely accused of treason, tried by a court convened to convict, and banished to the Siberian mines. All his property was confiscated, and his family thrown helpless on the world. She and her mother had to sew for bread; her brother, falsely accused of treason, had lost his position in the school of mines; and every hand extended to them with aid was looked on with suspicion.

Calmy, but with a force that told on and even thrilled the most hardened officer in the court, she told how Prince Gallitzin, on his return to St. Petersburg, sought out his old friends in the garret, and there renewed, as a man, the engagement that had been made as a boy. She told of her brother's arrest, and how her mother, the Countess Ruloff, was seized for trying to enter her own apartments, after going out to look for her son. Bravely she upheld the honor of her own house; and there was a convincing grandeur and power in her manner when, in reply to the questions of the presiding officer, she refuted the intimations that ever Prince Gallitzin, by word or act, in her hearing, did ought that was not becoming a patriot, a noble, and a soldier.

As Helen Radowsky listened to this telling evidence, heard Elizabeth Ruloff confess her love for the prince, and frankly avow they were betrothed, her whole manner changed. The glow of involuntary admiration in her eyes gave place to a glare of hate. Her figure was still bent forward, but the attitude was changed from one of attention to that of a tigress crouching for a spring.

'If he lives she will be his wife! He loves her, as she loves him. His eyes have burned into my soul and withered it. His name has been the horror of my life! Oh, Heaven I oh, Heaven! I am going mad!'

Her thoughts were interrupted by the loud voice of the crier:

'Helen Radowsky will take the stand.'

Looking neither to the right, nor the left, she went up and sat in the witness seat, with an air of unmistakable resolution. Bold as she was, she did not dare to meet the calm, dark eyes of the prince; but she felt the dark eyes of the prince; but she felt them—felt them looking into her heart and reading its terrible secrets of passion, vengeance, and perjury.

She wondered herself at her calmness, as the court and the audience at her story. She tried to create the impression, and succeeded, that Prince Gallitzin paid his addresses to her. She told of her visit to his palace; of his driving her home; of his calling to see her often, and of his leaving, on one occasion, the package of incendiary papers, which she exhibited to the court, and which powerfully corroborated the story Varwitch had told the day before.

When she had concluded her direct testimoay, the warmest adherents of the prince felt his cause was lost. Without looking at him she answered the questions of the prince in cross-examination.

She acknowledged she was the daughter of the Polish Count Radowsky, but denied that she had vowed vengeance against the Gallitzins; denied that she was a Nihilist, and courted investigation; denied the story of the dagger, but confessed the prince gave her a weapon for her own protection; and with dramatic effect, she drew it from the folds of her dress and held it up before the court.

The prince saw that his efforts to extort the truth but reacted against himself, so he ceased.

Count Kiseleff next gave in his testimony, vague, suspicious, and damaging—all the more damaging for the frequent complimentary allusions to the prince.

'Lushkine, a man whom I placed as a watchman in the Prison of the Exiles, is here with a note which Prince Gallitzin asked him to convey to the lady Elizabeth Ruloff. I have read the letter, and as it contains treasonable utterances, it might be well for his excellency the presiding judge to produce it in evidence.'

With this remark the crier shouted for 'Lushkine!' And as he did not answer at once, all the cries began to shout for 'Lushkine!' and to institute a search for the peasant; but he was nowhere to be found. The presiding judge growled; told Count Kiseleff to punish the man, and to be sure and produce him on the morrow. In the meantime he asked that Ruryk, the orderly of General Gallitzin, be called.

The orderly strode forward, anger in his eyes, and defiance in every movement of his tall figure. The prosecution hoped to prove by him the intimacy of the prince with Vladimeer Ruloff, but attempt failed at every point. The blunt soldier felt he was fighting for his master's life, and reckless of everything but what he thought would subserve that end, he kept on. The judge checked him; the board maddened him by questions, until, in his anger, he rose and invoked all 'the Cossack's curse.' And that night Ruryk was a prisoner with his master.

CHAPTER XXXII.

A STARTLING SITUATION.

Russian newspapers are free to publish the news and make editoral comments on it —with this proviso, that the news be approved by the government censor, and the editorials be laudatory to the Czar, and in favor of all the acts of the authorities.

Of course, the journals gave much space

to the trial of Prince Gallitzin, and those that expressed any opinion about it were compelled, against all private conviction, to say he was guilty, and to hint that he had forfeited his life. Of course there was much that was complimentary about the prince's record, his accomplishments, his youth, and the antiquity of his illustrious family.

The papers hinted that Cupid had blinded the prince of his duty, and strongly declared that Vladimeer Ruloff had taken advantage of the prince's blindness to bring him to ruin. With this conceded fact as a text, the papers denounced Vladimeer in unmeasured terms. He was 'a traitor to the country of his birth;' 'An ingrate to the friend he had deluded, then betrayed;' 'A coward who fled the country, leaving his mother in prison, and his victim in the valley of the shadow of death.' All this and much more was said in the papers; all this and much more was said by the people in the excited city.

Vladimeer read this with a tingling cheek. Vladimeer heard this, and at times came near throwing off his disguise and announcing himself; but prudence led him to suffer out of sight, and to push forward his plans beyond the keen of curious observation.

'Of course, Count Kiseleff was furious when the old peasant, somewhat under the influence of liquor, called on him that night. He threatened to imprison him. He rose to strike him, but was deterred by a wild gleam in the peasant's eyes, and the twitching of his soiled but supple fingers about the handle of the knife in his belt.

'Pardon, excellency, pardon. I met a man from my village, during the noon recess of the court, and took a glass. I am not used to drinking; it went to my head; and I thought it would be b tter for me to remain away than to make a mistake. I will be on hand in the morning with a clean beard. Trust me again, excellency, and forgive me this once.'

'You are a dog!' hissed the count.

'Yes, I am a dog. But trust me again, and I will make for you a great discovery.'

'A great discovery!' sneered the count.

'Aye, excellency, a very great discovery,' persisted the peasant.

'What is it?'

'I can tell you, within twenty-four hours, where Vladimeer the Nihilist is concealed.

'You can?'

'Aye, that I can.'

'Tell me now.'

'I would, excellency, but I know not. See, here is a note written in his hand; a man gave it to me to carry to the Countess Ruloff. But supposing it was from her son, I first brought it to you, my master.'

The count snatched the paper from the cringing peas nt's hand, nd read :

'Courage, mother! I am yet in Saint Petersburg. Before long I shall announce myself. Then th world shall know of the plot that sent my father into exile, and is now aiming at the life of Prince Gallitzin. We have friends working for us, working out of sight. So keep good heart.'

' And you were to give this to the Countess Ruloff ?' said the prince, after reading it over for the third time.

' Nay, excellency, to h:r daughter, *for* the countess,' replied Vladimeer.

' And where is the man who gave you the note.'

' I am to meet him in the morning. He is the man from my village with whom I drank to-day.'

The count softened at once on hearing this ; and he gave Vladimeer a coin in tokep of complete forgivenes :.

' Bring your friend to me as soon as you find him,' he said, on parting, ' and I will reward him.'

' I will, excellency. I will bring him even into the court,' chuckled Vladimeer, as he hobbled off, bowing over the coin.

That night Vladimeer called on Mr. Cushing, the American, who, with characteristic energy and shrewdness, had set himsel about cleaning up the mystery that surrounded his friend Prince Gallitzin, and unveiling the plot of which he felt him to be the victim.

In the mean time Mrs. Cushing and her daughter, through the American minister's intercession, had been enabled to visit Madam Ruloff in the prison hospital, and to convey to her delicacies and medicines of which she stood much in need.

' I tell you what, my young friend,' said Mr. Cushing that evening, ' it's my candid opinion that you ought to make a clean breast of your connection with the revolutionary element ; at least with that part of it that is n w attempting to ruin the prince. This Helen Radowsky is head demon, and I know all about her meetings and her doings.'

' You do I' exclaimed Vladimeer.

' Of course I do. I gave her free passage on one of my vessels from London, and I've had an eye on her ever since. She's beautiful as a snake's eye, and smart as lightning ; but, as I said, she's got the fiend in her, big as Mount Washington in my country. Now, my opinion is, if she and her accomplices are arrested, some one of them will make a confession. My advice is for you to be ahead of them, for, sure as you live, Gbourko is after them,' sa d the matter-of-fact American.

' But he cannot be af'er me ; that is, he cannot be aware that I am still in Saint Petersburg,' said Vladimeer.

' I must confess hat your disguise is about perfect. But be advised by me, and don't trust to it. A bold course is the best.'

This conversation, and much more of the same nature, occurred in a corner of the public reception-room in the Hotel America.

Vladimeer, as he rose to go, said—and he meant it—that he stood ready to suffer, even death, if he could release his friend ; and then he hinted about the organization of soldiers, students and citizens who were pledged to attempt the rescue of the prince.

' It won't work,' said Mr. Cushing, retaining Vladimeer's hand at parting. ' Mark my words, it will be throwing away valuable lives for nothing. He must escape by stratagem, if he is convicted. Now be careful, and do not rush under your disguise.'

That Mr. Cushing's advice was sound Vladimeer soon had cause to know' ' As he was on his way to lodgings—his duties at the prison ceased when the prince was transferred to the Admiralty Buil lings—he met Captain Freehoff, and obeying that officer's motion to follow him, he was led into a private room in the out-of-the-way eating-house.

The captain closed the door, and shaking Vladimeer's hand again, he sank his voice to a whisper, and said :

' It is fortunate—most fortunate—that I met you this evening.'

' Why, is there anything unnsual up ?'asked Vladimeer, his fears and curiosity excited by his friend's manner.

' There is a great deal up I Your disguise has been seen through, and you must either change it or leave at once,' replied the captain.

' Who has discovered me ?'

' Michael Pushkeene.'

' You are sure ?'

' I am certain. You know that I have not attended any meetings for some time, and I don't think I ever will again. This evening—indeed, not twenty minutes ?go—I met a friend whom Mr. Cushing has placed on the track of Helen Radowsky. This man, through Miss Radowsky's servant, whom he succeeded in bribing, secreted himself under a lounge in the sitting-room, where Count Kiseleff, Pushkeene, and Varwitch assembled with the mistress of the house. He heard them going over their plans from beginning to end, and heard the count say that Vladimeer Ruloff would soon be captured. In proof of this he repeated an interview he had

had with an old peasant in his employ—Lushkine—'

'I can explain all that,' said Vladimeer, eagerly, and he went on to tell of his interview with Kiseleff and the note he had showed him. In explanation he said : 'I wished it to become known that Vladimeer Ruloff did not fly like a craven coward from the city, but was here in defiance of the law.'

'Kiseleff left, and the others remained talking. Suddenly Michael Pushkeene sprang up, and clapping his hands and shouting with laughter, cried :

'I have made a discovery—a startling discovery !'

'What is it ? asked the others.

'We all know Vladimeer Ruloff is wonderful at dis u e. My life to a kopek i tha peasant be not Ruloff ! Not a word to the count ! We can get the prize that is offered, and, at the same time have him out of the way.'

'Those people,' continued Captain Freehoff, ' are now after you, and the only way to escape them is to keep in concealment or change your disguise.'

'I can do neither ; but depend on me to avoid them. To-morrow morning I go to the court and give in my evidence. Be there to hear me, Captain.'

CHAPTER XXXIII.

THE LAST DAY OF THE TRIAL.

It was expected the trial would close this day. It was generally believed the prince could make no defence ; and so well-known were his services and reputation that, if he attempted to prove them, the court would concede their truth without witnesses.

General Gortschakoff was there with his beautiful niece ; for, despite his disapproval of her recent conduct, her influence over him was wonderful ; and in compliance with her wishes he came. Seeing him in court, the presiding officer supposed he came to testify; and knowing how valuable the great man's time was, he whispered to the chief crier to call him at once.

The chief crier elevated his voice and shouted :

'His excellency Prince Gortschakoff will take the stand.'

And, delighted at the thought of being able to utter the great man's name aloud, and in his hearing, the whole army of deputy criers elevated their little white rods, on which the deformed eagles were uncomfortably roosting, and shouted in chorus :

'His excellency Prince Gortschakoff will take the stand !'

The old diplomat was for a moment, visibly confused ; but recovering himself, he walked up to the witness stand and said, as he sat down :

'I was not aware that I was to be called.'

'I supposed,' said the presiding officer, with an obsequious bow that was in striking contrast with his treatment of the other witnesses, ' that your excellency came to testify. Your excellency's name is prominent in the charges.'

General Gortschakoff waved his hand to indicate that he was ready to answer any questions that might be asked.

In order to prompt the presiding officer, Count Kiseleff took a seat near that functionary ; and his floral face looked more than ever self-satisfied and complacent.

General Gortschakoff, with evident feeling, told of his acquaintance with the grandfather and father of Prince Gailitzin. He told how he had been delighted by the doings of the young soldier in the Balkans ; and how, when he returned to Saint Petersburg, he sent for him and with his own hands gave him his commission as general. and by his own efforts had him appointed to the head of the secret police.

He, General Gortschakoff, was familiar with the prince's writing. Through Varwitch he had obtained many of the incendiary papers written in the prince's palace. He recognized the papers shown him as the ones he had seen. He could not credit them until the prince confessed to him that he had, of his own volition and without any authority, released from the Prison of the Exiles Madam Ruloff and her son Vladimeer, the a fter a notorious Nihilist, and now a fugitive with a reward on his head. This one act constituted a crime that it would be fatal to permit to go unpunished, for it was a direct, a vicious interference with one of the first great prerogatives of the throne.

The old diplomat said nothing about his efforts to have the prince wed his niece, though he did dwell at some length on the young soldier's efforts to have the case of Count Ruloff reviewed, or a pardon granted.

General Gortschakoff was about to step down, when Prince Gallitzin rose and said :

'Permit me to ask you a few questions.'

General Gortschakoff bowed, folded his lank fingers, and looked—up at the ceiling.

'Do you know this man Varwitch well ?'

'I do not,' replied the general.

'Do you know that he is expert in imitating the writings of any person, and every person ?'

'I do not.'

'Do you know Count Kiseleff ?'

'I do.'

'Is he an expert at imitating writing ?'

'I do not know,' said General Gortschakoff, adding, with a laugh : ' But I should say not, for he is credited with writing an abominable hand.'

Count Kiseleff laughed and blushed, as if this were a compliment.

' Do you remember everything you write?' asked the prince.

' No, but I could not fail to recognize anything I had ever written.'

' Is that your writing?' the prince handed him the note sent by Kiseleff the night before the arrest, asking him to fly from Saint Petersburg at once.

Prince Gortschakoff read the note, and then answered :

' I hoped you would fly ; but I positively deny having written this note.'

' But it is in your handwriting.'

' I must confess it looks to be ; but I did not write it.'

' Nor order any one else to write it ?'

' Emphatically, no.'

General Gortschakcff descended from the stand, and Count Kiseleff's face became purple and his lips ashy.

' Call Lushkine,' said the presiding officer.

' Lushkine !' was shouted with unusual vigor of lung, and the hundreds of people began to look around.

A man with matted hair and beard rose. and throwing off a heavy cloak. which had so far partly concealed him, walked briskly up to the stand.

He was sworn and asked his name.

' For the present I call myself Lushkine,' he replied, with an unmistakable peasant accent.

' You know Count Kiseleff ?'

' I have been in his employ since the day before Prince Gallitzin's arrest. I was recommended to his favorable notice by the Countess Alexandrina, from whom I had been asking aid.'

' He got you a position in the Prison of the Exiles.'

' Yes, for a few days.'

' You saw Prince Gallitzin in his cell ?'

' Several times.'

' And he gave you a note to convey to the Countess Ruloff, or her daughter?'

The witness hesitated, and the vast audience bent forward to catch his answer. Helen Radowsky's eyes were devouring him, Varwitch tugged at his beard nervously, and Pushkeene crouched as if about to spring forward.

With maddening deliberation the witness fished up from an inside pocket a note, and unfolding it, handed it, without a word, to the presiding officer.

' This,' said the presiding officer, ' is filled with treasonable utterances, and is in the handwriting of the prisoner. I will place it before the board.'

' Hold !' cried the witness. ' That letter goes not betore the board !'

' Why not ?' demanded the presiding officer.

' Because it is a forgery !'

' A forgery !' was repeated by the officers, and whispered by the astonished people.

' Aye. a forgery ! Prince Gallitzin never saw that note.'

' Then how came you by it ?'

' It was given to me by the Count Kiseleff.'

' I deny it !' shouted Kiseleff, now beside himself with fear and rage.

' Let the witness tell his story. You can contradict him afterwards,' said the presiding officer.

' Count Kiseleff.' continued the witness, ' asked me to furnish the prince with writing materials, but he would not use them. Then Count Kiseleff gave me this note, and paid me to swear it had been written by Prince Gallitzin. It was written by Varwitch at the request of the count !'

' Hold, sirrah !' shouted the presiding officer. ' Who are you, madman, that dares to make this charge against a Russian noble ?'

' I am that noble peer,' replied the witness, rising and standing proudly erect.

' This man is insane, or worse. Remove him, officers !' commanded the head of the court.

' Hold, till you have seen who I am !'

The outer vestments dropped off. The beard and matted wig fell to the ground ; and the youthful, soldierly figure of Vladimeer Ruloff stood revealed to the court and the vast assembly.

The amazing surprise, the suddeness of the act, the startling transformation, and the awful daring of this man, with a price set on his head, held the people breathless and spellbound for the moment.

Prince Gortschakoff gasped and rubbed his eyes ; and the presiding officer began swallowing bushels of the largest sized Adam's apples.

As for Count Kiseleff, he could not have collapsed more suddenly had he been struck by a bolt from heaven. In a few seconds more the court would have recovered from its surprise, but the fates and the Countess Alexandrina willed it otherwise.

The brave girl sprang from her uncle's side, and running to Vladimeer, she grasped his hand and pressed it to her lips. Then turning to the court with fire in her grey eyes, and the flush of dauntless heroism on her rounded cheek, she said, in tones of thrilling music :

'What Vladimeer Ruloff says I stand ready to prove by my oath ! I saw Count Kiseleff give him that letter, and I read it not five minutes after.'

'This is not evidence. The officers will command order, shouted the presiding officer pounding with his gavel to enforce order, for a murmur of applause, that threatened to break into an uproar, ran through the assembly.

The criers shouted and brandished their staves ; and the countess resumed her seat beside her now utterly astounded and bewildered uncle.

'As first assistant to the chief of his majesty's secret police, I call on the gens-d'-armes to arrest at once the traitor Vladimeer, the Nihilist !' cried Count Kiseleff, now recovered sufficiently to command his tongue.

'I came here to surrender myself, and if need be to die, in order to show to my master, the Czar, the conspiracy that would rob him of the bravest, truest,' noblest man in the empire. Before you take me hence let me say that the key to that conspiracy is now in strong hands. Let those who have wronged my father—Count Ruloff the patriot—and who would now make the Czar accessory to the murder of Prince Gallitzin, confess before the revelation comes. For true as the Czar reigns over Russia, and a just God over all, the day of vengeance has come !'

The soldiers now appeared and carried Vladimeer off. But so great was the excitement that the court decided to shut out the people and conclude the trial in secret.

CHAPTER XXXIV.

DESPERATE DISEASES REQUIRES DESPERATE REMEDIES.

It was not till he had reached his own palace that General Gortschakoff recovered from his surprise and fully considered the audacity of his niece's action. Then indignation, anger, and something like humiliation possessed him. He sought out the countess in her apartments, and demanded to know ' Why she had acted in this unusual and disgraceful manner ?'

'The terror of cruel laws and unjust edicts has made it unusual to oppose wrong openly—and this is why the people organize to oppose in secret. As to the *disgrace*, my uncle, I never before heard it was a disgrace to uphold such heroic manhood as Vladimeer Ruloff has displayed, nor to unmask such villainies as Count Kiseleff has shown himsel. capable of,' replied the countess.

'Your impulses have blinded you to the count. But tell me, have you not yet forgotten your foolish, childish attachment for Vladimeer Ruloff ?' he asked, softening down as he looked at her fine, brave face.

'I have not. You might as well ask me to be false to the memory of my dead mother because my love for her was childish—'

'But Vladimeer Ruloff has forfeited his life, and before one week will be in a felon's grave.'

'And in that grave,' she responded, ' my heart and my hope will be forever buried. You can control the empire, my uncle, and fashion treaties between states—you have studied such matters ; but when you attempt to dictate the affections of a woman's heart you are on foreign ground, where your authority is a shadow and your efforts futile.'

'By all Saint Peter, if I were to draw you out, I doubt not I should find you a Nihilist,' growled the general, as he arose to leave the apartment, with the feeling of a man who was being beaten.

'If Prince Gallitzin be a traitor, and Vladimeer Ruloff a Nihilist, I am both ; and under the mild rulings of your master I should be in the Prison of the Exiles, and not sheltered under the roof—screened by the wings of the all-powerful, and hitherto the all-good and wise— Prince Gortschakoff.'

It would be downright treason to hear more. General Gortschakoff hastened out, and on his way to the room where he gave audiences he met Count Kiseleff.

'What am I to do—what am I to do ?' cried the distracted count.

'Do ! Why, face your accusers as an innocent man should,' replied General Gortschakoff.

'But will the oath of Vladimeer, the Nihilist, be taken as against me ?'

'Until Vladimeer Ruloff is tried and convicted of the crimes of which he is charged, his word is as good as that of any man in Russia. He has outwitted you, and by his amazing audacity placed you at a great disadvantage. A great pity the empire could not have the services of such a man. But as long as you are innocent, my dear Count, you have nothing to fear, absolutely nothing.' And General Gortschakoff bowed himself away.

But Kiseleff did fear ; Kiseleff was in an agony of dread, and for the very reason that he felt himself to be unutterably guilty, and that he well knew Vladimeer Ruloff had not uttered a word that was not the truth. But he was not so completely beside himself as to lose the power of thought and action. Like all persons of his nature. danger and trouble but sharpened his wits, increased his cunning, and roused him to action.

There was no moment to lose. Already his name was being unfavorably discussed in the hovels and palaces of Saint Petersburg. If Vladimeer Ruloff were permitted to give in his evidence against him, ruin would follow. Down deep in his heart he invoked curses, the most awful, on the head of Vla i neeer. He wished him dead and in the infernal regions.

'Ah, if he were dead, I would be out of danger.'

His fear and his anger blinded him, or he would have seen that any one of his fellow-conspirators might become, in an instant, as dangerous as Vladimeer ; but, then, not one of his fellow-conspirators had been given such evidence of the approval of the Countess Alexandrina, whom he loved and was still resolve l to win.

As soon as it was safely dark, Count Kiseleff, with his form enveloped in a cloak, started for the residence of Helen Radowsky. He found that remarkable young women in a state of white anger. She had just been notified that her services were no longer needed as teacher to the imperial children, and in addition to this, a messenger had come from Ghourko, to tell her that she must leave Saint Petersburg within ten days.

To the count, who came to invoke her aid in his own troubles, not to bestow sympathy, this news was not encouraging. Yet he tried to appear cheerful ; and with that assumption of influence that characterizes little men he told her that he would have the order revoked at once, and that he would see that she was reinstated in her position.

'I care nothing for the place, nor do I wish to remain. But whither can I go, without taking my crushed life with me !' There was a cry of mingled woe and wrath in her voice, like that of a hunted animal at bay.

'That is nonsense. You are young and beautiful, talented and cultured—the world, with fame and fortune, is before you,' he said, coaxingly.

'Did you come to comfort me ?' she asked, with a sneer.

'No ; I came to save you,' he answered.

'Rather to save yourself.'

'Our interest are one, in this matter, and there is but one way to avert the danger— one act that can save and free us.'

'What is that ?' she asked.

'The death of Vladimeer Ruloff,' he whispered.

'But he is in the hands of the authorities, and his death must follow,' she reasoned.

'True ; but to help us it must come at once. I can guess well at all your doings in the past, and this cool, desperate man will uncover them. He knows of our relation, and the proof he can bring is too strong to be refuted by denial. Only his death can save us, and even that must be accomplished at once.'

'His death !' she mused.

'Yes, his death ! Is his life any more precious than the Prince Gallitzin's ?' he asked.

'Nay, nay !' she exclaimed. ' The life of Prince Gallitzin is worth a thousand such !'

'Yet you, and you alone, have given over to death the prince to gratify your own revenge. Are you not ready to sacrifice a less valuable life to save your own, and that of Varwitch and Pushkeene ?'

'Pushkeene is a traitor. Varwitch has the blind fidelity of a Siberian mastiff. But tell me, how could this end be accomplished ?'

'I can have Varwitch admitted to Vladimeer's cell in the garb of a black priest.'

'Yes.'

'Varwitch is a very strong man.'

'He is very strong,' she replied.

'Then he can plunge a dagger into Vladimeer's heart, and secrete on the body a letter in Vladimeer's writing, showing a settled purpose to die by his own hands if arrested again—'

'You are skillful in plots, Count Kiseleff. Let me call Varwitch. Address yourself to him.'

She went out and speedily came back with Varwitch, whose face wore a heavy scowl, and whose breath smelled of brandy. To him the count told his plan, and great was his joy at feeling his hand wrung, and at hearing the deep, hoarse voice replying :

'Lead me to the place at once, and I will do it !'

CHAPTER XXXV.

BACK IN PRISON.

Ruryk the Cossack had been held at the Admiralty Building until the arrest of Vladimeer Ruloff. They were taken together to the Prison of the Exiles, and would have created a great excitement on the street had the people known of the event.

They were placed in a close carriage, and escorted by Freehoff's lancers.

The gallant captain of that gallant but decidedly rebellious body managed during the ride to communicate with Vladimeer.

'I am afraid you made a great mistake,' said the captain, leaning over and speaking in at the window. "I cannot see that you have helped yourself, or friends."

Perhaps not, Captain; and I question if it was in my power to do it at once; though I have started the ball, mark my words. But the next greatest joy to helping one's friends is to strike down one's foes. If Kiseleff ever recovers from the blow I dealt him this day, I do not know the Russian people. But that blow was weak compared with the one that is to follow,' replied Vladimeer.

'I hope you are right,' said the captain. 'One thing is certain—you have given the lie to your traducers and proved the journals defamers. All Saint Petersburg is ringing with the praises of your skill and your daring. Even General Gortschakoff acknowledged, on leaving the court, that nothing more startling and thrillingly dramatic could be found in all the annals of Russia. The Grand Duke Alexis was present, and it is said he left the place expressing, in his hearty sailor way, unbounded admiration for your daring. Keep good heart, and all may yet be well.'

'I hope so. But tell me Captain, are not Ruryk and myself your prisoners until you have turned us over, and recovered for our precious bodies a receipt from the governor of the prison?'

'You are,' replied the captain.

'Then you have the power to let me see my mother and sister before I am taken to the cell?'

'I will see that it is done,' answered the captain, riding from the carriage to the head of the line.

The instant they entered the prison court Captain Freehoff sought the governor, and asked as a personal favor that Vladimeer Ruloff and Ruryk be taken to the hospital before going to their cells.

The governor gave a reluctant consent; he had not yet recovered from the offence given by Prince Gallitzin when Vladimeer and his mother were released.

Madam Ruloff was sitting on the edge of her cot, talking to Elizabeth and Mrs. Cushing when Vladimeer entered,

At sight of him all sense of sickness and weakness vanished. With a heart-cry of 'Vladimeer, my son! my son!' she sprang forward, and was caught in his arms.

Through Mrs. Cushing, Madam Ruloff and her daughter had learned of Vladimeer's re-arrest, and all the incidents preceding it. And the good American lady tried to cheer them under the blow with the belief that it was the very best thing he could have done.

It would be a waste of words, if not something of a sacrilege, to attempt to describe the interview between Vladimeer and his mother and sister. It seemed at the moment as if the vengeance of the Czar had imprisoned every one they held dear in the world.

Madam Ruloff did not ignore Ruryk in the excitement of the moment, but took the faithful Cossack's hand, and tried to give him a hope that she could not give herself. The brave fellow was affected to tears. He told the maiden he was ready to die for her and his master, whom he never expected to see again.

The fifteen minutes granted by the prison authorities soon flew by, and the followed was indescribably sad. All the sadder, indeed, for the heroic effort each made to suppress demonstrations and feign a calmness and hopefulness that was a bitter mockery.

But the heart bowed down by successive burdens of woe does not feel the thrusts that open old wounds, as it did the thrusts that first set those wounds to bleeding. There is a limit set by a merciful Heaven to the capacity for pleasure; and there is a point beyond which even torture inflicts no pain; but that point is only reached when the weary victim, becoming indifferent to life, strains his eyes to pierce the dissolving mists between him and eternity.

Vladimeer Ruloff again stood before the swarthy secretary and watched him for the second time writing down in the chained book his own decription.

'They must go to one cell,' said the swarthy secretary,' the prison is nearly full. If things go on as now, it will take ten such prisons to meet the demand;' and he looked as if he hoped the prisons would be erected, and that one secretary might do the recording for all.

The cell to which they were taken was on the first floor, and had a little grated window, through which one standing on tiptoe could look into the central court.

An extra bench was brought in, a loaf of black bread and a pitcher of water furnished, then the man, with the many keys in his belt, locked the door and went off, whistling with the light-heartedness of one engaged in the most congenial work.

To the credit of Ruryk the Cossack be said, he gave no thought to himself. Had he been ordered out that night for execution, he would still have been troubled for his master; and next to him he seemed most anxious for Vladimeer.

'Ah!' sighed Ruryk. 'If the prince had only taken my advice, he would be to day a greater man than the Czar, instead of being on trial for his life.'

'I think he may be acquitted,' said Vladimeer, hoping to keep up the Cossack's drooping spirits.

'No, no sir! They have met to convict. I have heard them speak. They say they must strike a blow at the liberal nobles. Their first blow, like death's favorite target, will be a shining mark.'

Impetuous though Vladimeer Ruloff seemed to his friends and foes, he was under all a cool, strong man, with an unbending will and a spirit that no oppression or suffering could daunt. He set about cheering up his companion, and with such success that Ruryk became a changed being, and grew so hopeful and confidential that he told Vladimeer of a little love affair.of his own, and announced his intention to marry when his master was again free and honored. It came out that the object of his affections was Catharine, the white-capped waiting-maid of Helen Radowsky. In his opinion, Catharine was not only a young woman of superi r physical graces and domestic accomplishments, but she was cast in a self-sacrificing, heroic mould that would no. have an opportunity to make itself manifest.

They had quite forgotten, in the earnestness of their conversation, that they were in a prison, when the key was heard to grate in the lock, the door partly opened and the turnkey whispered in:

'A priest of our holy church desires to speak with Vladimeer Ruloff.'

'Show the man in,' replied Vladimeer.

'He wishes to see you alone.'

'Th re are two of us here, s that is impossible. My Cossack friend will either go to sleep or hear his counsel, as the priest chooses,' laughed Vladimeer Ruloff.'

The turnkey was heard to call to some one in the corridor, and in a few seconds a short, stout man wearing the black serge dress and his face covered by the cowl and hood of the monks of the Greek church, entered the cell like a solidified shadow.

Vladimeer Ruloff and the Cossack rose and bowed to the priest.

'My children,' said the man, in a cautious husky whisper, 'I will not detain you with religious counsel to-day. I come rather to minister to your physical wants. I am a friend of the exiled Count Ruloff and of Wladislas, Prince Gallitzin, whom may Heaven protect, for he has been sentenced to death this night—'

'Sentenced to death!' exclaimed both,

'Aye! so say t e people and the press. I have brought you papers, which you can read when daylight comes. Here they are, folded about some wine and food.'

The priest took the parcel from within his dress and laid it on the bench.

'Ask not my name. I am a friend, and will see you on the morrow. See that my kindly offices come not to the notice of the prison authorities, or it would go hard with me.'

The mysterious man shook hands with the prisoners, tapped on the door for the listening turnkey, and went out. He passed through the reception room into the court and through the vault-like arch to a waiting carriage. The instant he was in and the door closed, he took off his vestments and burst into a loud, hoarse laugh, to the evident annoyance of Count Kiseleff, who sat opposite.

'You have not told me what you did. Speak, mar, this is no laughing matter,' said the count.

'To you, no; to me, yes. I saw them, told them the news, and left them papers to prove it, and wine and food to comfort them. Ho, ho, ho!' And Varwitch held his sides and laughed again. Recovering himself he continued: 'The dagger! Why did we think of such brutal butchery, when subtle poison can do more effective work? It takes Helen to refine on all our plans. Oh! she is a wonderful woman! Earth never saw such an angel—of darkness. Satan himself must be jealous of her resources.'

'But did they eat? did they eat or drink before you left?'' asked the count. .

'No; they had not time.'

'But, you are sure they will?'

'What! Do you think they will neglect white bread, cold fowl and wine, for black bread and brakish water! Only the monks do that. They are eating now, and drinking the health of their unknown friend, the black priest. Hurry on the horses! I, too, am thirsty. I must have brandy! Ah! working in blood makes one thirsty, and making others cold in death fills one with a fever. Drive o , drive on! Take me to Helen!' shouted Varwitch, with the phrensy of a madman.

CHAPTER XXXVI.

SENTENCED.

Where one man s will—as in Russia—is law, trials are apt to be the merest farce; and a charge made at the instance of the Czar is equivalent to a conviction. The case of Prince Gallitzin was no exception to the rule; and no man knew better than he how empty and meaningless was the h llow mockery of a court. But he was young and hope_ ful, with every inducement to cling to life and, above all, that strong assurance of his own innocence, which he imagined would impress itself on the members of the board of m litary justice.

It was midnight after the close of the trial, and the great hall in the Admirality Building was illuminated, showing the officers were still in session.

Word had gone abroad that the board had found Prince Gallitzin guilty of all the charges and specifications, with a few minor exceptions; and that they were reviewing the evidence against Vladimeer Ruloff and Ruryk the Cossack, with the intention of-sentencing all three at the same time.

So swift is the execution of these sentences that men have eaten their breakfasts peacefully, and without fear of danger, with their families, and before midnight have been on the way to the Siberian mines.

A court martial has frequently heard charges made that day, and tried, and sentenced, and shot the accused before night.

'Prince Gallitzin will be sentenced to-night!' 'When will he be executed?' 'He will have his choice to be hanged or shot!' 'He will die as fearless as he charged the Turkish batteries of Plevna!' These were a few of the whispered exclamations that ran from lip to lip, as the awe-stricken crowd looked up at the windows, facinated by what was in their own minds rather than by anything that met their eyes.

Groups of students met on the outskirts of the crowds, and away from the observation of the police ; and exchanging whispered reports, vanished to meet at some other point.

When they could speak without being observed by their officers, the mounted Cossacks and many of the foot soldiers spoke in the hushed tones that soldier- use when creeping forward under cover of darkness to surprise some stronghold.

There was a feeling of danger and trouble in the air, and men of the steadiest habits sat up late that night, without being able to assign a cause for the singularity.

The restaurants and drinking shops were crowded, but there was not much eating, and less drinking. The ringing laugh gave way to hushed comments, and the hearty greeting was made manifest only by the tighter grip of the hand.

From cellers and garrets the ragged rabble swarmed out ; but their impudent defiance had given place to a morose silence, amounting almost to dignity.

The sky was overcast ; and the wind swe p ing in from the Baltic and Bothnia, was laden with rain-freighted clouds, against which the illuminated clocks in palace and church towers burned like monstrous eyes. The hourly tolling of the bells swept through the city with a muffled, funeral sound.

At midnight the rain began to fall, but the people on the streets did not heed it ; rain and darkness seemed fitting accompaniments to the awful solemnity with which all were filled.

Prince Gallitzin, pale and calm, sat writing in the room to which he had been assigned. His hand was as steady and his pulse beat as strong and regular as if he did not know the verdict of ' guilty,' had been rendered, and that at any moment a mesenger might appear to summon him for sentence.

The clock in the Admirality tower boomed one, and the sound was still trembling in the air, when the door of the prince's room opened, and an officer, the secretary of the court, came in, with an open paper in his hands. Taking a military position before the prince, he coughed nervously, and said ;

'I am authorized to conduct your excellency to the court.'

'And you have reached a conclusion?' The prince arose, and folding his papers on which he had been writing, laid them carefully away.

'We have, excellency—' The man hesitated, and ceased his embarrassment by another cough behind his hand.

'You have found against me?'

'We have, excellency,'

'And I am summoned for sentence?'

'Yes, excellency ; and deeply do I deplore it,' said the officer.

'I believe you, my friend. But my respect for the c urt has increased. You have proved yourselves good soldiers by implicitly obeying your superior officers.'

The prince's winning smile robbed his sarcasm of his edge. As he went up through the guarded passages, the soldiers came to a salute, and looked after him with that expression of adoration which soldiers and saints feel for the object of their worship.

'Wladislas, Prince Gallitzin, or Novgorod you will stand before the court,' said the presiding officer, as the prince and his escort came into the solemn assembly.

The prince bowed, and advancing to near where he had sat during the trial, held himself proudly erect ; but in his noble bearing there was not a trace of blustering defiance.

'We, the board appointed to try you on the charges and specifications which were read to you in this court, find you guilty of all t e charges and not guilty on two specifications, which we find foreign to the case. This is the verdict of all.

The presiding officer paused, and all the members of the board coughed and nodded their a; proval.

'It only now remains, to ask you, before sentence is passed, if you have any reason to offer against the justice of our findings, or any excuse that may tend to avert your fate.'

'I have no reason to offer that will be acceptable to this board, or to our imperial master the Czar, whom may heaven defend, To all the charges, excepting that of releasing innocent people, imprisoned through my oversight, or through the forging of my name, as I now believe, I pleaded ' not guilty,' and gave my proofs, so far as this august body permitted me. I can render no excuse that will avert your sentence, for that is decided on, and your asking me is a hollow form, that adds not dignity to this mockery of a trial,' said the prince.

'Vladimeer Ruloff. whom you released, has this night been convicted of treason by us, and we have sent for him and your orderly, Ruryk, to receive sentence. You have all been working secretly together.'

'And Madam Ruloff?' asked the prince.

'We have found nothing against her. She is free. It only remains now for me to pass sentence in due form.'

The presiding officer coughed again, then sinking his voice to a tone of fitting solemnity, he said:

'Wladislas, Prince Gallitzin of Novgorod, you have been found guilty, by this honorable board, of treason, on twelve charges, against our imperial master the Czar. It becomes my painful duty, therefore, to pass on you the sentence of death, to be executed tomorrow, the first day of June, at the hour of high noon. As a soldier and a citizen you have the privilege of electing the mode of execution. Choose, therefore, between the halter and the musket.'

'It is comforting to know that this choice is left me. A soldier never chose the halter, and I am surprised that it is offered. I ask that the detail for my execution be selected, not from my countrymen the Russians, but from the Warsaw-Legion of Polish Contingents. I desire this for two reasons; first, from a feeling of national pride; and in the second place, the Pole is our foe, whether conquered or not; and to a conspiator from that land I am indebted for my fate.. Let the countrymen of Helen Radowsky complete the work she has pushed through to the death.

CHAPTER XXXVII.

THE PARTING BEFORE DEATH.

Count Kiseleff, let Varwitch out in front of Helen Radowsky's house, and then drove rapidly off, as if fearing to be seen in that suspected vicinity.

Varwitch did not go into the house at once, but hastened to a drinking shop, and bought a bottle of fiery, Hungarian brandy. He poured out a large glass full and drank it down raw. He concealed the bottle, in his pocket and ran back, muttering to himself like an insane man.

Helen Radowsky, dressed as if for traveling, but with a cold glitter in her eyes, and a deathly, pallor on her cheeks, let him in.

She was alone; the white-capped maid had deserted her.

'What drinking again?' she hissed, and closing the door she laid her hand on his shoulder and dragged him into the sitting-room.

'Yes, Helen! Yes, my love, my life; try some—you need it. Oh, there is nothing like brandy to banish dull care—'

'You are a cowardly dog!' she cried; and this is the way you show your love for me, now that my life, is in danger, and I should be flying, under your protection, from the city!'

'Haven't I sold myself to satan to show my love for you, Helen? Didn't I commit two murders to-night, under the garb of a monk, to show my love? Won't Prince Gallitzin have his handsome body pierced by bullets to-morrow, just because I was determined to show my love? Come, Helen, give me one kiss to show your appreciation; just one kiss.' He reached out his arms, but, with a shudder, she drew back from him.

'Not now; wait, wait! Go get horses! We must be flying. Go, Peter, if you love me still: go, for we are betrayed!'

'Betrayed!' The word seemed to sober him for the moment, and staring into her blanched face, he asked: 'Who has dared to betray us?'

'My maid and—'

She hesitated, for she heard the noise of many feet without.

'And who?'

'And Michael Pushkeene!'

With a sulphurous oath, Varwitch drew a pistol, and brandishing it aloft, swore he would shoot Pushkeene, the moment he came in sight.

Hark! the clatter of sabres and a thundering, authoritative knock at the door.

'The guards, Varwitch! Let us fly!'

She seized his wrist and dragged him into the hall, just as the door crashed down, and a swarm of soldiers, Pushkeene in their midst, rushed in.

'There they are! Seize them! seize them!' cried Pushkeene; but drawing back from the glare of Varwitch's eyes.

'You traitor and dog!' shouted Varwitch. 'I will keep my oath.'

And before the soldiers could leap forward to prevent, he raised his pistol and fired; and Michael Pushkeene sprang forward with a bullet in his brain.

For a moment Helen Radowsky fumbled at her breast, but as the officer in command approached, she became suddenly calm, and demanded to be told why she, a peaceful woman and good citizen, was subjected to this outrage.

'You are charged with Nihilism,' said the officer; 'and,' looking down at Pushkeene's body, 'I can swear your friend Varwitch will have to answer for murder.'

Shouting that he would never surrender, Varwitch was speedily overpowered, bound, gagged, and taken out to a waiting van.

Helen Radowsky followed, leaning on the officer's arm, which she pressed, as if for protection, and all the time she was pouring into his ears, her low, musical protestations of innocence.

'To the Prison of the Exiles,' said the officer ; and the escort moved on, with the prisoners in their midst.

For hours after the sham priest left them, Vladimeer Ruloff and Ruryk the Cossack sat in awful silence, neither able to give utterance to the feeling that oppressed him.

'Let us hope that daylight will bring better news,' said Vladimeer at length. 'In the meantime it might be well to take such rest as this wretched place affords.'

He was about to lay down, when the parcel left by Varwitch came in his way.

'Oh, Ruryk ! here is the food and wine left by our good friend the priest. Are you hungry ?'

'No, sir,' replied Ruryk ; 'but after you have drank a sufficiency of the wine, I would not object to a little.'

Vladimeer uncovered and uncorked the bottle. He tasted it, and declaring it was delicious, he raised the bottle, with the intention of taking a long drink.

Another instant and he would have swallowed the fatal poison : but his hand dropped on hearing a knocking at the cell-door, and the voice of the turnkey, as he fumbled at the bolts, calling out :

'Wake up, Wake up ! An order has come to send you away ?'

Vladimeer had secreted the bottle under the bench by the time the door opened and the turnkey made his appearance.

'Where are we to be sent to ?' he asked.

'I know not,' replied the man. 'But there is n ed of haste. Come !'

They entered the gloomy receiving-room from the prison just as the soldiers came in from the court, with Helen Radowsy and Varwitch in their midst.

Had they been spirits, or the actual dead rising up before him, Varwitch could not have been more horrified. He gasped, and would have fallen had not a soldier caught him.

'Are you the dead ?' he asked, when they came nearer.

Vladimeer did not speak to him, but Ruryk looked as if he could die ever so much happier if he could fasten his iron hand on Varwitch's throat for the fraction of a minute.

'Well, Helen Radowsky,' said Vladimeer,

'and so you, too, end your work in this place, to which you have cruelly sent the innocent.'

'I come to prison under a mistake,' she said, with a freezing laugh, 'but I will be free to-morrow. Do you know where you are going ?'

'To Siberia, perhaps,' said Vladimeer, turning away.

'Ha, ha, ha ! No such good fate. You are going before the tribunal to hear the sentence of death pronounced.'

'Why didn't you take the poison ? I played the friend, after all !' roared Varwitch ; and before the official could interfere he drew out the brandy bottle and drained the last drop.

Helen Radowsky did not wait to be searched, but took everything from her pocket—money, gloves, and a few trifles such as ladies carry. But when she was led to her cell her white hand was clasped to her breast and her fingers were wound about the jewelled hilt of the Gallitizin dagger.

CHAPTER XXXVIII.

LOOKING INTO THE FACE OF DEATH.

The dread tribunal was still in session when Vladimeer Ruloff and Ruryk the Cossack were ushered in.

The proceedings were brutal in their briefness and more than barbarous in their brusqueness.

The meaningless questions were asked Vladimeer, but not having heard the evidence nor the charges, he bravely scorned the offer to make a defence that would avail nothing.

He was a noble, and had been trained as a soldier. He, too, was offered the choice between the rope and the bullet, and chose the latter. One favor he asked, and it was granted—that he might be permitted to die beside Prince Gallitzin.

The offence of Ruryk called for the knout and imprisonment, but he stoutly maintained that he was as guilty as his master, and in his determination to share the prince's fate he hinted at a great many—imaginary —crimes that he had been guilty of again and again.

He was taken at his word, and never a martyr heard sentence of death with a feeling of greater exultation. Whether for convenience in guarding, or a feeling of humanity—it could hardly have been the latter— the two condemned men were taken down to the room where the prince, with his habitual calmness, was writing his last letter on earth.

The prince sprang up and embraced Vladimeer, kissing him on both cheeks, and showing more emotion than he had manifested during the whole trial.

'Ah! my master,' exclaimed Ruryk, after he had pressed the prince's hand to his bearded lips and wet it with tears of affection, 'I told you I should be with you even in death.'

'That you did, my brave Ruryk. Well, we have looked into the fleshless face too often together to shrink back now,' said the prince.

'I will still be your orderly, my master, even up there,' said the soldier, raising his eyes.

'Nay, my Ruryk, up there you will be my equal, the equal of all the kings who have gone before, or who may come after.'

'I would not be happy in such a heaven. Saint Peter would let me have my own way. I would rather be the orderly, on earth, of Prince Gallitzin, than first aid to the Czar. Death cannot change me.'

They sat down, and Vladimeer surprised the prince by telling him of the arrest of Helen Radowsky and Varwitch, which he saw ; and of the death of Pushkeene, of which he had heard the guards speak.

'Deluded wretches!' said the prince, 'their arrest comes too late to undo the wrong they have wrought. But let us treasure no hate against them at this hour.'

They talked on until the rising sun of their last day shone in at the windows.

They had eaten breakfast when the guard opened the door, and Madam Ruloff, Elizabeth, the Countess Alexandrina, and Mrs. Cushing and her daughter Belle rushed in.

It was a sacred scene, which the guard felt was not for his eyes, so he rested on his musket, with his bronzed face turned to the window, where his tears could not be seen.

They were admitted through the efforts of the Countess Alexandrina, that they might see and bid farewell to the condemned men for the last time on earth.

The rain had ceased and the wind died out, but still one black cloud, like a great pall, hung over the imperial city of Saint Petersburg. The rising sun shone out for a few minutes, then veiled his face.

The commotion on the streets was greater than on the day before.

In addition to the troops regularly stationed in the city, other regiments had been called in from the surrounding garrisons.

On all the great streets artillery was planted, and the caissons, filled with fixed ammunition, and the fire buckets at the mouths of the brass pieces, told the people that this exhibition was not for idle parade.

The rumor of disaffection in the Cossack ranks had reached the war office, and as a matter of precaution these fiery warriors were assigned a position where they could not witness the fate of the last descendant of their dethroned kings.

The streets were lined with gens-d'armes; the ranks growing heavier and more formidable in the direction of the Admiralty Building.

Mounted officers, with anxious faces, galloped here and there, forgetting for the once that they were not exhibiting themselves to the ladies in the windows.

At ten o'clock the bell in the tower of Saint Peter's began to toll its strokes—one, two, three—coming every five minutes, as if measureing the last seconds of the condemned men's lives.

A proclamation had been issued warning the people against gathering in groups on the streets, but for once the imperial edict was openly set at defiance.

The three thousand students in the city were on the streets, all in motion, here, there, and everywhere, and evidently objects of great interest to the swarming police.

While all was painful tumult and uproar on the street, the scene in the room where the three condemned men were confined was deathlike in its calmness.

Through General Gortschakoff, or rather through his niece the Countess Alexandrina permission was granted the friends of the prisoners to remain with them from ten o'clock in the morning until the hour when they were to be removed to the place of execution.

Pale, exhausted, and with an expression of blank despair on her face—which it would have been a mercy for the death-angel to have kissed away—the Countess Knloff sat by her son, his arm about her, and trying from his abundant courage to give her strength.

On the opposite side of Vladimeer sat the Countess Alexandria, pale at the thought of her approaching loss : defiant against the cruel laws that were soon to rob her of her idol.

The manner of Prince Gallitzin had not changed. He bore himself with that sweet dignity, and heroic fortitude, that so conspicuously distinguished all his acts. He sat holding the hand of the beautiful Elizabeth Ruloff, and talked in the calm, cheerful way so calculated to beget confidence. But no rose came to her white cheeks, no tear to her eye, no tremor to her cold hand. She was turning to ice under the strokes of that distant bell. Her heart beat slower ; she seemed to be dying from the cruel bullets, before they were belched from the guns at the breasts of her dear ones.

Mrs. Cushing and her daughter came as general comforters, but with well-bred discretion they saw their efforts would be out of place here, so they silently held themselves apart.

Catharine, Helen Radowsky's white-capped maid, still white-capped, came in at the eleventh hour, to the great delight of Ruryk, who had been thinking about her all the morning.

The chilling whispers in which conversation had been carried on, stopped on the entrance of an officer, aid to the Czar.

'I come,' he said, removing his hat, ' to say that General Gortschakoff desires to speak with Prince Gallitzin.'

'Admit him at once,' said the prince.

'But, your excellency, he would see you in another apartment,' said the aid.

'My respects to General Gortschakoff, but my time is too short, The few minutes left me are precious to this dear one,' he said, turning to Elizabeth Ruloff.

The aid withdrew, and soon after the slow, shambling step of the old diplomat could be heard.

He walked into the centre of the room, and looking only at the prince, he said :

I bear to General Gallitzin a message from our master the Czar. The old man's voice trembled.

The prince rose, and made answer :

' My master's messages are ever welcome.'

' I come,' continued General Gortschakoff,' authorized by his imperial majesty to commute the sentence of you and your companions from death to exile, on one condition.'

' Name the conditions said the prince.'

' That you will make and assign a confession of your past misdeeds, that we may be the better able to root out the people organized to destroy the government.

' Does General Gortschakoff come here to insult dying men ?' demanded the prince.'

' Such, I assure you, is not my purpose.'

' Then bear back to his majesty, whom may Heaven long spare, these my last words. Wladislas Gallitzin, conscious of his own innocence, has no confession to make. And he declines to lie, even to save his own life.'

' The prince speaks for me,' said Vladimeer, feeling in his heart a twinge as he recalled his own secret indiscretions.

' I go with my master,' joined in Ruryk.

' I have accomplished my mission. I regret that it has not resulted in more good,' said General Gortschakoff, turning to leave.

He stopped near the door and said, as if thinking aloud :

' It deeply grieves my heart that this should be the fate of the last of the Gallitzins.'

' General Gortschakoff's sympathy is appreciated,' said the prince.

' Will you,' he said coming back, ' give me your hand at parting ?'

' Willingly, for I treasure no ill will against the highest or lowest subject in all his majesty's realms,' said the prince, coming forward and wringing the proffered hand.

' And you too, Vladimeer Ruloff ?'

Vladimeer took his hand, and as he held it he said :

' If by thought or word I have erred, it it was not because I hated Russia, for which I was ever ready to die; but because perjury, conspiracy, and I will add tyranny, tore my soldier father, Count Ruloff, from us, and sending him into exile, threw his family impoverished on the world.'

To this the prince made no response, but waving his hand at the room, went out.

He entered his waiting carriage and between lines of soldiers was whirled away to his own palace. As he descended from the carriage, he looked up at a neighboring clock. It was half-past eleven, and he shuddered as he thought the condemned would be on the way to execution within half an hour.

Down the street came the clatter of flying hoofs and a mass of shining lances.

' Freehoff's Cossacks !' shouted the people, on the sidewalks.

General Gortschakoff turned, just as Captain Freehoff threw himself from his horse.

' Hold ! hold, your excellency !' cried the captain.

' What is it ?'

' Miss Radowsky and Varwitch, now in the Prison of the Exiles, have made a written confession of the plot to destroy Prince Gallitzin. Here it is ;' the captain drew out a roll of paper, and handing it to the old man, continued : ' They have also told where other papers could be found, particularly those on which the evidence was built up against Count Ruloff.'

' What !' cried the general, glancing over the papers.

' It is the truth !'

' Yes, yes. But, gracious Heaven, it may be too late !' shouted the general. ' Away to the palace and announce my coming to his majesty. Do not wait an instant. I will follow !'

' But, let me stop the execution !'

' Away, I bid you ! that is the royal prerogative !'

With the alacrity of a young man, the general sprang into his carriage.

' To the palace ! On like the wind ! To the palace ! to the palace !' he shouted.

The people, seeing the flying carriage, supposed at first that the prince and his friends were escaping. But the Gortschakoff livery dispelled the pleasant illusion.

Reaching the palace, the old man got out, and ran passed the guards. He stopped not at the ante-room, guarded by a grim soldier with drawn sword, but burst into the reception room.

'Where is his majesty!' cried the general.

'He retired by the advice of his physician, and left orders not to be disturbed,' said the attendant.

'I p u t see him! As you v lue your life, announce Prince Gortschakoff at once.'

Under the firm conviction that the general had taken leave of his senses. the attendant hurried off, and the old man dropped panting into a chair.

In the meantime the hands of all the clocks in the city flew—hitherto it had been their invariable habit to creep—to the hour of high noon.

The artillery band, with their instruments draped in mourning, played a dirge at the head of the rapidly forming line. The prince's own regiment, with arms reversed, went solemnly into position—left in front, as is the custom at military funerals.

Down the streets, the hush of the crowd marking their advance, came a company of the Warsaw Legion of the Polish Contingent, the selected executioners, with their polished rifles carried at a 'right shoulder shift.'

Hark! The booming of a gun from the parade ground, the signal for the advance, will come in five minutes.

Unable to move, the Countess Ruloff has remained back with generous Mrs. Cushing and her daughter.

The condemned men have come out on the great platform—Elizabeth clinging to the prince's arm; the Countess Alexandrina holding the hand of Vladimeer the Nihilist; and Ruryk and Catharine walking side by side.

What a sea of anxious, pain-marked faces! What an awful stillness! How quiet even the horses seem to stand.

The hands of the clock have touched twelve, and the Titan strokes of a hundred b 1 s announce that the hour has come.

A few hurried words; a kiss; the brief, suppressed cry of a women; the unsuppressed cry of the mob, like tortured wild beasts; and the panting is over. The three men have walked firmly down. With heads erect, and measured step; they take their place in the centre of the line.

Forward!' blares the bugle at the head of the line. 'Forward!' repeat the officers along the line. The band strikes up the 'Dead March in Saul;' and the funeral procession—of living men—is in motion.

On, on, on. The crowd grows denser, and the streets nearing the parade-ground narrower, and the gaunt, gray houses higher.

The line stops. The band stops. A horseman presses his way back; and word is passed from company to company to load. She students have barricaded the streets. The windows on each side are torn away as if struck by lightning. Fresh apertures in the walls, and ten thousand rifles in the hands of ten thousand men, half of them Cossacks who have deserted their commands, are brought to bear on the troops in the street.

The news of a revolt flies through the city. and the citizens, all secretly armed, cheer, and in wild torrents pour down the streets to the point of attack, shouting with fury:

'Gallitzin!' 'Gallitzin of Novgorod!' 'To the rescue of Vladimeer the Nihilist!'

Soldiers who blanched not before Turkish guns turn pale now.

A shot, a blow, would be the signal for a conflagration that all the power of the Czar could not quench.

The sound of flying hoofs, and Freehoff's lancers dash after the procession, though the bugler at the captain's side is blowing a 'halt!' with all his strength of lung. The captain urges his horse to the commanding general's side, and whispers something that has a most exhilarating effect on that officer. He rises in his stirrups and shouts so that the mob can hear:

'Prince Gallitzin and his friends, on fresh evidence, are found to be innocent! Our master, the Czar orders me back!'

Such a cheer as followed never was heard on the banks of the Neva; and it rolled along the streets, a great wave of sound, and beat against the walls of the palace of the Czar. The soldiers tossed up their caps in the line and caught them on their bayonets. The band tore off the crape from their instruments, as the line came to a 'right about face,' and struck up 'See the Conquering Hero Comes.' A hundred students took the horses from General Gortschakoff's carriage, as that old man drove up, and unheeding his protestations, they placed therein the prince and Vladimeer Ruloff, and mounting Ruryk on the box, they started up the Russian hymn, the crowds along the sidewalk joining in, and back they went to the Admiralty Building.

In a short time the journals had their extras flying through the streets, setting forth the conspiracy, and lauding Prince Gallitzin and Vladimeer Ruloff as fulsomely as they had denounced them a short time before.

The Countess Ruloff and all her friends— they were not many—were still at the Admi**ality Building. Elizabeth and the Countess Alexandrina were among the first to hear the news ; and when, in response to the vociferous demands of the crowd, all showed themselves, and cheering was renewed ; and the bells started pealing as if determined at once to exhaust all their capacity for sounds before they stopped.

CHAPTER XXXIV.

IN WHICH THE CURTAIN IS RUN DOWN AT

THE CLOSE OF THE LAST ACT.

A conspiracy is like a bubble—brilliant, perfect, apparently clear and solid—but prick it with the needle of truth, and whiff—there is nothing.

It breaks all over leaving no sign of the formation on which it was erected.

Varwitch, in his confession, stated where papers could be found that would prove his ability to imitate any handwriting he ever saw, and he told of a hundred cases where he had availed himself of this dangerous talent. He boldly avowed his opposition to the existing government, and prayed for its speady downfall. More, he told of his reasons for taking service with Prince Gallitzin, and how, under Helen Radowsky's instructions, and the aid and countenance of Count Kiseleff, he marked out the plan which, he believed, would destroy the prince. He laid bare his part in the conspiracy against Count Ruloff, and showed that it was a part of the Nihilist scheme to turn the Czar against the most trusted of his nobles.

The first result of this confession has been shown ; the second result was the immediate arrest of Count Kiseleff, who was sent soon after to Siberia ; and the third result was to prove all Varwitch's statements beyond a doubt.

Anxious to remedy the grevious wrong he had done, the Czar dispatched at once for the return of Count Ruloff; and that gentleman passed—near the Ural mountains—Count Kiseleff going in an opposite direction.

Varwitch made his confession in obedience to the request of Helen Radowsky. But how that unfortunate but remarkable young woman came to change at the eleventh hour has never been learned.

In charity let us hope that her better nature, glimpses of which we have seen, asserted itself, and that, realizing that she had been betrayed as a Nihilist by Pushkeene, and that conviction must follow, she determined to close her brief career by an attempt at justice.

Two days after the release of the prince and his friends, the papers stated that Helen Radowsky was found dead in her cell with a curiously wrought dagger buried in her breast. Prince Gallitzin at once hastened to the prison and discovered it was her father's dagger—the one he had given her.

He had the body decently cared for, and the fatal weapon buried with her.

Among her papers—written some time before her arrest—was a sheet on which, with intense expression, she avowed her love for the man whose ruin she was planning.

By the intercession of Prince Gallitzin and his friends, Varwitch's sentence was commuted to imprisonment for life ; but the night before he should have been sent off he was found to be dying, and in obedience to his last request, he was buried in the same grave with Helen Radowsky.

And now, what would be expected to follow the many stirring and trying events we have recorded ? First, Count Ruloff is back with his family, restored to his honors, and his estate restored to him ; but in this year of grace, 1879, he prefers to live with his family in France.

Making a virtue of a necessity, Prince Gortschakoff consented to the marriage of his niece with Vladimeer, no longer called ' the Nihilist.' They, too, are living with Count Ruloff.

Prince Gallitzin, the hero of our story, is still the hero and the idol of the young soldiery of Russia. But the day following his marriage, to the beautiful Elizabeth he left Russia, and, at the present writing, is travelling on the Pacific coast with his friends the Cushings. It need not be added that Ruryk is with him, nor that the white-capped servant has placed herself for life under the faithful Cossack's protection. And still within the wide realms of the Czar the revolutionary fires smoulder; and still other tragedies are being enacted that must pass into oblivion.

We have attempted an actual picture of Russian life, showing no desire to hold the failings or the virtues that undeniably exist on either side. While writers write, and liberty is possible, and love exists so long, in some form, the story of ' Vladimeer the Nihilist' will be repeated. But never in the free land where this is written and read, and ended.

THE END.

www.ingramcontent.com/pod-product-compliance
Lightning Source LLC
Chambersburg PA
CBHW022010050726
47499CB00008BA/2822